MW01129436

NIGHT OF PLEASURE

A SCHOOL OF GALLANTRY NOVEL

DELILAH MARVELLE

DELILAH MARVELLE PRODUCTIONS

Portland, Oregon

Delilah Marvelle Productions, LLC
Delilah@DelilahMarvelle.com
Portland, Oregon
www.DelilahMarvelle.com

Publisher's Note: This is a work of fiction. Names, characters, places, and incidents are a
product of the author's crazy imagination. Locales and public names are sometimes used
for atmospheric purposes. Any resemblance to actual people, living or dead, or to busi-
nesses, companies, events, institutions, or locales is completely coincidental.

Book Layout ©2014 BookDesignTemplates.com

Night of Pleasure/Delilah Marvelle -- 1st ed.
ISBN-13: 978-1497315990
ISBN-10: 1497315999

To my husband Marc.
You proved to me love at first sight
is not only real, but that it lasts.
Thank you for coming into my life.
I love you.

This book wouldn't be in anyone's hands if not for a team of amazing people I adore and trust. A special smooch and big thank you to the ever fabulous Jessa Slade aka Jenna Dales, Maire Claremont, Kim and Debbie Burke, Ronnie Buck, Kim Wollenburg, Jessie Smith, Cynthia Young, and Carol Ann MacKay.

PROLOGUE

Trust that fate has a plan.

It may not be a very good one, but it has a plan.

-The School of Gallantry

London, England – March 14, 1823
The Banfield House at Grosvenor Square, early afternoon

If only his mother knew the difference between a cough and pneumonia, his life would have been so much easier. Not that he was complaining about the fact he was missing his oral exam on the Principles of Sound Doctrine. It had saved him from memorizing eighteen pages of some lonely chaste man's pathetic idea of salvation. He was his own salvation. And being lonely and chaste wasn't at all what he aspired to be.

He was too good-looking for that.

Sitting on the hard wood of a gilded straight-backed chair, which the tails of his coat did little to cushion, Derek tugged at the high collar pinned tightly around his throat. It was a mandatory garment for all Eton students, even the eldest Upper Boys, such as him. While the rigid

1

collar was confining and irksome, it was not as irksome and confining as the corridor where he and his younger brother Andrew had been forced to wait for the past hour and a half.

After standing, leaning, and pacing, he opted to sit. As did Andrew. Three doctors had already come and two had already left, both of them looking bewildered. This was no surprise. The doctors always left bewildered after being called in by their mother who imagined various deadly diseases that didn't exist.

Feeling like his collar was choking the sanity out of him, Derek sat up in his chair and announced to his fourteen-year-old brother, "I'm about to do something I shouldn't."

Andrew perked. "Fabulous. What are we doing?"

Derek reached out and mussed Andrew's head of dark hair before playfully shoving it. "Why do you always think everything involves you? My collar needs to come off, is all. I've had it on since seven this morning." He yanked on the end of his cravat, unraveling it, and draped it over his shoulder. Removing the rigid collar buried beneath his linen shirt by unfastening the pins, he stripped it and whipped it to the floor. "May the devil and the Head Master go with it." He unbuttoned his tawny waistcoat to ensure more comfort and stretched back, letting a booted heel hit the floor.

"And I thought I was a rebel." Andrew raked back his tousled hair. "Mother won't be pleased seeing you unkempt."

Derek dug into his pocket and pulled out a tin of hard ginger candy. "No one is here to notice. I'm fine." He opened the tin, flicked a piece of the spiced amber candy into his mouth and held it out to Andrew. "I bought these off Stanwick during Long Chamber hours. His uncle owns a confectionary shop out in Surrey. They are my definition of incredible." The strong pine-pitch taste already stung his tongue. He loved how it amplified his senses. "Take one."

"*Only one?* Off with you. I'll settle for three, if you don't mind." His brother grabbed three with a scoop of fingers, leaving only five behind and popped all three into his mouth. He clacked them against his teeth and paused, his eyes watering. "Dirk me…I…you could have…warned me."

Derek smirked and clicked the tin shut. "Greed is punishing you. I told you to keep it to one."

Andrew coughed, hitting his own chest twice and swiped at the tears leaking from the corners of his eyes. "You and your…damn need for… *spice*."

"Spice makes a soul breathe in deep. Live a little."

"More like *die* a little."

Steps echoed in the distance, making Derek slip the tin back into his coat pocket.

They both glanced toward the sound.

Three figures cut through the sunlight gleaming through the long row of windows at the far end of the adjoining corridor.

Derek groaned. "Damn it, I just—" Scrambling to his feet, he swiped up his collar, skidded back and fell into his seat, trying not to choke on the candy floating in his mouth. He gagged and swallowed it whole without meaning to.

Andrew let out an impish laugh, still clacking all three candies against his teeth. "Serves you right. As our cousins say, never take off a collar unless you're in bed entertaining a woman."

Derek laughed and kicked a foot out toward him. "Quiet, half-man," he chided out of the side of his mouth. "What do you know about enter- taining women? You can't even handle a piece of candy." Unable to get the stiff collar back around his neck, he rolled his eyes and shoved it be- hind himself. Buttoning his waistcoat, he focused on wrapping and tying his cravat around the natural short collar of his linen shirt. "Who are they? Can you see? Do you know?"

His brother leaned sideways in his chair and squinted. "I can't deci- pher quite yet. But they don't appear to be carrying medicine chests. So they can't be doctors."

"I told you it couldn't be anything serious. If she kept it to only three doctors, I foresee us being back in school by tomorrow." Still trying to finish tying his cravat beneath his chin, Derek tossed out, "Is it family?" They had a lot of cousins – eighteen – half of whose names he couldn't remember. He didn't try. Most of them only came around when they needed money anyway.

Andrew pointed with his chin. "No. They don't look like any of the magpies related to us. Too well dressed."

Derek paused as the figures emerged from the blurring brightness of the vast corridor. A tall gentleman dressed in a fine wool morning coat, grey trousers and gleaming knee-high boots made his way toward them. The pulsing silence was amplified by the sound of his boot heels against the marble. While his chiseled face looked young enough to pass for an Oxford student, his wavy black hair was silvering at the temples, hinting he was in his early forties.

Walking in exquisite refinement alongside the gentleman was a young female of about sixteen. Her regal face was a pale oval in the stripes of sunlight and shade that glimmered across her profile as she passed the last row of windows leading toward them.

Derek's hands fell away from knotting the last of his cravat. If she had been walking alone, he would have whistled.

A pleated green bonnet was assembled over an intricately knitted black braid that looped upward into her bonnet and back down, fashionably draping one slim shoulder. A daffodil gown frothed and flowed with her graceful movements as snowy white satin slippers peered out with each measured step. Chin perfectly set – not too high and not too low – she carried herself with a sweeping, swaying elegance that reflected years of lecture dedicated to feminine poise.

In his opinion, she could have easily passed for a debutante of eighteen if there had been more...well...*bosom*...in her corset. She was almost as flat as paper. Which was sad, really. A sizable pair of high-perched breasts would have made her a triumph.

Was it ungentlemanly for him to notice her breasts or lack thereof? Yes. Yes, it was. But he'd been confined to an all-boys school since he was thirteen, and being almost eighteen, whenever he had a chance to cast an eye at a pair of bosoms, no matter their size, he did.

Andrew tilted closer. "Who are they?" he whispered.

"I have no idea." He didn't know much about their father's personal life. But he did know one thing. Their father only associated with the best. "Get up," Derek instructed. "If they got past the butler, they have an appointment and we should acknowledge them."

Andrew and Derek both stood, clicking their boot heels in unison.

The footman who had been leading their visitors, directed the gentleman and young lady to the closed doorway of their father's rooms before proceeding back down the vast corridor.

The young lady glanced at Derek and upon seeing him, quickly pivoted her head toward him, showcasing a shimmering glint of emerald earrings that swayed against the inside of her bonnet. Full raspberry-colored lips parted as stunning, soulful blue eyes captured his.

Derek could do nothing but half-breathe and stare. If perfection had a name, it would be hers. Whatever that name might be. Her pale skin was flawless and the brightness of those pretty eyes against the ebony of her braided hair made her look ethereal. Something out of a dream. *His* dream. One that whispered of long summer afternoons spent lying on sun-warmed grass with his head resting on her lap and her hand brushing away strands of his hair as she leaned down to kiss him on the lips with just a little bit of tongue. Followed with a lot of tongue and their clothes laying everywhere.

An expensive wool coat and broad shoulders abruptly blocked Derek's view of her.

It was her father.

Derek cleared his throat. "Good afternoon, sir. Welcome to the Banfield home. The household is rather harried today, for which we apologize. How might I be of assistance?"

The towering man removed his black leather gloves in smooth sweeps, searching his face with piercing blue eyes. "The name is Mr. Rupert Grey." An American accent tinged that deep voice as the faint scent of cognac teased the air. "Are you *the* Honorable Derek Charles Holbrook?"

A frisson of unease skated down Derek's spine. How and why did this man know his full name? "Yes, sir. I am."

The man skimmed Derek's appearance and tucked away his leather gloves into his coat pocket. His features softened. "Look at you. All grown. I haven't seen you since you were a tot." He held his gaze. "You look like your mother."

Derek blinked. He always thought he resembled his father.

The man turned and inclined his head enthusiastically toward Andrew. "You must be Andrew. A pleasure to meet you, sir. I have heard so much from your father about your writing adventures. You had yet to be born when I last traveled through London." Patting Derek's shoulder, he returned his gaze to him. The teasing scent of cognac pricked the air again. "I can't believe you're actually shaving." He tapped a finger against Derek's cravat. "Tend to that cravat, will you? It's lopsided and there is a young lady present."

Derek scrambled to straighten it.

Mr. Grey smiled and drew back his hand. "Your father asked that I call on him the moment I got into London. I was surprised to hear he is bedridden. Is he not well?"

Who was this man? "I have yet to know anything, sir. I haven't seen him. But I'm not overly worried. He has always been a man of good health."

"Quite right. Your mother and her penchant for doctors has certainly seen to that."

It was more than obvious this man knew his family.

Reaching back, Mr. Grey guided his daughter forward. "This is my daughter, Miss Clementine Grey. I would rather not impose on your father by having us both call on him as I originally intended. Might I leave her in your care for a small while, Mr. Holbrook?"

Miss Grey perused Derek's bright blue school coat and its gilt buttons.

Derek adjusted the coat in an effort to better display his broad chest, which he knew to be twice the breadth of boys his age. "Yes, of course, sir. It would be an honor."

"Excellent. Thank you." Mr. Grey angled a quick kiss to his daughter's cheek beneath the wide rim of her bonnet. "I will be just beyond that door visiting with George. Mind yourself."

She said nothing.

Striding toward the closed door, Mr. Grey opened it and edged inside, closing the door promptly behind him.

Knowing he and Miss Grey were finally alone (as his brother didn't count), Derek peered at her. The faint scent of marzipan drifted toward him as if he had just walked into the kitchen at Christmas. It suited her and made him want to nestle her against his chest before a fireplace late at night.

Compared to his still-growing size of five feet and ten inches, she couldn't have been more than five feet and two inches herself. The yellow ribbon at the end of her glossy black braid had been pressed, looped, and tied to perfection.

She turned her head toward him and looked up, the white satin ribbon on her oval bonnet shifting. Well-lashed eyes that were the shade of a bright summer sky just before nightfall stared up at him.

He stared down at her, his head, his heart and his body pulsing. He'd never felt anything like it, but those alluring eyes made him want to grab her and bite down. Hard. He inclined his head. "Good afternoon, Miss Grey. How are you?"

She blinked as if weighing what she was supposed to say.

It was darling that she appeared to struggle for words. He had never been one to struggle with anything. Although it *had* been a while since he'd associated with any prepossessing ladies worthy of his time. Eton, as well his parents, kept him from associating with any females to prevent what they called his 'untamed and unnecessary, sinful lusting' after he groped and exchanged one too many tongue-involved kisses with a certain debutante about half a year ago. He understood their concerns. But unlike fresh-faced Lady Beatrice, who had only made him sigh in mere reverence, this sultry Miss Delectable Grey made him want to bite his own knuckles in a form of indecent lust no amount of praying would change.

Stepping aside, he gestured toward the chair he vacated. He paused, realizing his collar was still sitting on it. He grabbed it and shoved it into his coat pocket with a gruff, apologetic laugh. "The Head Master makes me wear it. It's annoying." Clearing his throat, he gestured toward the chair again. "It isn't by any means the most comfortable of chairs, but there is no need for you to stand. Take my seat, Miss Grey. I insist."

She lowered her chin. "Thank you, but please don't insist," she replied in a refined American accent, her lips rounding as if every word mattered. "I was confined to a carriage for much too long. I would rather stand, thank you."

Damn. He'd heard Americans speak before, but not with such dazzling sophistication and purpose. It was enchanting. She was enchanting. His mouth quirked. "I completely understand." He shifted toward her. God was she beautiful. He wanted to grab that face and tongue her until neither of them had the ability to breathe for weeks. "Traveling can be quite tedious. Wouldn't you say?"

"Yes, it can be," she offered.

He smoothed his cravat. "I actually know a thing or two about traveling."

She held his gaze. "Do you?"

He grinned. "I most certainly do. I was the only heir in the history of our family to have ever been born abroad and on a ship. I've been to countless places. Almost too many to name." He decided to name them anyway. "Spain. Italy. France. Germany. We even went as far as Africa, although I wasn't old enough to remember. My parents love to travel and take us everywhere. Sadly, my brother and I haven't traveled in some time. He and I study over at Eton throughout the year, which doesn't allow for it. But I'll be graduating in a few months. In fact, I'll be eighteen by the end of this year. Which means in three years, I'll be legally available for marriage. How about you?"

She stared disapprovingly. "Please don't talk to me anymore, Mr. Holbrook. I have no interest in entertaining your incredibly poor sense of humor." She then gave him the shoulder and stood squarely facing the closed door.

His grin faded. Him mentioning his availability for marriage was probably pushing a bit too hard given they just met. "Right. I'll uh…take the seat then. Given you won't be…using it." Pushing back his coat tails with the back of his hand, Derek sat and refrained from hitting his head against the wall behind him. He was usually popular with the females and could easily charm the stockings off their toes by tossing out a smile.

Eton had apparently bankrupted him of all appeal.

Black leather ankle boots and gangly legs dressed in black breeches nudged in closer from beside him, scooting over the chair. Andrew's dark eyes darted over to Miss Grey as his ink-stained finger came up and tugged on the oversized collar fastened around his own throat. He angled in. "You overdid it," he whispered so she wouldn't hear. "It was like watching Father try to dance with his cravat tied over his eyes. Entertaining but not in the least bit practical."

Being practical had never made anyone smile. Derek glanced at Miss Grey before quickly leaning toward his brother and whispering, "Go for a walk or something. So she and I can be alone."

Andrew's eyes widened. "Don't you *dare* get us into trouble. Knowing what you and Lady Beatrice did in that alcove at Mother's own party, the poor girl needs a chaperone." Theatrically clearing his throat, his brother tilted toward Miss Grey, with an elbow on his knee and offered in a manly tone, "Forgive my brother. He imagines himself to be quite the *bon homme.*"

Damn his brother for not leaving.

Miss Grey smoothed her skirts and said to her toes, "If only he imagined himself to be a gentleman."

Andrew laughed and pointed. "If only! He knows nothing about control. Absolutely *nothing.* Ask Lady Beatrice." He shoved an elbow into Derek's side.

Derek shifted his jaw and elbowed his brother back, reminding him they were related.

Andrew stood and rakishly adjusted his school coat. Rounding their chairs, he snapped out an ink-stained hand toward her in greeting. "Allow me to introduce the real gentleman in this family. I am Mr. Andrew Mark Holbrook, youngest son to the Honorable Viscount Banfield, who is also known amongst his peers as 'The Laughing Viscount' due to his inability to control his jolly nature in public. It's a Banfield trait. We all have our own control issues, or so I've been told more than once." He grinned at her. "I wish to genuinely welcome you into London and into our grand home."

"Uh...thank you. That was certainly quite the introduction." She paused and glanced at his ink-stained hand but didn't take it.

Andrew still held it out.

She still didn't take it.

He edged it closer to her. "It's a hand."

She quirked a brow. "I know what it is."

"No. You clearly don't. You're supposed to take it when it's offered. It's a form of greeting here in England. What? Do they not shake *hands* in America?"

She gave him a hard pointed stare and countered, "It's a dirty hand. What? Do they not have *soap* in England?"

Derek snorted. Now *that* was good.

"It's ink," Andrew drawled in agitation, wagging his hand closer toward hers. "I write novels. As the Lower Master always says, ink stains are the sign of an intellectual and no amount of soap can erase true brilliance."

She tsked. "You're being incredibly rude by insisting I touch a hand that clearly hasn't been washed in days."

Andrew flopped his hand to his side and trudged back to the chair and sat, rolling his eyes at Derek. "You can have her." He shoved his dark hair out of his eyes, huffed out a breath, and glanced toward the closed paneled door. "When are we going to see Father?"

"When the doctor or Mother says we can."

"And when will that be? It's been over an hour. How is it this Mr. Grey was able to prance right in and we're left out in the corridor with his *daughter*?"

Derek sighed. "I don't know. But if it were serious, we would have been told by now. You know how Mother is. She *invents* diseases."

At a sound from within, they both straightened, casting hopeful glances at the closed suite leading to their father's rooms. Derek could hear the faint bass of Doctor Shire's voice, two other voices, his father's gruff laugh and the chink of china. The voices were indistinct and the heavy mahogany door remained shut.

Derek bit back a smile, knowing his father was most likely telling the doctor to prescribe him a bottle of champagne and three slices of almond cake. As always.

Miss Grey stared disapprovingly. "Your father is ill and you're smiling?"

Derek broadened his smile into a grin knowing she had been watching him. That only meant one thing. She liked him. "Don't think the worst of me. My mother does this to us every year. The man gets a cough or a fever and the whole world has to know about it. She once kept him in bed for two weeks after he nicked his left arm with the edge of his fencing sword because she was incredibly worried an infection would end up leading to the amputation of his entire left arm. She called in *eight* different doctors for an opinion I could have very well given her myself. She is very much like that. The complete opposite of my father. He worries about nothing and she worries about everything."

"How curious." Her brows drew together. "So whose opinion do you share, Mr. Holbrook? Are you more like your mother in that you worry about everything? Or are you more like your father in that you worry about nothing?"

It would seem this treasure was trying to get to know him. "Actually, Miss Grey, I fall in between. The only thing I ever take too seriously is the impression I make on a lady." Oh, yes. It was time to let her know just how interested he really was. For although he might have been earlier blindsided by her glorious presence, he'd never been one to remain blindsided when he genuinely wanted something. And he most certainly wanted something: her and him against the wall around the corner.

He stood, dug out his tin of amber mints, and flicked it open. He held it out to her. "Keep it to one. They're very strong but well worth the unexpected bite." It was the ultimate test. If she could handle the heat of his candy, she could handle him.

She peered down at the small tin that hosted the remaining amber hard candies. "What are they?"

"If ginger and licorice ever fell madly in love and married, their children would look exactly like this. It's an acquired taste." And yes, he was also referring to himself.

She leaned in and lifted her gloved finger above the tin as if to take one, but edged her fingers back and quickly lowered her hand. "I really don't care for spiced candies. They usually overwhelm me. I prefer simple candies. Plain sweets. Do you have any honey sticks?"

Honey sticks? This one desperately needed some excitement in her life. And he was more than willing to give it. "I'm sorry, love, but I don't do honey sticks. Plain sweets do nothing for me. In my opinion, being *overwhelmed* is far better than being *underwhelmed*." He edged in closer until their faces were only two hands apart and her skirts brushed his trouser-clad thighs. The fullness of those lips taunted him as he rattled the candies in the tin. "I can assure you, it's worth trying." He held her gaze. "I promise you'll never be the same."

Her lips parted as she lowered her gaze back to the candies and perused each one as if they were different, even though they were the same. "I suppose I don't mind trying one. How strong are they?"

"Your very knees will wobble." He took one out of the tin with his bare fingers and brought it to her mouth, gently tucking it between those already parted lips. "Now imagine me crawling onto your tongue." He pushed it in, letting her moist lips graze the tip of his finger.

Her eyes widened.

Ah, yes. *That* was the reaction he was hoping for. He grinned, clicked the tin shut and put it into his pocket. Holding her gaze, he sucked on the finger her lips had touched, trying not to be too obvious about it, and asked, "What do you think?"

She glanced at the finger he had sucked, her cheeks flushing. Her lips remained overly puckered as she winced against watering eyes. "I...sakes alive...it's very..."

He still grinned. "Intoxicating. I know. If you bite into it, it adds more fire. Do you like fire?"

Her chest rose and fell more steadily. She waved a hand before her flushed face and pushed the candy around in her mouth and winced. "No. I don't— This is...I can't believe you actually like this. It's like piling on...*agony*. My tongue is burning."

That wasn't the only thing burning. Her flushed face was stunning to watch. He could only imagine what she'd look like after a kiss. He angled in very close to the side of her bonnet and whispered so his brother couldn't hear, "If you can handle the burn, you can handle me. How about we disappear for a small while into the library? I promise we won't do anything you don't want to do."

She choked and spit out the candy into her gloved hand.

He leaned back. "Are you all right? Is it coming on too strong?"

She scrambled away, her chest heaving. "I can assure you, Mr. Holbrook, it isn't the candy that is coming on strong." She tried to flick the candy off her glove, but it stubbornly clung to the kid leather. She panicked and shook her hand once and twice, but it still clung.

He closed the distance between them again. "You shouldn't waste it. They cost a shilling a piece. Come here." Taking her hand, he brought her palm upward.

She stilled and their gazes locked.

Still holding her gaze, he used his lips to fully take up the candy into his mouth, dragging his lips across the expensive leather of her glove so he could taste more than just candy. "You're beautiful. Do you know that?"

She gasped and yanked her hand away, her uneven breaths quaking. Setting a trembling hand to her corseted waist, she dragged in several deep breaths as her mouth opened and closed. No sound or breath came out. It was as if she were having trouble breathing.

Derek froze, realizing she *was* having trouble breathing. Jesus. "Are you all right?" He leaned in close, grabbing her arm. "Do you need water? Should I call out the doctor?"

She stumbled back, her chest rising and falling in uncontrolled panicked breaths. "N-no. I...I'm fine. Please don't—"

"Fine?" he echoed, veering in and taking her waist. "You are not fine. You're barely breathing. I want you to sit down. You've been standing too long. Now come over here."

She leaned away. "I can't...breathe with you—"

"You need to sit down," he insisted, pulling her close enough for his legs to get buried in her full skirts. "Now sit down." He tried tugging her toward the direction of the chair only to realize she was still tilting back against his arms. He tried to straighten her with both hands. "What are you doing? Why are you resisting? I'm trying to—"

"Stop it!" She shoved him, startling them both.

He stumbled against her skirts and realizing he was about to fall, instantly released her arm and waist so she didn't get hurt. Letting the weight of his body fall away from her, he fell against the chair he'd been trying to get her into, flipping it over. The back of his head hit the marble floor, stunning him, as the end of the chair dashed his forehead and clattered off to the side. He lay there staring up at the ceiling trying to figure out if he should ever get up again knowing he had officially made an idiot of himself.

Andrew snorted. "And *that* is how Romeo committed suicide."

It was like performing before a live audience.

Miss Grey scrambled toward Derek. "Oh God." She knelt beside him, her skirts blanketing a part of him. "I…I'm so sorry. I didn't mean to hurt you. I didn't mean to—" Her trembling hands jumped to his face, feathering it with quick touches. Her eyes widened. "The chair marked you. I shouldn't have pushed you. I shouldn't have—"

Derek decided to lay there and revel in those touches for free. It was so nice.

Her features twisted as several large gasps escaped her. "Oh God, I…I hurt you. I—"

Maybe reveling at her expense was not wise. "You didn't hurt me, love. I'm fine. I fell out of a two-story window once. This is nothing." He sat up, draping an arm against his knee and smiled. "I appreciate your concern, though. It takes away the sting of humiliation." He rolled away then jumped to his feet, snapping out a hand toward her. "Allow me to help you up."

She gaped up at him, her braid swaying against her shoulder. "There is a sizable welt on your head."

He paused and dabbed a hand to it, unable to even feel it. "It's nothing. It doesn't even hurt. I'm fine."

She pushed herself up and straightened, several large breaths escaping her. "I shoved you a bit too hard." There was still a slight quake lingering in that refined voice as she searched his face. "I'm so sorry. I truly am."

Touched by her genuine concern, he softened his voice. "Had I known my advances were going to keep you from breathing I would have asked you to sit down first."

Andrew coughed and glanced at the closed door across from them. "As I told you before, Miss Grey, my brother knows *nothing* about control." Pushing up onto his feet, Andrew straightened and trudged across the corridor over to the closed door. "I don't know about you, Derek, but I'm going in. It's been over an hour."

Their mother would throw a boot at them for going in and interrupting her long list of questions for the doctor. "*Andrew.*" Jogging up from behind, he grabbed the collar of his brother's wool coat and yanked him back before he could get to the door. Derek released the collar. "You know full well Mother gets ruffled when we nag at her about her imaginings. Leave it be. The sooner the doctor can dispel whatever ails Father, the sooner we can get back to school."

Shoving his fists into his pockets, Andrew huffed out a breath. "Who says I want to go back to school? I hate it there." He turned and scuffed his way down the tiled corridor, staring at his boots with each step. His dark hair fell into his eyes. He swiped at it, clearly annoyed.

Falling into stride beside his brother, Derek nudged his shoulder into his. "Are the Lower Boys bothering you again? Or is it one of the Upper Boys from my side this time?"

"No. I wasn't thinking about that at all." Andrew came to a halt, his sharp features tightening. "What if Father dies?"

Derek's stomach dropped. "Don't be ridiculous. You heard him earlier. He was in there laughing."

"Yes. Exactly. He sometimes tries to laugh off even the worst. You know that. I started thinking about this entire situation." Andrew chewed on his fingernail. "I mean...don't you think it's rather odd that this-this…Mr. Grey, a man our father hasn't seen in ages, would suddenly show up in London and be visiting with his daughter?"

An amplified sense of dread and panic made Derek smack his brother's hand away from his mouth. "Bad things only happen if you will it. So cease willing it."

Miss Grey rounded on them from behind, her skirts rustling. "Not to argue the point, but I'm afraid bad things happen even if you don't will it, Mr. Holbrook."

Derek paused, capturing her gaze.

"When my father and I were in Spain a few months ago," she went on, "a bearded man tried to grab me at knifepoint outside of our hotel. Do you think I willed it? No. I didn't. Fortunately, my father took that man's head straight to the pavement and hit his skull enough times to paint it red. Apparently, he was a Prussian revolutionist who thought kidnapping me would somehow change a law he didn't agree with. That idiot is still in prison."

Derek stared. "You were almost kidnapped? At knifepoint?"

She nodded. "It happens quite a bit given who my father is. If it isn't a knife coming at us, it's a pistol. And if it isn't a pistol coming at us, it's a brick. As Papa says, people can't keep their opinions to themselves. But beside that, my point is, bad things happen. All the time. That is why I like to spend most of my days in my room painting. That way, I assure my own safety."

By God. Who was she?

Voices echoed, making them all turn in unison toward the now open bedchamber door.

A somber Mr. Grey emerged followed by his mother.

Lady Banfield's dark eyes solemnly darted over to Derek. She lingered, her hands clutching the sides of her indigo morning gown. Her pale face was mournful and her usually playful eyes were faded, the rims swollen and red from tears. All those brown, stiffly pinned curls that were routinely immaculate were frayed and lopsided, making her look much older than her seven and thirty years.

He stiffened. "Mother? Is Father—"

"He wishes to speak to you, Derek," she offered in a strained tone. "I have been advised by his doctor to call for a priest. Be prepared, my darling. Your father is having difficulty breathing and may not last beyond the night."

Derek stared, listening to his mother's words that made absolutely no sense. The longer he stared and tried to focus, the louder her words echoed in his own head. His father wouldn't last the night and was DYING. Everything momentarily blurred. He turned his gaze to the staggered gilded paintings of his ancestors and their calm, refined faces that lined the walls of the corridor. They seemed to smear. Mocking him.

"Quickly," his mother prodded. "He is waiting."

The doctors had to be wrong. They had to be. "What about Andrew?" he whispered.

His mother's voice softened. "You're the heir to the estate, Derek. Andrew will see him once all matters of the estate have been addressed. Now please. His strength isn't what it should be." She gestured toward the open door. "Go to him and close the door."

This wasn't real. His father must have been misdiagnosed.

Hurrying past his mother, Derek jogged to the open door where Mr. Grey still lingered. The choking stench of vomit, urine and mulled wine pierced his nostrils. Derek almost retched but forced himself to breathe in and out of his mouth to control it. Edging into the darkened room lit by lamps and candles, he closed the door.

The heavy curtains had been tightly drawn over the windows facing out to the garden.

Sparse light and dark shadows shifted across the massive four-poster bed displaying a grim, gaunt, sweat-ridden figure propped against a wall of pillows. His father stared out at him with hollow dark eyes, looking nothing like the strapping, jolly, and boisterous man Derek had last seen during Christmas and Twelfth Night holiday.

This was not his father. It was the ghost of what had been. Derek couldn't breathe. This was not recent. It had all been happening while they were away at school. His mother was either cruel or deeply misguided to have kept his father's illness a secret this long. Especially after countless years of calling in doctors when he wasn't ill at all.

Viscount Banfield, whose exposed arm was bandaged from bloodletting, weakly patted the space beside him with a pale hand. The lace-edged linen of his nightshirt fluttered with the movement. "Closer." His chest heaved. "We...we mustn't waste time."

Derek hurried past their family doctor, Mr. Shire, who folded a damp towel over a small handled porcelain bowl filled with fresh blood. Mr. Shire set the bleeding bowl onto a sideboard, wiped both hands onto a crimson-spattered apron and proceeded to gather various glass bottles of tonic which he organized back into his portable medicine chest.

Lingering beside the bed, Derek lowered his gaze to his father's veined hands that trembled as they unsuccessfully attempted to grasp the linen. His father, a fit, well-muscled man of four and forty, who only a few months earlier had been dancing, boasting and riding, couldn't even grasp the linens.

Glancing at the doctor, Derek choked out, "Isn't there any other medicine you can give him? There must be something more you can do."

Mr. Shire paused from fastening the medicine chest, his grey bushy brows coming together above his gold-rimmed spectacles. "I have done everything within my means."

Derek glared. "No. You haven't, sir. If you had done everything, he would be recovering. If you had done everything, he would be—"

"Derek, cease." The viscount dragged his linen up to his waist, his breaths wheezing. "You...you mean to hold him accountable? He cannot make me breathe."

Oh God. Derek tried to remain calm.

"Thank you, Mr. Shire," his father announced. "You may...may retire."

"I will remain close at hand, my lord." The doctor removed his apron, bundled it and took up his medicine chest. He left the room, closing the door.

His father gritted his teeth, his breaths uneven. "I have actually known about my condition for...for some time. I simply didn't want you and Andrew to...to worry." He drew in several more breaths. "I had your mother swear that...that she...she wouldn't...say anything. God knows how difficult it has been for her, especially with you...you boys in school." Sweat-soaked, shoulder-length dark hair clung to the sides of his father's flushed, unshaven face. He shifted. "The priest will be arriving within the hour. Do you...do you understand?"

Derek pinched his lips hard in an effort not to cry.

The viscount pointed. "Just because I'm dying before I have greyed...doesn't mean my life wasn't golden. So no tears. I...I don't want to see any tears." His gaze became penetrating and full of purpose. "I need you to be strong."

Derek's eyes burned as he struggled to obey. The pain of impending loss ripping at his chest was almost too vast to contain.

His father paused. "What happened to your...forehead?"

Derek swallowed, knowing that while he'd been romancing Miss Grey, his father had been in here suffering and unable to breathe. "I was being stupid. I earned it. It's nothing."

"Ah." His father crackled out a few phlegmy coughs, clearing his throat thickly before continuing. "Pardon my level of...of seriousness, but I...I wish to discuss a matter of importance regarding the estate."

Derek tried to focus but all he kept seeing were those trembling hands and that suffering, gaunt face. It haunted him. He was never going to know this great man in the way he always wanted to. Man to man. Over cards. Over brandy. Derek was graduating from Eton in only a few months. It meant nothing now.

"Are you...you listening?"

Derek searched his father's face. "Yes. I am."

"Sit."

Derek sat on the bed, angling closer.

The viscount smiled and held out a trembling hand.

Grasping that large cool hand, Derek met those tired dark eyes that still tried to smile. Derek struggled to maintain his composure as slightly larger fingers gripped his weakly. The skin was dry and overly rough. Nothing like the hand he'd arm-wrestled with during Twelfth Night months earlier.

The viscount shook Derek's hand. "For the sake of your mother and...and brother, be...be everything you are and...and more. As for Rupert, whom you have already met, he will be...be staying in London to assist you through the hardship my...my death will bring." His father pushed out several ragged breaths, shifting against the large pillow. "He will be contributing money to the...the estate over the next few years." His hold tightened and he smiled with quaking lips. "He has agreed to...to join our families. I wish to congratulate you on...on your betrothal to...to Miss Clementine Henrietta Grey."

Derek's heart skidded to a halt. Holy God.

"Mind you, she is still...very young. Only...fourteen."

Derek closed his eyes in disbelief knowing how he'd behaved. He'd thought she was closer to his own age and could handle it. No wonder she had panicked.

"Rupert insists that she...she wait beyond the typical debutante years to...to ensure she is well versed for her role as...as an aristocratic lady. You will therefore wait seven years until...until she is a full one and twenty."

Derek opened his eyes. His throat tightened, wondering how he was ever going to face Miss Grey again. "Who is Mr. Grey to you?"

"A dear friend." Several phlegmy coughs escaped him. His father cleared his throat and let out a gruff laugh. "'Tis a...a funny story as to how we met. Your mother and I...we...we were on our honeymoon out-side of Paris when the coach we were traveling in was robbed at...at gunpoint by a fellow who barely reached my...my shoulder." He smirked, clearly amused, even for the state he was in. "We were left with no money, no trunks and...and your mother's French...her French wasn't enough to save us. Fortunately, Rupert was at a...a tavern where we ended up. He assisted us. Sadly, with the amount of...of traveling he does, our close association has...has dwindled to mere letters. Rupert, you see, is a very...influential diplomat well known all over the world. Very important man." His father hesitated, dragging in more unsteady breaths. "This union will allow the estate, its lands and...and our legacy to survive difficult times. Do you...understand?"

Dearest God. "Is this about money?" Derek half-whispered in disbe-lief.

His father lowered his gaze and adjusted the linen. "It was my duty to ensure we...we all lived well. Perhaps we lived too well. Aside from our own expenses, none of...none of your cousins were ever capable of fi-nancially...supporting themselves. I had to...to bestow them all with yearly allowances and...and I'm afraid it depleted quite a bit of our funds."

Derek's eyes widened. "You've been giving yearly allowances to all eighteen of our cousins and their children? Father, how could you—"

"They are family, Derek. And...and we *always* take care of our family. No matter the burden it brings. I...I expect you to be as generous as...as I was. Continue to give whatever they...they need."

It was a mess. All of this. What defined need? A new house? A new carriage? His cousins weren't living in straw huts and starving. "Will Mr. Grey's assets even be capable of sustaining the burden of generosity you speak of?"

"More than capable." The viscount adjusted the bandage on his arm with trembling fingers. "Rupert is worth...well...an astounding amount.

You and he will negotiate the financial aspect of the…the marriage contract when it is time. He assured me it will be generous."

Derek fingered the middle button on his coat. "Does Miss Grey know of our union?"

"She was informed of it shortly before arriving in London." His tired eyes brightened. "Did you get a chance to…to meet her?"

He was such an arse. "Yes. I did meet her."

A small smile cracked those lips. "Respect her and…and your bond will be…unbreakable. My own marriage was…was arranged as well and it…it was…beautiful." His father hesitated. "Promise me that you will…you will honor this arrangement. Promise me."

Derek searched those ragged, pleading features. Just as his father had never denied him anything, he was not about to deny his own father peace. He loved the man too much. "Our families will become one."

A shaky breath escaped his father. "My secretary and…and solicitors will guide you until you come of age." He searched Derek's face. "You…you have always made me proud."

Derek's lip trembled, knowing his father was saying good-bye. Those words were too staggered and not at all reflective of the playful, witty man who raised him.

"Embrace your blessings and…and always take life with a smile."

A tear traced its way down Derek's cheek. He couldn't hold it in. A sob escaped him.

"Oh, now, now, none of that. You…you must live up to what I have given you. Honor me by…by showing the world you can laugh even at the worst times. As I have done." The viscount adjusted his head against the pillow in between rasping breaths. His mouth curved into a playful but broken smile. "Do tell me. Is Andrew still…still writing those female penny novels about romance and…and love? Has he started wearing a bonnet yet?"

A strangled laugh escaped Derek at the unexpected quip. "No. Not yet."

His father tsked in a manner an old woman would, wobbling his head. "I worry about that one. The Lower Master forever complains about...about him. Where is he? I...I want to see him."

A shaky breath escaped Derek. Opening the door, he stepped out of the room. Seeing his brother against the nearest wall, Derek managed, "He wishes to see you. His breaths are short and uneven. Try not to make him talk too much. I made him talk too much."

Andrew scrambled away from the wall and darted into the room.

Mr. Grey and his mother intently spoke to each other in grief-stricken whispers. Knowing his mother had kept this from him, regardless of his father's insistence was...unforgivable. All the hours and days and weeks lost. To school. To nothing. He should have been with his father.

Miss Grey quietly lingered barely a few feet away.

He swallowed hard and eased himself against the wall beside the door in an effort to remain standing. "I'm sorry about my earlier behavior, Miss Grey. I..." He dug deep into himself and smiled at her, even though he wanted to collapse and cry. "Who knew I was proposing to a girl who was already mine?"

She pulled in her chin. "You didn't know about our engagement?"

This was not how he imagined his life turning out. His eyes burned but he managed to keep his smile from wavering. "No. I didn't. I just found out."

She slowly wandered toward him and lingered before him. "Why are you smiling?"

Painful though it was, he broadened his lopsided smile. "Because as my father always says, grief only bites your soul if you let it."

She stared. "You are dishonoring your grief by even saying that."

Maybe. But it was how a Banfield had always handled a crisis: with a smile.

Unable to maintain his façade, he said, "Forgive me. I must go to him." He swung away and entered the darkness of his father's room so he didn't have to focus. Rounding the bed, he paused beside his brother and chanted to himself not to cry.

The viscount dragged in several uneven breaths and searched Andrew's face. "Do not remember me like this. For this is not...not who I am. I...I want you to remember the man who...who dances and...and laughs and...and..." His weathered lips parted as his shadowed eyes stared straight out and through them. "Andrew?" His father reached out. His trembling hand blindly drifted through the air between them. "Derek, I cannot see."

Andrew scrambled back.

Oh God. "Andrew, take his hand." Derek frantically grabbed his brother's hand and forced it into that outstretched hand. There was only one thing he knew he could do for his father. The one thing his father loved most. "Tell him a quip."

Andrew glanced up at him through tears, his eyes widening. "A quip?" he echoed.

"*A quip,*" Derek insisted. "You know how he loves them. Tell him anything you might have heard. Because I can't think of anything right now."

"I uh...know one." Stumbling against the side of the bed, Andrew tightened his hold on that hand and offered, "Two London girls living at the docks with their families had been sent by the kindness of the vicar's wife to have a happy day in the country. On their return and upon being asked about their experience the girls said, 'Oh yes, mum, we did 'ave a 'appy day. We saw three pigs killed and a gentleman buried. But sadly, no one died of the pox.'"

A gargled chuckle grabbed the air. "That is...this is by far the...the best quip yet," their father rasped with a smile, blindly touching Andrew's face with quaking fingers. "Bless you both for...for always...making me..." He unevenly sucked in breaths as his hand fell onto his chest. His eyes fluttered closed as he struggled to breathe. His chest quaked.

Derek edged closer. "Father?"

That chest rose and fell but his father otherwise didn't respond. It was as if his mind had drifted from his body. His breaths loudly wheezed and rasped.

Andrew laid his head on their father's arm.

They listened to those gasping breaths not knowing what to do. Their mother quickly came into the room, leaned over the bed and brushed away the damp hair clinging to their father's forehead.

Mr. Grey and his daughter lingered off to the side.

The priest soon entered, read words from the Bible in a monotone voice that promised salvation, and receiving no response other than wheezing breaths of Lord Banfield, he departed.

Their mother let out a sob, touching the hand hidden beneath the linen. "George?" she whispered. "George, do you hear me?"

He didn't respond. His breaths kept wheezing.

Derek edged away, his vision blurring as tears slipped down his face. Those breaths continued, yes, but the father he knew was gone. A part of him refused to forgive his mother knowing it. How could she have left their father to suffer like this alone?

Andrew swiped his reddened eyes with the sleeve of his coat and darted out of the room.

Their mother frantically looked around. Clapping a trembling hand against her mouth, his mother hurried out of the room and down the corridor. *"Dr. Shire!"*

It was a known fact that a Banfield never cried in front of anyone. They laughed, they danced, they played and maybe even shouted at a few people who deserved it, but everything else was reserved for when one was entirely alone. They usually suffered in silence and alone.

A male hand gripped his shoulder. Mr. Grey quietly walked over to his father's body that still quaked for breaths and gently laid a hand atop of that resting head. He drew in close and murmured something in that ear, as if sharing one last conversation with his friend. Slowly taking

NIGHT OF PLEASURE | 27

back his hand, he straightened and walking past Derek said, "I adored him." He blinked back tears and sniffed hard. "I'll be in London a few weeks to help you and your family through this. Whatever you need, it's yours."

Derek ruthlessly struggled to keep himself from crying before a man he didn't know.

Mr. Grey patted his shoulder one last time and strode past toward his daughter. "Tine, I will leave you to give your condolences to Mr. Holbrook. Meet me out in the corridor when you are done. We should let his family share their final moments alone with him." He left the room.

Miss Grey walked up to Derek. "I'm so sorry."

Derek didn't meet her gaze. He waited for her to leave the room. So he could cry.

She edged closer. Reaching up, she awkwardly embraced him with one arm, the scent of marzipan and soap filling his breath. She buried her head against him, her bonnet bumping into his chest. "I don't usually embrace people." She adjusted her arm against him. "But you need it."

The unexpected gesture and genuine warmth she offered despite the way he treated her made him bring his arms around her. He released a much-needed breath that kept him standing and savagely tightened his hold knowing his father would soon be gone. Unable to keep it in and feeling as if he could be himself in her arms, Derek sobbed and sobbed and sobbed. He dug his fingers harder into those soft shoulders, biting back the need to scream and felt as if he were betraying his father by letting out his grief. Even as a child of six, when he found himself wailing about skinning his knee, his father always nudged his chin up and said, *'If a tear could save the world, I would tell you to use it. But given it can't, I am telling you to save yourself and smile.'*

Miss Grey stiffened against him, her hands rigidly gripping at his school coat.

Realizing he was holding her too tightly, he loosened his grasp. "I'm sorry," he choked out against her bonnet. "I'm sorry about the way I treated you earlier. I didn't mean to—"

"I'm fine." She rocked him for a long moment, setting her cheek once again against his chest. "Don't apologize."

Something told him he was going to love this girl for the rest of his life. She cradled him as if he deserved it. He swallowed and tightened his hold again, settling into a sense of calm knowing what his future would bring: her.

They rocked each other in silence.

She eventually pried herself from his arms but didn't meet his gaze. "I'm so sorry for your loss, Mr. Holbrook. Losing a parent is never easy. I should know. I'll leave you alone with him. Please let my father know if you need anything." She quietly walked over to the door and lingered for a moment before her steps echoed down the corridor.

A gargled breath trembled from his father's body, startling Derek. Knowing his father needed him, he stumbled toward him. Sinking against the side of the bed, Derek grabbed his limp hand, his hands trembling in an effort to hold onto his father's warmth. "I know you always tell me to never cry. So don't think I'm dishonoring you. I'm not. I simply need to honor you in my way. And crying is my way of—"

A deep anguished sob escaped him knowing his perfect world wasn't perfect anymore. Perhaps it had never been. Perhaps the laughter they always shared in had hidden the worst in all of them. Regardless, it was now up to him to uphold the family name. For the world, for Andrew, for his mother and cousins, he would be what he was expected to be: strong, responsible and reliable. But for Clementine, he would be everything he already was and wanted to be: hers.

LESSON ONE

Meaning well and doing well are two very different things.

-The School of Gallantry

February 26, 1830 – early evening
Essex, England – The Banfield country estate

To the Right Honorable Viscount Banfield,
I regret to inform you that your brother owes me a substantial amount of money after a generous investment I made in the publication of his recent book. I thought I might solicit my original investment and humbly expect the full one thousand two hundred pounds to be delivered into my hands by the end of this month. If you choose to ignore this letter, or the amount owed, I will ensure your brother's crass association with the Duchess of Winchester will be made known in every last respectable circle. Her husband, from what I am told, is an excellent duelist well known for—

Derek didn't even bother reading the rest of Lord Trent's letter. He doubted he'd get anything more out of it. One would think after his own antics prior to their father's death, he'd be used to handling his brother's tomfoolery.

One would think.

Glancing at the closed door of the study, Derek Charles Holbrook, Viscount Banfield, tore the parchment in half. Tossing the torn missive into the flames of the hearth beside him, he watched the paper blacken and curl until it frayed into grey ash that collapsed against the coals.

He groaned. One thousand, two hundred pounds? Christ. He'd have to sell every horse in the stable, including the harnesses, the saddles, the whips, the hay, and all the help.

Air. He needed air. He needed—

Jogging across the study, he unhinged the iron latch and folded out the windows facing the open fields and frost-covered gardens below. A cold breeze laced with heavy flakes of snow drifted into the study. He dragged in a deep breath in a valiant attempt to focus.

Old lanterns creaked and swayed against the wind, dimly illuminating the vast walking grounds that were blanketed in white just beyond the ancestral home. An ancestral home that had been dependent all these years on Mr. Grey's generosity. A generosity Derek would never intrude upon by asking for more money even if he needed it. Because aside from the unending honor of marrying Clementine, he was also getting three million to do it.

He was still recovering from the amount.

Whilst his father had once been dubbed the 'Laughing Viscount,' Derek was now being dubbed the 'Golden Viscount' by snide audiences due to the ridiculous amount of money he'd soon be marrying into. Of course, those snide commentaries only made him hit his chest in pride, because he *was* golden. Hell, he was getting something not even three million could buy: Clementine.

Unseeing, Derek gripped the window frame, white-knuckled, as a cold breeze picked up strands of unbound shoulder-length hair and whipped it around his face. Swirls of heavy snowflakes stung his skin, fluttering the gold and crimson brocaded curtains that had decorated the window long before he was born.

Unbuttoning his evening coat, Derek latched the window shut. He pulled out a black ribbon from his inner pocket, then raked back and tied his hair tightly, adjusting his queue. Striding back over to the writing desk, he sat and eyed the pile of eight financial ledgers sitting crookedly atop each other. If he paid his brother's debt in full using whatever money he had, he wouldn't be able to pay the gamekeeper or the land agent who were both awaiting funds.

He'd done a piss-awful attempt of teaching Andrew about cause and effect. After their father died, he tried to be everything to his brother. Only it made Derek realize he'd taken his father's *noblesse oblige* too far.

He pushed all of the ledgers aside.

Seeing his square tin of ginger hard candies, he grabbed it and opened it. Empty. He'd already eaten them all and knew full well there was nothing left in the confectionary box where he usually stored extra. He groaned, tossing it back onto the desk and rose to his feet. He'd have to ride out to Stanwick's confectionary shop again and deal with all the women there. Women who didn't know how to keep their eyes and giggles to themselves. There was *nothing* wrong with a grown man liking candy.

The sound of running steps from down the corridor made him lift his head.

The door of the study rattled. "Derek?" Andrew called out. The door rattled again. "For God's sake, why is the door locked? What are you doing in there? *Flogging the bishop?*"

Derek glanced back at the locked door outlined by candlelight and rolled his eyes. As if he had time to masturbate anymore. Stripping off his evening coat, he flung it onto the chair and stalked over to the paneled door. Turning the key, he unlatched the bolt and yanked the door open, doing his best not to start yelling.

Andrew snapped out a letter with the wax seal facing up. "It's from Miss Grey. For it to have arrived at this time of night and by courier, no less, means it must be of *unmitigated* importance." Andrew grinned, those notorious dimples appearing on each of his lean, shaven cheeks. "Does she ever write anything naughty to you? And if so, do you oblige? Do you two fornicate through letters? Is that how you two—"

"Oh, for God's sake—" Derek snatched away the letter. "Her father reads all of the letters I send. So I can't readily frisk her with my own words. I have to keep it tame. Which is damn difficult, I assure you." Smoothing the parchment against the palm of his hand, knowing she had touched it, he carefully tucked it into his inner waistcoat pocket for later.

Andrew pointed. "Aren't you going to read it? She sent that by courier."

"She always sends her letters by courier."

"So you mean I could have left it on the side table and gone to bed?"

Derek huffed out a breath. "We need to talk."

Adjusting his coat to better display an expensive embroidered blue waistcoat, Andrew propped himself against the doorframe. "Of course. What would you like to talk about?"

"Your life."

"Am I in trouble again?"

"What do you think?"

Andrew hissed out a breath. "Whatever it is, I'm sorry. I didn't mean to do it."

Like hell he didn't. It wasn't the first married woman Andrew had gotten involved with. "I just finished going through all of the correspondences for the week. Lord Trent claims you're involved with the Duke of Winchester's wife. Is that true?"

Andrew groaned. "I haven't even been here a day. I was going to tell you."

It took every ounce of muscle in Derek's two arms not to grab his brother by the lapels of that coat and shake him until his brass buttons fell off. "Can I ask *why* I'm always the very last to know anything?"

"You're not the very last. Mother is. Besides, it happened *months* ago. It isn't even worth talking about."

Derek swiped his face to maintain composure. "So you bedded her."

"I thought we were in love. But then I found out…we weren't."

"Andrew, what the hell are you doing? Aside from the fact she is married, her husband is the Prime Minister's left hand!"

"I know! Don't you think I know?! She called on me, after we met at a gathering her husband hosted and we…*it happened.*"

Derek slowly shook his head. "I don't even know how Lord Trent knows about your involvement with the duchess, but he plans to expose you if I don't pay the investment he made into your career. And I'm not paying him. Even if I had the means to – which I don't – I wouldn't. Because you would learn nothing if I dig you out of this mess. It's all I ever do for you these days. Dig, dig, dig. I might as well be walking around with a bloody shovel."

Andrew squinted. "He says I owe him money?"

"Over a thousand. What in God's name are you doing with all the money I'm sending you from the estate every month? You get more than enough to— Why are you borrowing money from titled men? Can you answer me that? Why?"

"I already paid him. Hell, I had to borrow money from *another* titled man to do it."

Jesus. "If you paid him, then why is he saying you didn't?"

Andrew rolled his eyes. "Because he's a damn Boretto man in desperate need of attention, is what."

"Last I knew I don't speak Italian. What the hell is a Boretto man?"

"You're older than I am. How could you not know what a Boretto man is?"

"Don't chastise me or I'll put your head under my arm and twist."

Andrew sighed. "It's an older gent who fancies young men."

Derek's lips parted. "Lord Trent is a sodomite?"

"Has been for years."

"And how the devil do you know that?"

"Aside from a few unwanted advances? Brayton told me."

"Brayton? Who the hell is Brayton?"

Andrew touched his head. "Sorry. Lord Brayton and I started sharing living quarters about a week ago after Trent had asked me to take him in given there appears to be a family feud of some sort. I haven't known this Brayton long, seeing he just got into London, but *bloody hell* you should see the man. He makes criminals with pistols cross the street. Apparently, he was living in various monasteries around the world and got tired of it. He hasn't been around women in twenty years. And it shows. It's hilarious."

Only in London. "So you don't owe Lord Trent any money?"

"No. That three-legged ingénue is merely upset that I refused his offer of becoming his mistress." He sighed. "He gets jealous of my associations with women all the time. It results in stupid threats, but he never follows through on any of them. Leave it to me. I'll talk to him."

Derek stared. "Are you and he involved?"

His brother gave him a withering look. "I'd sooner stick my cock into a hornet's nest. Do I look a male pillow to you?"

"I'm getting tired of being the last to know *everything*. We're not brothers. I'm your goddamn criminal lawyer." Derek shifted from boot to boot and glared. "Who else are you associating with these days? Who else do you owe money to? Because I'd like to write this all down. For future reference."

Andrew searched his face. "You seem...tense. Did something happen? Are you all right?"

It was clearly time to let this go. Because Andrew always did what Andrew wanted to do. And as long as the city wasn't burning, who was he to care? Derek adjusted the ribbon on his queue. "I'm just tired. I've been putting in a lot of hours trying to organize all the ledgers before April."

"Why before April? What happens in April?"

"You aren't the only one who has secrets. Mr. Grey finally let me set the date for the wedding." He flashed a smile. "I'm getting married this April. And you're the first to know it."

Andrew snapped straight. "Oh, damn. You don't say? Well...congratulations." He hesitated. "Are you still concerned about your lack of experience? Or did you finally gain some?"

Derek awkwardly stepped back. "I ended up hiring a woman when I was back in London." He had to. He couldn't very well be a virgin to a virgin and unleash all of his passions on her like a wild animal in need of raw meat.

His brother angled closer. "You hired a prostitute?" he demanded loud enough for his voice to echo throughout the corridor and beyond. "Whatever happened to your vow of never touching another but Miss Grey?"

Derek shoved him and glanced toward the corridor behind them. "Jesus. *Quiet.* Are you trying to announce my sins to the world?"

"You needn't worry. Mother retired over an hour ago." His brother quieted his voice. "You didn't pick up a random woman off the street, did you?"

"What do you take me for? An idiot in need of the pox? I went over to a high-end establishment on Moon Street. They ensure the women are clean and more importantly, they let me bring my own condom. Because I sure as hell don't trust theirs. They barely wash them."

Andrew pulled in his chin. "I went there myself not that long ago. Hopefully, we didn't ride the same goddamn horse or I'll—" He shuddered. "Her name wasn't Nancy, was it?"

Derek rolled his eyes. "No. Her name was Elizabeth."

"Thank *God.* Or I'd gag." Andrew's mouth quirked playfully as if he'd already moved on. "You should have bypassed the grotto and gone straight to the duchess. It would have been free and she comes with a long list of instructions."

Unbelievable. There could be a knife to his brother's throat and he'd still make a joke of it. Andrew was definitely their father's son. Because when the weight of responsibility threatened to choke *him*, Derek didn't have it in him to laugh quite as easily. That was who he used to be. He'd long since learned that being stupid at the wrong time came at a high price.

Turning on his heel, Derek strode back to his desk and shook his head. "Let me know when you're interested in being serious." Trying to distract himself, he dug out Clementine's letter from his waistcoat, broke the seal, and unfolded the parchment, square by square. "I'll acknowledge you in the morning. I have a letter to read."

It had been almost eight months since he'd heard anything from her. *Eight.* He was beginning to worry that his last letter had been overly amorous. Of course, they all were. He called her 'beautiful' and 'dearest' and gushed on and on about how he couldn't wait to see her. He even signed it 'My whole heart goes out to fetch you.' He couldn't help it. He had been sharing all of his personal thoughts with her since he was eighteen. And the best part? She genuinely listened. Even if she didn't always reply in a timely manner.

Andrew seated himself on the edge of the mahogany desk with a long hefty breath, clearly intent on staying. "Women exhaust me."

"Are you certain you aren't exhausting them?" Derek tossed back.

Andrew snorted and straightened the haphazard pile of ledgers with the back of his hand. "It's not like you would understand. You've never been involved with a woman."

"You forget who you're talking to. I was kissing women long before you even knew what a kiss was." Derek sat and turned Clementine's letter over in his hand, admiring the way she wrote his name and address.

"I can't believe you actually hired a prostitute. You waited seven years and couldn't wait another few months?"

Derek tried not to feel guilty. "I just didn't want to bumble my way through my own wedding night." He bit back a knowing smile. "It was a hands-on five hour tutorial on what would make Miss Grey moan. Very educational." He tilted back in his leather chair. "Now if you don't mind, I need a few moments to read this. All right?"

He snapped the letter straight. That elegant script he adored and knew all too well lured him into her world. The suffocating burdens of the estate and everything expected of him by the world fell away as he imagined Clementine's voice. It was a voice he hadn't physically heard since 1823, but one he still remembered as if she'd spoken to him yesterday.

Dear Banfield,

Your last letter took some time to reach me, given I was traveling again. It must have been lost as there are half a dozen postmarks, and signs of enough wear to indicate it might have traveled to the moon. I was happy to receive it, along with all of your warm thoughts. I was very sorry to hear that your poor mother's cat died after being mauled by a neighbor's dog. It would seem not even our cats are safe in this world. Please pass along my condolences, which I will be able to offer in person soon. As you well know I will be leaving New York in a few weeks, for which I am most grateful. I have never been all that fond of Broadway Society as the people here seem to think their money makes them right. By the time you receive this letter, I will already be en route to London and if the weather is fair and willing, Father says we should arrive in early April. I look forward to seeing you again after all these years. There is certainly a lot for us to discuss.

Sincerely,

Clementine Henrietta Grey

He grudgingly folded the letter. Twice. All of her previous letters had been much warmer and chattier. He couldn't quite make it out, but it was as if she had cooled to him. He'd waited eight long months to hear from her – *eight* – only to receive a mere 'Sincerely' and a 'There is certainly a lot for us to discuss.' In his opinion, there wasn't anything to discuss. He was going to damn well tongue the lips off that woman the moment they were alone.

Opening the drawer filled with all of her letters, he set her latest atop his regulated pile and paused at seeing the oval miniature portrait she'd sent. Painted blue eyes peered up at him. Black ringlets of long hair framed her pale face, accentuating the detailed brush strokes against the small canvas. The first time he'd seen it, he'd stared at it for hours unable to believe she'd grown even more beautiful.

Andrew leaned across the desk. "Why not pull her portrait out and set it on your desk?"

Derek slammed the drawer shut. "I stare at it enough already."

A bright mockery invaded that stare. "Admit it. You were soft for her from the moment you and she met."

That was a fucking understatement. Over the years, he'd grown to not only mindlessly yearn for her but had come to genuinely love her for always letting him write whatever words he needed to. Good days. Bad days. And everything in between. Her letters, though not as many as his own, insinuated she had become everything he had always imagined her to be. Intelligent, witty, overly proper and kind. Everything that made his blood zing. The memorable ten weeks they spent together back in '23 carried him through every single one of these seven years. On their last day together, when she set her own pale cheek and a gloved hand against the carriage window in quiet farewell, it hinted at what their married life would be: absolutely darling. Like her.

Andrew rumbled out a laugh. "Oh, come now. There is no need to look so depressed. Being soft isn't always a bad thing. It simply means—" He let out a whistle and veered his forefinger down onto the desk. He hit it. "You're no longer in control. She is."

Derek leaned back against his leather chair. "That is exactly what I'm afraid of. I'm marrying a woman worth eighteen million. How the hell does a man impress a woman who has everything?"

His brother shifted against the edge of the desk and methodically removed a piece of lint from his trousers. "By giving her the one thing no amount of money can buy: a cock full of Banfield seed."

Derek burst into laughter. "You ought to be arrested for your way of thinking."

Andrew grinned. "I learned from the best. Something tells me she'll be pregnant in less than two weeks. If it's a boy, name it after me. If it's a girl, still name it after me. Call her *Andrewlina*."

Derek swiped his face at the thought, rose to his feet and walked toward the window before swinging back. "She won't even be here in two weeks. I'm telling you, the wait is burning me alive."

"Tickle her portrait and you'll be fine." Sliding off the desk, Andrew tugged on the sleeves of his coat. "Unfortunately, I have to retire. I'm heading back to London in the morning. I promised Brayton I'd show him around the city." He sighed. "What time is it?"

Derek glanced at the clock on the mantle of the hearth. "After midnight. I have to get up early and finish going through the ledgers. Again. I'm going to hire a new bookkeeper because none of the ledgers are making sense." Trudging over to the desk again, Derek opened the drawer where he kept all of Clementine's letters and rifled through them, plucking out his favorite. The one where she described New York during the winter. He tucked it into his waistcoat pocket, to take upstairs with him, then pulled out her small portrait, tucking that in his pocket, as well. He liked sleeping with her portrait. It was better than a pillow. He closed the drawer and pointed at his brother. "You didn't see that."

Andrew walked toward him. "By God. You're more than soft for her."

Derek edged back. "Maybe. What of it?"

His brother shrugged. "I'm not poking you in the rib about it. I'm incredibly happy knowing the arrangement turned into something meaningful to you. Most men end up grouching about whatever their parents arrange. So uh..." He cleared his throat. "I actually have my own announcement to make. I was going to wait until morning, but I can't." Andrew edged in, a boyish excitement overtaking his features. "Out of all the people in my life, you're the only one who never shuts the door. No matter what I do. Hell, if it weren't for you, Mother would have disowned me by now. You keep all of my secrets. Every last one. Even the worst of them."

Now he was scared. He leaned back. "Are we talking about the worst here?"

"Far from it." Andrew glanced toward the open doorway and lowered his voice. "I've *finally* met the woman I was destined to meet. I'm talking about a woman who reaches deep into your being and dredges out things from your soul you didn't even know existed."

It was as if his brother was referring to Satan. "Do I know this woman?" he drawled.

"No. But I was hoping you'd be willing to meet her. Do you have time to come out to London in the next two weeks and host a luncheon for her and her mother? It would mean the world to me." He sounded hopeful.

By the Saints. His brother had never asked him to meet any of his women. Maybe this was it. Maybe his brother was finally going down the respectable path of being a married man. *Amen.* Derek grinned, reached out and shoved that head. "I'd love to meet her. Why the hell didn't you tell me about her sooner? Who is she?"

"I don't think our mother should know about her quite yet."

Derek's grin faded. "So you're saying Mother wouldn't approve."

"You know how she is. Prim and proper this and prim and proper that. Like everyone else in our circle. She would never understand.

You're the only one I can trust in this." Andrew hesitated. "If I show you something, do you vow not to tell Mother or anyone else about it?"

This was anything but promising. "I really don't think—"

"Do you vow?" Andrew pressed. "On your golden name?"

He was too soft. Derek thudded a fist to his chest. "It stays here. What is it?"

Eyeing him, Andrew pushed up his coat sleeve and linen shirt, exposing the skin beneath. Raised uneven welts that created the word MENTULA were burned across his inner arm. It appeared fresh and was Latin for...

Fear scrambled Derek's mind and innards. A shaky breath escaped him as his gaze snapped to his brother's face. "What the hell are you doing to yourself? What is this?"

Pulling down the linen sleeve and the coat, Andrew grinned. "It's my promise to her. I let her burn it into me. Hurt like hell but it was worth it."

"You let her burn the word PENIS into your arm?"

Those eyes widened. "*Penis?* No, no. Mentula is an endearment. I asked."

Derek snorted. "It is *not* an endearment but an insult. Have you ever read the texts of Priapeia?"

Andrew glared. "So you're better read than I am. What of it?"

"What of it? Jesus, I'm trying to— What rational woman burns a man's arm with the word penis and claim it's an endearment?"

"She—" Andrew cleared his throat. Twice. "A few weeks ago, I hired this incredible birch mistress out of an exclusive brothel I'd never been able to get into until now. Her name is Elsa. And I love her."

Derek's eyes widened. "You're in love with a birch mistress you just met?"

"Ey, now, real passion, when one finds it, burns fast. Not everyone can be like you and let things simmer for seven years." Andrew pointed to the sideboard. "Can I have a drink?"

Saint's blood. Maybe *he* needed a drink. "You're one and twenty, Andrew. You don't need my permission to drink."

"Amen for that." Striding over to the sideboard, Andrew pulled out a decanter of brandy and a glass. He filled it, tossed it back and set the glass down with a hard chink. "You would like her. I know you would. Much like you, she loves to fence and is incredibly good at it."

Derek dragged in a breath. He'd never met a birch mistress, but he'd heard more than enough about the strength of their arms to make his cock shrivel and invert. He had to get his brother out of this. Any woman burning the word penis on a man's arm meant she would most likely slice it off next. "We need to talk."

Andrew swung toward him, his features hardening. "Don't give me that."

Derek sighed. When it came to his brother, he always had to appeal to sensibilities the boy didn't have. "Andrew, setting aside your own safety, and whatever is left of your arm, society would damn well turn its full wrath and judgment against our mother, Miss Grey, and every female ever born and related to the Banfield name. Including all of our female cousins, many of them who are looking to get married. What are you doing?"

Andrew was quiet for a moment. "I was going to ask her to marry me."

Christ. "You can't marry a-a...*birch mistress.* Never mind what society will think, our poor mother would ask for a blade to fall upon. She can't even say the word 'kiss' without going into convulsions."

His brother closed his eyes. "Elsa isn't a whore. She doesn't have sex with men. Even I haven't had that privilege. Men hire her for torture. Nothing more."

He couldn't believe his brother was rationalizing torture. "You've lost your mind."

Andrew opened his eyes, a calm settling over his features. "No. I've found it. Through physical pain, I have finally learned to better understand and appreciate my own blessings."

Mother of heaven. Andrew didn't know what he was talking about. No one knew him better than he did. As a boy Andrew would wail if a splinter so much as touched his finger and refused to even wrestle, saying it was too rough for him in nature. Never mind the woman being a prostitute, his brother was about to permanently shackle himself to the art of pain. He had to do something. He had to— "No. I'm sorry but this is…no. This is not who you are. And I won't have some woman erasing your mind by making you think burning the word mentula on your arm is normal. Because it's not. Hell, if I had to guess, she is taking advantage of you. You're the brother of a titled gentleman bringing in close to a thousand a year. And that measly thousand, as you damn well know, will become a full ten thousand once I marry Miss Grey and increase your yearly annuity. Does this woman know this?"

Andrew didn't meet his gaze. "Maybe."

"*Maybe*? Did you or did you not tell her about your finances?"

"Yes. I did. All right? I did. What of it?"

Shite. "Is that why you've been borrowing funds? Because you're giving *her* funds?"

Andrew still didn't meet his gaze. "I'm assisting her with sizable debts."

A cold knot formed in Derek's stomach. His brother always gave too much of himself to the world. And sadly, too many people took advantage of that. "You can't keep doing this to yourself. You can't let women— You're done with this." He pointed at his brother, his ability to stay calm waning. "You are *not* to see her again. Or I will bloody have her arrested for what she did to your arm. Do you understand? I want her name and the address of this establishment. Now."

Andrew's startled face snapped toward him. "Why? What do you plan to do?"

"I plan to take a carriage to London and talk to whoever the hell she is working for. Because it's fairly obvious by her *endearment* and the money she is confiscating from you that she is taking advantage of your affections. Like all the others."

Andrew angled toward him, intently searching his face. "She isn't like the others."

"This isn't the first time you've been financially swindled by a woman. I can easily name ten others. Remember Miss Lester? That shop girl you fell madly in love with and who needed a hundred pounds? After you gave it to her, did you ever see her again? No. She disappeared and never even bothered to give you a reason why or a thank you."

"This is different."

"No. Forgive me, Andrew, but it's rather obvious your heart needs a new chest if you think it acceptable to be burning and whipping yourself in the name of impressing a woman. Because I know you. You weep at the sight of blood. Marry a birch mistress, indeed."

Those dark eyes flared. "Yes, well, unlike your spoiled ruby American heiress, she doesn't hold out a hand. She bloody smacks it."

Derek shifted his jaw, feeling a muscle ticking angrily in it, and edged toward his brother until they were boot to boot and almost nose to nose. "Are you insulting my woman? To my face, no less?"

"You insulted my woman first."

Derek didn't move. "End it. Or I will."

His brother stared him down. "I thought you, of all people, would stand by me in this."

"You thought wrong. I'm not supporting your damnation."

Andrew shoved past, slamming Derek with his shoulder. He stalked toward the open door of the study. "Tell Mother I'll see her in two weeks. I'm heading back to London tonight. I'm not staying here. I can't."

Derek swung toward him, his throat tightening. "Andrew, how can you not understand my concerns? When it comes to women, you're— *irrational.*"

A hand snapped up. "Yes, I suppose it must be nice to know Miss Grey is all yours without you having to try."

That stung. Derek stalked after him. "Don't you bloody toss that at me! I've stood by you in everything. You damn well know that! But you can't expect me to—"

"No. I suppose I can't." Andrew came to a halt. "Which is why it's time I stand on my own. I'm asking that you not send me any more money from the estate. Because I will admit, you are right. I'm not handling my finances well and spend far more than I should. But I'm done with that. I'm asking that you hold onto all my money for a full year. Invest it for me. That way, when Elsa and I are ready to start a family next year, I will have a sizable investment to work with."

Derek quickly made his way toward him. "How the hell are you going to live if I invest all of your money? You'll need *something* for monthly expenses."

"My novels will pay for that."

Derek's eyes widened. *"How?!* You haven't sold any in months. It would be like me wanting to make money off the paintings I used to do when I was twelve."

Andrew set his shoulders. "I appreciate the moral support. I wish you the best at your wedding, and I'm sorry I won't be there." He swung away and disappeared out into the corridor, his steps angrily hammering farther and farther away.

Derek seethed out a breath and jogged out into the corridor, skidding to a halt. "Now you're just being bloody spiteful. I'm trying to give you sound advice. I'm trying to—"

"Like always, Derek, you are only trying to run roughshod over my life and everyone else's. Why are you trying to control us when you know that isn't who we are?" Andrew kept walking. "Go back to your superior way of thinking and your superior way of life that includes your superior American princess. I'll simply head back over to the large steaming pile of shite I made for myself and roll around in it."

"Why are you always so goddamn— *Where are you going?* We need to sit down and talk about how marrying this woman is going to—"

"Going to what?!" his brother yelled, swinging toward him, his eyes ablaze. "Plunge me into hell because I'm looking to make a respectable woman out of someone you and the rest of society thinks is a whore? Well, what if I were to tell you that I was the real whore here? Not Elsa, but I? And what if I were to tell you *this* particular whore wants a better life outside of all the beds he's been rolling around in since he was eighteen? What then?"

Derek swallowed. "I never called her a whore. Not once. And you damn well know it."

"Invest the money for me," Andrew bit out. "In the meantime, don't bloody call on me with your lectures. You're not my father." His brother swung away and disappeared.

Derek fell against the nearest wall and stared up at the gold-painted ceiling far above his head. They were alike in so many ways. The only difference was that he'd been fortunate enough to have been born heir and handed everything he could ever want. An impending great fortune of three million, a title, good health, the respect of everyone in his circle, a brother he could always confide in, a mother who thought the world of him, cousins who thought the world of him. And Clementine. A beautiful woman who was about to change his life by gifting him with the one thing he'd always wanted: a family of his own.

Not the one his father had envisioned for him. No. But the one he envisioned. Where his son could cry in his arms whenever he needed to without being scolded. Where his daughter could come to him and admit to wanting to be a scientist without being scolded. And where his wife embraced him, not because of an arranged marriage that required her to, but because she wanted and needed to be in the only place she had ever truly belonged: in his arms.

LESSON TWO

When you finally meet the person you are destined

to spend the rest of your life with, do not panic.

Unless, of course, it is warranted.

-The School of Gallantry

London, England – in a carriage on its way to the Banfield House at Grosvenor Square
April 26th, 1830, late afternoon

The precise moment as to when Clementine Henrietta Grey's life had become a jaded fairy tale would have been at birth. She was, after all, the eldest and *only* child out of eleven to have been born breathing. As such, her father ensured every breath she took was of immense value. He certainly had the means to afford it.

Her father, Mr. Rupert William Grey, was renowned throughout all of New York, Madrid, Moscow, Paris and Hamburg as 'The Commander of all Political Assets,' capable of putting any man into governmental power. He had held that golden chalice of esteem since 1810, after he had turned a sizable investment of half a million into an astounding two

49

million. It wasn't planned. After getting drunk one afternoon, he signed papers he shouldn't have, letting his broker overinvest in the wrong stock. Fortunately, it resulted in the largest payout the stock exchange had ever seen. He'd been investing in stocks and large parcels of land all over New York City and the world ever since, growing his sizable fortune one crisp dollar at a time until it came to be what it was today: eighteen and a half million.

Ever since her father's financial assets had more than tripled over the years, everyone's interest in *her* had tripled over the years. Men from all over the world had been calling on her father in a desperate effort to appeal for a matrimonial arrangement that might put Grey assets into their lint-filled pockets.

But her father, bless his dear misguided heart, was determined to marry her off to a mere third generation viscount in desperate need of money. Her father was deeply sentimental. He had adored his now deceased friend, George, the former viscount, and wanted their families to become one. He had always claimed the Banfields were the definition of happiness and perfection and what a family needed to be.

She respected her father's sentimentality, but knew happiness and perfection was a matter of opinion. Her father *claimed* to have had the perfect marriage. Yet almost every silk wall in their house had to be repeatedly replaced over the years from all of the objects that had been smashed against them. He and his wife ruthlessly argued about everything for years.

Until the woman died.

Clementine remembered that night. Her mother's sobs and shrieks could be heard throughout the house, much like the year before and the years before that, as her father had quietly assured Clementine yet again that there would finally be a brother or a sister for her to hold. He assured her that out of the countless babes that had been lost this one would survive and allow them to create the happy family they always deserved.

NIGHT OF PLEASURE | 51

Her father had been overly hopeful. Neither the babies or the happiness had survived. And though it was ghastly to even whisper it, Clementine was glad her mother didn't survive. She had never liked her mother. The woman was cold in both mind and heart and had wobbled around pregnant year after year, bitterly blaming her father and the rest of the world for the fact that she was a woman. Was it part of life for a woman to get married and get pregnant? Yes. Yes, it was. Could a woman aspire to be more than a wife and a mother? Yes. Yes, she could.

She simply had to plan for it.

Thunder cracked overhead, causing Clementine to jump against the cushioned seat of the carriage. Her heart skidded, and, for a gasping moment, she was crawling beneath the breakfast table as a brick came crashing through the window of their New York home.

She hated the feeling of having her emotions amplified.

At least here in London no one knew who they were. Her father had no political affiliation with the Whigs or the Tories or Parliament itself. That made her like the idea of London very much. No one was going to try to kill them for supporting the wrong political party.

Not that she was going to stay in London long enough to care.

She glanced toward the blackened sky beyond the windows. Large drops of rain slowly splattered and tapped against the glass. Within a few breaths, the window was smeared from a deluge and the cobbled street they rode on became a blur of water spraying everywhere as people draped their coats over their heads and darted beneath building doorways.

Tightening her gloved hold on the beaded reticule set in her lap, Clementine glanced toward her father.

His horsehair top hat was pushed back from his dark brows as he casually angled the leather bound book he was reading toward the glass window in an effort to get better light despite the dark sky. He turned the page and kept reading, squinting at the text.

"You shouldn't read with so little light," she commented.

"Don't nag me, dear." He attempted to lessen his squint by holding the book further away from himself. He angled his head and squinted all the same.

She lowered her chin. "If I didn't nag you, you wouldn't have any eyes left in your head. Where are the reading glasses I bought for you?"

"Tine, I'm far too young for reading glasses. I'm only fifty-two." He kept reading.

He was such a child. He always had been. By all accounts, he really shouldn't have been allowed to raise a daughter. He consumed more cognac than any human ought to gulp and shared all of his cheroots with her as if they were bonbons. Even worse, his political alliances with un-popular men he financially supported usually resulted in someone want-ing them dead.

Another crack of thunder made her jump.

He lifted his gaze, revealing sharp blue eyes. "Are you all right?"

She let out an exasperated breath. "Yes. I'm fine." Annoyingly, thun-derstorms reminded her of angry mobs. And in particular, one stormy night three years ago when a group of riled men had broken into their home and tried to smash everything after her father supported a Catho-lic man who had been elected mayor. It was the first time she'd ever fired a pistol. And the last. She wasn't very good at aiming and had shot holes into everything but the men destroying her home. She had far bet-ter luck using vases against their heads. "Thunderstorms unnerve me, is all."

He slapped his book shut and set it on the upholstered seat beside him. "I imagine seeing Banfield again is what really unnerves you."

That much was true. She had been writing letters to Banfield since she was fourteen, after she had left England to go back to New York back in '23. And with every passionate letter he wrote, she couldn't help but linger on the memory of an overly-flirtatious young man with play-ful brown eyes who, from their first meeting, seemed wildly intent and overly eager to make her his to the point of sending her into a panic.

Whilst his letters had proven to reflect that he had matured and grown into an intelligent man, he simply expected too much. She repeatedly tried to tame him over the years through letters by getting him used to the idea that they were merely companions assigned to a lifelong duty (which she planned to abandon) but it only resulted in him stubbornly signing all of his letters with '*My whole heart goes out to fetch you*'. Unlike him, she wasn't one to gush about her emotions. In her eyes, such uncontained passion led to very bad things. She only hoped Banfield was prepared to accept the truth she was set to deliver: they weren't getting married.

Her father sat up, dug into his coat pocket and removed the silver casing holding his cheroots. Snapping it open, he held the case out. "Did you want one?"

She stared at it, wanting to say yes, but promised herself she wouldn't. She'd grown a bit too dependent on the habit and as a result, smoked every time something bothered her. Which pushed her through *a lot* of cheroots. "No, thank you. I shouldn't."

Her father slid one out. Sticking it into the corner of his mouth, he shoved the silver casing back into his pocket and dug out a flint and a match. Striking the match, he cupped the flame to the end of his cheroot and puffed. "All of the wedding arrangements have already long been taken care of by Banfield and his mother. From my understanding, you'll be getting married this upcoming Monday."

She sat up. "*What?*"

He chuckled. "No need to panic. We will manage. Banfield got ahead of himself in planning everything. We were supposed to arrive earlier in the month and the boy was overly excited. Let him be. I find it charming."

What was so charming about a man shoving aside all etiquette by not including his own bride in any of the formalities involved? A bride who wasn't even going to be at the wedding. Gad. It was a mess. She still didn't know how she was going to tell her father about it.

Waving away the flame to extinguish the match, her father tossed the burnt stick into an ash pan attached to the seat and dragged in a long breath before letting smoke out through his nostrils and mouth. "Whilst I don't doubt Banfield invited a jolly bunch, maybe we ought to have the footmen deliver invitations to random doors throughout London and see who shows up. Wouldn't that be fun?"

Her father's idea of fun had always been the opposite of her own. "Yes, and why not invite the Zoological Society, including the animals themselves? At least that way we would know what to expect from all of our guests when they arrive."

He wagged the cheroot at her. "Stop nagging. Can't the father of the bride have ideas?"

"When they belong to you, I worry."

"Yes, yes, and I love you, too. I'm certainly not going to miss all of your spoilsport nagging. Banfield can have it."

She tightened her hold on her reticule. "Begging your pardon, Mr. Grey, but my nagging kept your hands out of the sideboard all these years."

He grunted. "Men drink, Tine. It's what we do."

"No. It's what you do. Because rational men don't drink four decanters of cognac in the middle of the day then stumble around looking for more. You may think me to be naïve, but I'm not *that* naïve. I was the one who pulled every drink from your hand since I was ten. Every drink. And you know it."

Her father said nothing. He rolled the cheroot in his hand, staring down at it.

It was like seeing the broken man she grew up with. She softened her voice. "You are doing infinitely better."

He shrugged. "I'm trying."

She reached out across the distance between them and touched his knee to acknowledge his pain. She wasn't one to give affection, even to her own father, but whenever he needed it (like he clearly did now), she delivered. "I know you're trying, Papa. And I'm very proud of you for that. You haven't faltered in over eighteen weeks."

He cleared his throat. "About that. I uh…I drank some cognac with Banfield yesterday. More than I should have. He offered it during contract negotiations. I felt awkward saying no."

She groaned. "Papa. You didn't have to drink it just because he offered it."

He winced. "I know. I…" He puffed out a breath, deflating both cheeks. "Fortunately, I didn't let it get out of hand. I stopped myself right after I emptied a full decanter."

Which, sadly, was light drinking for her father. She sighed. "So now I have to worry about you again? Is that what you're telling me?"

"No. I'm fine. My valet knows to keep all the decanters filled with water and I already paid off everyone in the hotel to ensure they don't service me anything stronger than tea."

That was something.

The carriage rolled to a halt, causing her to sway against the movement. The torrential rush of rain drowned out all sound. She paused and glanced toward a looming four-story aged limestone home bordered with iron black gates bearing a crest of a sword placed over a sprig of heather. Footmen holding umbrellas scurried to open the gates.

The carriage rolled through, drawing closer to the massive limestone home beyond.

She leaned toward the window, her lips parting. Ivy, living and dead, covered most of the limestone and fingered the very sills of each narrow window. It made the house look old. Not at all what she remembered. Set against a thick, dark sky heavy with rain, the structure had no welcoming light glowing through any of the countless windows. It was like visiting a cemetery. "This isn't Banfield's house, is it?" She tried not to sound appalled.

"Yes. It's his London residence. Don't you remember? We visited him almost every day for ten weeks back in '23."

Most of the ivy had not only grown but died. Despite what her father thought, she remembered the house very well. She remembered it being so much more inviting and manicured. Perfect. Not this. "Have you been sending him money?"

"Of course I have."

The unkempt dead ivy said otherwise. "How much?"

"Clementine, please. You make it sound like I've been neglecting the boy."

She pointed at the house. "Something has clearly been neglected. How much have you been sending him? I have a right to know."

"A full thousand every June, every year. Why?"

"*Only a thousand a year?* Papa, how did you expect him to upkeep a house like this and a house in the country on a thousand? My clothes cost me more than that. How—"

"He never asked for more. If he had, I would have gladly given it. I simply didn't want him to think he had access to unlimited funds until the marriage contracts were signed." He lowered his voice. "As popular as he has always been in his circle, he could have very well taken off with someone." He paused. "Don't tell him I said that."

She wished to God she had been more aware of the funds he'd been distributing to Banfield. Her father, whilst generous, had a tendency to get protective of his money. "He is the son of your closest and dearest friend whom you swore to protect from ruin. How could you—"

"Don't lecture me, Tine. He is getting three million in return for your hand. *Three million.* That is how I am honoring and protecting the boy. As for you, Miss Clementine Henrietta Grey, I damn well hope you're no longer associating with that Persian nonconformist. It was fine to socialize with him as a friend back in New York but you're about to be a married woman. And married women don't align themselves with Persian bachelors."

She decided not to say anything. That Persian nonconformist, after all, was her closest and dearest friend who was going to ensure she hopped on the next boat to Persia. She glanced toward the old Georgian house. An old house that dredged up memories she wasn't ready to face. She could almost taste him through that spiced candy that had burned her mouth well enough to make her think she still tasted it. All of her fears, all of her emotions and all of her buried insecurities unfurled itself into the one thing she never expected: Banfield.

Her throat tightened.

It was why she was leaving him. She was a woman of control and he was a man of no control. Their union would never amount to anything but the misery she grew up with. Lowering her gaze, she opened her reticule and dug out her personal silver case of cheroots she always carried. She promised herself she wouldn't smoke, but how else was she going to survive the afternoon? She needed it.

Flipping open the monogrammed casing, she pulled one out. "So when does Banfield get the money?" Setting the cheroot between her lips, she struck a match and lit it, gently puffing. Wagging the match, she tucked it into a small ash pan embedded onto the side of the seat. Inhaling the earthy smoke, she slowly blew it out, finally feeling at ease. "It's important that he get the money soon." Before she left to Persia.

Her father rolled the lit cheroot against the tips of gloved fingers. "I'm simply awaiting his signature on all of the contracts. Once they are delivered to my solicitor, the money is his."

She was so relieved. It was the least she could do for Banfield. "Thank you, Papa." She dragged in a puff, letting the warm smoke fill her mouth and paused, realizing there was a male figure standing in one of the windows of the house, staring out toward her. Her fingers stilled, holding the cheroot in midair by her lips right before the carriage window for all to see.

The man, whoever he was, could see her smoking.

She sensed it was Banfield.

She tossed the cheroot to the floor, crushing it with her heel. Her heart pounded.

The figure turned and disappeared.

The carriage clattered past the window and beneath a stone portico, silencing the rain as it came to a halt. She glanced back toward the window that was no longer in view. "Be sure to tell me when he signs the contracts and gets the money," she insisted.

"You really needn't worry." He smirked. "I'm good for it." He yanked his cheroot from his lips. "You should have been there during contract negotiations yesterday. That boy did nothing but talk and talk about you as if you were the Queen of England coming into his home to stay. He is incredibly excited about the wedding. Everyone is."

She lowered her gaze, regret pinching her. "I know."

He grinned and pointed. "Who says money can't buy you love?"

The poor man really seemed to think money *could* buy him love. She tried to rescue him from his stupid way of thinking, but realized he didn't want to be rescued. So it was time to rescue herself. For that was the one thing she could control. "I'll miss you, Papa," she murmured, a part of her already saying good-bye.

He smiled. "I'll miss you, too." His smile faded. He sighed. "I'll be leaving London shortly after you get married. I wish I could stay, but they need me back in New York."

A woman had to grow up and stand on her own sometime. This was her time.

The door to the carriage swung open. Footmen in red livery unfolded the stairs and stepped aside in unison, revealing a massive oak door with an iron lion head knocker.

Clementine tucked her silver casing of cheroots into her reticule. Dread scraped every inch of her soul. She really wasn't ready to face Banfield knowing what she was about to do. Because it wasn't like she wanted to hurt him. She liked him. Very much. Too much.

"Tine, the footmen are waiting."

She rose, pulling her cashmere shawl tighter around her shoulders. Gathering the fullness of her chartreuse morning gown from around her slippered feet, she extended her hand to one of the footmen waiting and was guided down. She stared at the imposing door that had yet to open, nervously fingering the reticule hanging from her wrist.

Her father flicked his cheroot off to the side and stood beside her beneath the portico.

The entrance door opened, revealing buffed black and white marble tiles and not just one but two sweeping staircases that rounded toward the same landing on the second floor of the house beyond. A dozen footmen in red livery and a balding butler dressed in black serving attire lined the inside entrance of the grand hall, their shoulders set and ready to serve.

Her father touched the small of her back, ushering her forward.

She walked inside, her steps echoing. Her lips parted in reverence. "I remember this." Her gaze lifted up and up toward the cathedral height ceiling leading into the home and a massive crystal and gold chandelier that illuminated the vast, ornate space of pale silk walls. She remembered how the façade of the home did not reflect the glory inside.

It always seemed so incredibly impressive for an entrance hall. Even the richest of New Yorkers, like themselves, usually kept their entrance halls simple. True American knickerbockers of old money, which is what they were, believed wealth was to be displayed in one's mannerisms, not one's living quarters.

The sound of approaching booted steps made her veer her gaze toward the end of the corridor where a very tall, broad-shouldered gentleman with a self-assured stride announced that he was the master of the house coming to personally greet his guests.

Her pulse thundered in her ears. It was Banfield.

Despite the sizable distance, she could make out a dark-grey morning coat, an embroidered blue and gold waistcoat, a knotted white cravat and black wool trousers that tapered snugly into a pair of polished leather boots.

As his well-muscled frame drew nearer and his rugged face came into full focus, her heart flipped. He'd grown into quite the man. Broader. Muscular. The portrait he'd sent didn't do him justice. He was ridiculously handsome. Those sharp, refined features reminded her of a dashing politician about to take the podium and address his people.

That smooth, long-legged stride and set, shaven jaw hinted that he was a man in control of not only himself but the world. Astoundingly, that golden-brown hair, which appeared to be fashioned at shoulder length, had been pulled back into a ribbon similar to what her grandfather might have worn back in the 1700's. She couldn't believe he wore a queue. No one wore a queue anymore.

It was as if he was trying to stand out amongst his peers. And he certainly did.

He came to a regal halt several strides away from her and her father.

The scent of freshly starched linen pierced the air between them.

A breath escaped her. He was so beautiful he belonged in a museum behind glass with the large brass inscription that read 'Adonis.'

Intense brown eyes skimmed her appearance. He searched her face for a moment and inclined his head, the black ribbon tying his hair cascading against his high collar. "Good afternoon, Miss Grey." His voice was deep and refined, laced with an opulent British accent that showcased several generations of tradition. "At long last we touch the same soil."

She respectfully inclined her head. "Good afternoon, my lord."

He lingered for a moment before averting his gaze to her father. His features playfully brightened. "Mr. Grey! Good to see you again. You'll be pleased to hear that all of the contracts were hand-delivered to your solicitor with all of my signatures not even an hour ago."

She almost sagged in relief. The sooner he got the money, the sooner she didn't have to worry about him. He'd be fine without her. More than fine. Yes, it would pinch his pride, but with three million, he could buy himself the sort of life he really deserved. The sort she knew she wouldn't be able to give him.

He set a hand against his lower back, taking on a formal, gentlemanly stance and cleared his throat. "My mother and I were disappointed that neither of you would be staying here at the house. There is no need to stay at a hotel." He captured her gaze. "I have rooms."

It was as if he were communicating that she needed to take the room next to his.

"We appreciate the offer, Banfield," her father countered with a quick smile, "but I already bought out an entire floor of rooms. It's paid for." Mr. Grey swept a hand toward her. "And here she is, as promised, Banfield. "Hasn't she grown into something magnificent since you last saw her?"

Leave it to her father to tell the man what he was supposed to think. She awkwardly caught Banfield's gaze.

His eyes had never left hers. Not once. "Indeed, she has." Something intense flared in that rugged face.

Her pulse quickened. That barely contained intensity reminded her of when they had first met. "I trust that you are well, my lord."

He still held her gaze. "Incredibly well, Miss Grey. It may be raining outside, but here inside, the sun is shining because you are, at long last, here."

It was getting awkward. He was beginning to sound like a medieval poetry book and was staring too much. "That is incredibly lovely of you to say, Banfield. Thank you." She swept out her gloved hand toward him in greeting and waited.

His shaven jaw tightened as those riveting brown eyes softened just enough to convey that he was touched by the gesture. Stepping closer, he grasped her gloved hand with large, bare fingers and brought it toward himself. "My warmth knows no bounds." Tightening his hold, he sensuously grazed his slightly parted mouth against the knuckles of her glove, still holding her gaze.

It was indecent. Not that he had ever been anything but.

His masculine lips pressed straight through the leather and lingered in a bold manner that whispered of unending rapture. She swallowed tightly, knowing the only respectable thing protecting her from his lips was a mere glove and her father standing two feet away.

Letting his fingers drag against hers, Banfield released her hand. "Your father mentioned we would be spending the afternoon together. I'm afraid the weather will make it difficult for us to enjoy the garden. Might I interest you in a tour of the home instead followed by a quiet meal?"

His muscled shoulders looked as if they might rip the wool of his coat if he moved the wrong way. "That would be lovely. Yes. Thank you."

"Excellent." He casually turned toward her father. "Will you be joining us, Mr. Grey?"

She prayed her father wouldn't stay. There was so much that needed to be said. So much Banfield needed to understand. Things her father would never understand.

Mr. Grey gestured toward the entrance door behind them. "No, thank you. I have a few errands to oversee on the other side of town."

A half-breath escaped her.

"I'll return at five o'clock."

Her momentary relief turned into dread. Because she didn't need five hours to deliver what could be said in a single breath. "Five? I can assure you, an hour is all we really need."

"*An hour?*" he echoed. "Don't be ridiculous. You need time to get reacquainted. Even five hours in my estimation is overly short after all the years you two have been apart." Her father gently patted her cheek. "Seeing all of the marriage contracts have already been signed and delivered, chaperones are no longer necessary. Why? Because I trust both the gentleman and the lady to respect each other. Enjoy the freedom."

Clementine cringed. Her father knew that aside from a few rebellious moments she had snatched with Nasser, she didn't trust men or their passions. Not anymore than society did. And she most certainly knew what sort of passions Derek was capable of. He'd proven that within the first five minutes of them knowing each other.

Mr. Grey made his way toward the door which a footman opened. Glancing back at her with a wink, he strode out toward their carriage waiting beneath the portico. The footman closed the door and positioned himself on the far wall, leaving the foyer in complete silence.

Her throat tightened. She highly doubted the next five hours were going to be pleasant.

LESSON THREE

If your lover's cat were to be discovered dead

in your garden, don't just throw it over a wall

and pretend you never saw it. Be considerate and

offer up genuine condolences.

-The School of Gallantry

L etting out a refined breath, Clementine turned toward Banfield, hoping she was capable of surviving whatever happened next. Doing her best not to fidget, she politely offered, "I can only apologize for my father. Apparently, he doesn't realize a tour of any sized house won't take five hours."

Banfield's mouth quirked, his dark eyes brightening. "I don't mind." He studied her face, unhurriedly and intently. "My butler will take your bonnet and gloves," he added in a low tone.

Her body felt heavy and warm. Whilst there was nothing indecent about removing one's bonnet and gloves before a man, for she did it all the time whenever making calls, his gruff tone might as well have asked her to remove her gown and corset. "Thank you."

She turned toward the waiting butler and fumbled to unravel the satin ribbon at her chin, painfully aware Banfield was watching her. A warm tingle uprooted the pit of her stomach, and although she tried to slow the rapid beat of her heart, it was of no use. She was as nervous now around him as she had been when she was fourteen. It was stupid. She had always hated the way he made her feel: breathless, out of control, and on the verge of bursting into flames.

Removing her gloves, she handed both to the elderly male servant. Sensing that Banfield was still watching her, she glanced toward him.

He swept his gaze over her pinned hair and smiled. "There is no need to linger here in the entrance hall. The main rooms are upstairs." He held out a hand toward the direction he wanted them to go and strode past. "Please follow me."

She tightened her hold on her reticule and made her way after him.

He said nothing more.

The silence was unnerving. They always had plenty to say to each other in letters. He, more than she. But now, their letters and the ten weeks they had spent together in their youth didn't seem to exist. Face to face, they were strangers. A man and a woman who were meeting for the very first time.

"How many rooms are there?" she offered, hoping to break the silence. She knew, of course, how many rooms there were in his house, given she had spent enough weeks in it, but a respectable woman had to start the conversation somewhere.

He cleared his throat. "Twenty, not including the servants' quarters in the upper attic. The country estate in Essex is twice the size of this and has twice the staff. The upkeep has been tedious, especially given all the renovations throughout the years. Something is always peeling, breaking, or leaking." He walked up the main stairwell, his bare hand smoothly trailing up the mahogany banister. His hand was large, those male fingers extending well beyond the shape of the banister itself. The effortless movement of his hand against the banister hinted at a playfulness he was clearly withholding.

Gathering her skirts, she made her way up the stairs after him, lowering her gaze to his backside hidden beneath his morning coat. She pinched her lips together, knowing she shouldn't be staring at his backside and lowered her gaze to his leather boots instead. His black boots had been polished to such perfection, she could see light refracting from them. Not even her father, who was notorious for wanting everything *mis en place*, kept his boots *that* polished.

Upon reaching the top of the stairwell, Banfield stepped aside and waited.

She came onto the landing, noting a long wall of ancestral gilded paintings. Nothing had changed. She remembered almost everything about the house after spending weeks going in and out of it. She didn't expect to miss it, but a part of her had. For it had been her home away from home for ten weeks. Ten incredibly overwhelming weeks of realizing at the age of fourteen she was going to be a wife to a very eager and very passionate young man who had no qualms about announcing what he wanted and needed. Be it in person or in his letters. He'd terrified her with his enthusiasm and the way he always charged at life. And at her. Over the years, although she'd come to admire that take-no-prisoners attitude, she had still decided she wouldn't let him make *her* a prisoner.

He gestured toward the right. "The receiving room is this way. It's where Mother and I welcome all of our guests during calling hours."

"I remember the receiving room quite well," she chided. "You certainly tried to hold my hand enough times in it."

His brown eyes captured hers. He shifted toward her. "Are you flirting with me?"

Annoyingly, her face grew hot. "No. I was merely stating a fact."

He tilted his head, searching her face. "You're blushing."

He was never subtle, was he? "Yes. I know. I can feel it."

He smiled. Still searching her face, he added, "You haven't changed, Miss Grey. Not one bit. The only difference between now and then is that you don't appear to be panicking."

What little he knew. Over the years, she had simply learned to control the panic.

He dug into his pocket and with his thumb, opened the lid off a tin she knew all too well. His eyes brightened and his tone softened. "Want one?"

She remembered three things about the day they first met. The way his finger had pushed itself into her mouth in a most ungentlemanly manner, the way his candy burned her tongue for life and the way he kept getting into her face which ultimately led her into shoving him and dashing a welt into his forehead. And that was all within the first hour of them knowing each other. "No, thank you."

"Are you certain?"

"Quite. I'm still recovering from the one I had seven years ago."

He smirked. "I thought you might remember that. Which is why...." He set an amber candy into his mouth, shutting the tin with a snap and shoved it back into his pocket. He reached into his other pocket and pulled out a piece of folded confectionary paper. Unrolling it, he held it out, presenting a small single stick of flaxen-colored candy. "I got this for you, seeing you like plain sweets. It's a honey stick."

Her lips parted. He remembered. She swallowed. Why did he have to be so terrifyingly adorable? It wasn't fair. She was trying to leave. Not stay. She gently took it. "Thank you."

"My pleasure." Crushing the paper into a ball with both hands, he shoved it into his pocket. "Tell me what you think." He lingered.

He clearly expected her to eat it now. She hated eating things in front of people. "I'll eat it later, thank you."

"Why not enjoy it now?" he pressed. "I travelled well over three hours to get that."

Lovely. Now she *had* to eat it. She sighed. Hesitantly bringing it up to her lips, she set her teeth against the honey stick and snapped it off. It rolled against her tongue, an unexpected tangy sweetness heightening her senses. She chewed, crunching through its stickiness and inwardly melted at the enchantment. She hadn't tasted a honey stick this good in years. It was…divine.

Realizing he was intently watching her, she tucked the other piece into her mouth and primly chewed and crunched, half-nodding. "It's very good. The best I've had in a while. Thank you."

He searched her face. "Christ. Watching you eat candy should be illegal." Adjusting his coat with the tug of the lapels, he turned and kept walking. "How was your trip?" he rumbled out.

It was like she had just emerged from a pulsing void of the fiery boy she had first met and the virile man he had become. A man who learned to control himself just enough to allow him out into public without a leash.

Pushing out a calming breath, she swallowed what remained of her candy and tried to keep up with his long-legged stride. "My trip was tolerable," she managed. "Crossing over the Atlantic is always tedious, I find, but unlike Papa, I never get ill."

"I'm glad to hear it." He glanced toward her in between enjoying his hard candy. "After the roar of the Season, you and I are heading out to Paris in early July." His voice dipped. "For a late honeymoon."

She cringed knowing she'd be in Persia by July. She also glanced toward him. "Don't you think the idea of a 'honeymoon' is over-popularized and archaic?"

"Archaic? God no. It's romantic."

"Romantic?" she challenged. "You mean you really think there is honey on the moon?"

He smirked and finished chewing his candy. "Well, now, maybe there is. Maybe the moon is over-populated with white bees and white flowers and we simply don't know about it because the telescopes blur reality."

White bees and white flowers? Now there was a thought. It actually made a girl want to go to the moon.

They walked for a long moment in silence.

He came to a sudden halt and swung toward her.

She tilted back.

"I got ahead of myself." He widened his stance and stared, clearly long finished with his candy. "The wedding is next week. Hope you're ready to soar. Because I know I am."

Ready to soar? Gad. Everything about him was so *intense*. Like his spiced candy. It was as if *everything* mattered to him. Being around him was like their first meeting, their weeks spent together and all of his letters meshed into one breath. It was overwhelming. She tried not to panic knowing she still hadn't heard anything from Nasser. He promised he'd already be in London waiting. "Uh…yes. I heard you got ahead of yourself." She felt like such a rogue.

Derek leaned toward her. "Are you all right?"

She edged back. "Yes." She couldn't just blurt out that their engagement was at an end. It wouldn't be in the least bit civilized or kind. She had to wait for the right time. Although heaven only knew when that would be given she had five hours.

He hesitated before saying, "The banns have already been read in Saint Paul's these past few weeks and my mother finished taking care of all the arrangements and invitations well over a month ago. I'm afraid it won't be a small wedding. My mother had a list of more than three hundred people."

Oh, God. The more people they invited, the bigger the scandal. "I say we keep it small. Very, very small." The less that was planned, the better off everyone would be.

His mouth quirked. "No chance at that. All the invitations have already been sent. Not only for the wedding but the masked evening ball that will follow it."

"A masked evening ball? For a wedding?"

"Yes. It was actually my idea. It's rather brilliant." His left brow rose a fraction. "That way, you and I can ignore the guests and do whatever we please." He grinned boyishly. Setting a hand behind his back, he guided her down the corridor again, now walking beside her. "A masked ball will also ensure a measure of peace given the amount of family I have coming to the wedding. We Banfields are rarely known to keep our opinions to ourselves, especially in public. With everyone wearing masks, we're guaranteed none of them will be able to recognize each other and all arguments will be left at home where they belong."

Ah, yes. She remembered those cousins. They were the obnoxious peasants in the family who had set an entire wooden crate of champagne on the late viscount's grave, because apparently, it had been the viscount's favorite drink. Not even a day later, one of them had come back to drink every last sip because the viscount certainly wasn't able to.

Banfield smirked. "I can tell by the look on your face that you're worried about dealing with my cousins. Don't be. I've learned to control them since coming into my title. It's called 'money' and they love it too much to argue with me about it." He perked. "By the by, my mother sends her apologies. She was hoping to be here to greet you but keeps a rather aggressive charity schedule that leaves her no time. I can assure you, however, she is incredibly enthusiastic about the wedding. Too much, I'd say. She plans on moving into her own townhome after we get married to give you full ownership of the house. Of course, that doesn't mean you'll be rid of her. She will most likely call often. Though hopefully not every day or you and I won't have any time for each other."

The more he talked, the guiltier she felt. She struggled to remember all the ways she'd imagined she might get *him* to break off the engagement. Instead of her doing it. But in his presence, she couldn't even focus long enough to think. "I remember her fondly," she managed. "How is she?"

"Incredibly well. She still misses my father, obviously, but unlike before, she has been attending more events and returning to her regular way of life." He was quiet for a moment. "You look exactly like your portrait. I didn't expect that."

"I hope you don't think I look *exactly* like the portrait my father sent. I thought it rather hideous."

He hesitated. "I meant it as a compliment."

"Oh, I have no doubt, and it's very kind of you, but you clearly didn't notice how far apart my eyes were. The painter must have thought he wasn't being paid enough."

A laugh escaped him.

It annoyed her. "I take it you find it amusing that he painted my eyes so far apart?"

He paused and held her gaze, growing serious again. "Well, no, I..." He cleared his throat and eyed her. "I'm beginning to remember that you don't have a sense of humor."

The way he said it jangled her stomach. It was as if he wanted to be entertained. "I do indeed have a sense of humor. Ask my father." She kept walking. After the life she'd led, she'd more or less learned that people who were constantly smiling were hiding their true intentions, and people who laughed a bit too much were idiots who thought the world was slathered with rainbows.

He strode up next to her.

With a full five hours on their hands, she had to stagger out their entire conversation and leave the worst for last. She dreaded his reaction. Trying to wave away the silence, she quickly asked, "Are there any fashionable shops in London you recommend? Ones that specialize in Parisian gowns?" It was the only thing she could come up with.

Renewed amusement overtook his face. "I don't usually shop for gowns."

She almost smacked a hand to her forehead. "Forgive me. Of course you don't. I merely thought that...well...maybe you pay attention to the shops your mother or female cousins go to. Women talk about these things all the time." That was one way to amend being stupid.

Still amused, he shrugged. "If they ever do talk about gowns, I certainly don't listen. I'm not a man of fashion. Never have been and never will be."

She wasn't too surprised by that admission. As dashing as he was, he certainly didn't appear to be devoted to the latest trend. His queue was proof of that. And his clothes, which were simple in its fabrics and stitching were also proof of that. It was unexpectedly endearing given he was a titled man. It was like he only wore a coat because he had to. Unlike most men who wore it because they wanted to announce to the world they were coming. She perused his wool coat and paused in astonishment, realizing the seams on the shoulder of his coat were uneven, as if the tailor had missed an inch.

His amusement faded as he also came to a halt. "Is something wrong with my coat? Why are you staring at it?"

She sighed, knowing she oughtn't let him publicly walk around in it. She reached out and gently tapped at the seam of his coat on his upper arm. "The seams are uneven." She pulled back her hand feeling the tension of his shoulder which had instinctively flexed in response to her touch.

His hand jumped to the seam as he glanced down, staring at it with a lowered chin. His large fingers pulled at the fabric. "I thought this was the best coat I had. It's why I wore it. I..." He dropped his hand, averting his gaze and said nothing more.

Sensing she had humiliated him, she inwardly winced. "I normally wouldn't have noticed, but with us being in such close confines and walking side by side, it—" She hesitated, realizing she was only making it worse and quickly said instead, "It's a grand coat, actually. I love the fabric and the color. It suits you."

He snapped his gaze back to her. "You're just saying that."

"What if I am? Can't you take a compliment when it's given?"

He gave her a sidelong glance.

She pushed her reticule up her wrist, thinking of a way to keep them talking. "So..." Five hours of this was going to be her undoing. "Might I ask what you've been busy with? Anything you didn't mention in your letters?"

He adjusted his queue with a quick hand. "Nothing I can think of. What about you?"

She shrugged. "I've started painting again. I haven't painted anything in years."

His brows went up. "Is that so? I used to paint when I was younger. Much, much younger. I abandoned it when I realized I had far more talent holding a fencing sword than a paintbrush." He shifted toward her. "So are you good with the oils?"

"So good Michelangelo would have wept," she confided.

He threw back his head and let out a peel of laughter that echoed in the corridor.

She lowered her chin. "Don't laugh. I'm quite serious. If I were a man, my art would be displayed in every museum around the world. Even in your king's palace. I'm incredibly good."

His laugh faded into a mere smile. "Are you now?"

"Yes. I am." She'd known about her talent since she was seven. She could replicate anything that was real or in her head. It wasn't anything she'd learned. She simply knew how to do it and her father, realizing her talent, eagerly set her before a canvas to practice every day. While her father would always puff out a chest in pride, her mother would only squint at it and point out all the flaws. It made her stop painting for a while. "My father always loved my paintings," she admitted. "He would hire renowned painters from Milan to come out and teach me. Unfortunately, none of the painters lasted beyond a few weeks as it was obvious I knew far more about painting than they did."

Banfield rumbled out another laugh. "I adore your sense of pride and accomplishment." He set his hands behind his back. "I will have to give your talent the admiration it deserves. When can I see some of your paintings? Did you bring any with you from New York?"

She hesitated. "Sadly, I don't have anything to display. I haven't finished anything recently, and those I did finish throughout the years are all scattered around the world."

"What do you mean?"

"As you well know, we always travelled abroad a lot. As a result, almost all of them were left behind at various homes we visited. There was simply never any room to travel with them. It bothered me when I was younger, but now I revel in knowing that my paintings hang in various homes all over the world. Like a true artist."

He observed her for a long moment, the rushing sound of rain against the windows and roof surrounded them in the vast corridor. "What if I were to ask you to paint something for me? I would *love* a painting depicting you as Venus standing in Rome. Life size. Hair down and minimal clothing." His tone indicated he was serious.

He was clearly asking for a classical half-nude. She felt her face grow hot. It became so hot she could have easily melted butter on her cheek. Why did he always have to make her feel so physically self-conscious? "You're being indecent."

His gaze fell to her lips. "You have always made it difficult for me to be anything but."

The corridor seemed to shrink and press itself against her skin. It was like being fourteen again. "Can we just get back to the tour instead of standing in the corridor like unwanted pieces of furniture?"

He shifted his jaw. "Of course."

They started walking again.

When they arrived at the entrance of the receiving room, he extended his hand. "After you."

Gad it was hot. "Thank you." She entered, her skirts trailing behind her. She did everything she could to keep her own hand from fanning her face. It was obvious controlling Banfield was going to be like trying to keep the devil out of fire. Nasser had better be in London or this was going to get problematic.

Clementine suddenly paused in the middle of the room, over-whelmed by remembering all that had once been so many years ago. A well-lit room whose pea-green silk walls were decorated with countless country paintings made her pause. There were a few new additions hanging in between all the old ones. They weren't by any means good, as the shadowing of the trees and streams were crooked and not at all well blended, but there appeared to be a genuine attempt to re-create a hom-age to landscape art. An array of old but distinguished furnishings in the room, from the gold and blue porcelain vases to the upholstered gilded chairs and couches whispered of the times she and Banfield had quietly sat in this room playing cards.

Half the time, he made up all the rules. One of his favorite games was plastering a playing card to his forehead in which they had to play 'commerce' without it falling. If he won a hand without the card falling, he got to hold her actual *hand* for a full minute. They spent a lot of time holding hands because of it.

She'd always had very muddled feelings about their relationship. She still did. A part of her wanted to stay. She wanted to give herself a chance to explore what she was capable of as a wife, but a much larger part of her had seen what strong passions could do to a marriage. She refused to ruin him *or* herself.

"Who painted all of the new additions in the room?" she finally asked.

"I did," he offered from behind, his low voice surprisingly close. Too close.

She turned and stumbled toward him, realizing his boots were stand-ing on the hem of her gown. "What—"

His large hands jumped to her corseted waist as he stepped off the hem. "Forgive me." Tightening his hold on the curve of her waist, he lowered his head to hers. "I was admiring your perfume. It's..." He searched her face, his mouth softening. "How are you?"

He lingered, his large hands skimming and then tightening on her waist. He heatedly lowered his gaze to her lips. He leaned in closer, the scent of freshly starched linen and his hair tonic piercing the air between them.

She froze, fully aware that his arms were not only drawing her body against his own muscled frame but that his rugged face was hovering above her own face.

His lips edged down toward hers. The scent of spiced ginger from his mouth now teased the remaining space between them.

Heaven forbid he unleash what he was holding in and kiss her. She'd be pregnant in a day. She slapped both hands over her mouth, bumping his arms and kept her palms firmly and rigidly in place. So he had no access to her lips. At all.

He stilled, the heat of his mouth grazing her forehead. "Are you trying to be adorable?" he rasped. "Or is this your way of telling me you're not interested?"

She felt faint against the heat of his breath fanning her face. Her hands trembled against her own mouth in an attempt to stay calm, her gaze staying trained on the brass buttons of his waistcoat. "We shouldn't," she managed through her hands.

His broad chest rose and fell unevenly. "You don't have to keep your mouth covered. I promise I won't lunge."

A whooshing breath escaped her as she lowered her hands. She stepped away and almost staggered knowing she had avoided being kissed. Ending up pregnant wasn't what she had in mind.

He still lingered very close.

She edged back. "Can you please move away?" She delicately half-motioned him toward the direction she wanted him to go. "You're standing a bit too close for my liking."

He glared. "Why not ask me to leave the house while you're at it?"

She awkwardly stepped back to ensure there was more space between them. "Please don't take that tone with me. You have no right to touch or kiss me."

"No right?" he echoed, angling toward her. "I'm pretty sure I just signed marriage contracts."

He would have to remind her of that. Of course, it wasn't a church document.

He shifted his shaven jaw and veered away toward the nearest chair. He set a hand onto the gilded back, observing her. "I wasn't even going to kiss you."

He was such a liar. "What were you going to do?"

He shrugged. "I don't know."

Oh, he knew.

"I didn't mean to stand on your dress," he casually added.

She set her chin. "Thank you for apologizing for your indecent behavior."

He pointed at her. "I wasn't apologizing for trying to kiss you. I was apologizing for stepping on your dress."

He was such a rake. "I thought you said you weren't trying to kiss me."

"I'm not a very good liar."

"No. You most certainly aren't." She turned and wandered closer to one of his paintings on the wall as a way of trying to distract herself from the conversation they were having. She paused and stared up at what appeared to be a family sitting in the shade of a battered oak tree by a smeared stream that lacked dimension. She inched closer to the gilded frame. One of the children appeared to have a third arm. She pinched her lips together in an attempt not to laugh. Who says she didn't have a sense of humor? "Was there a reason you painted an additional arm on this poor child?"

"Christ, don't look at that," he waved her away from it. "I...some of the paint splattered and I decided to make use of it. As I said, I wasn't very good and thankfully I haven't touched the paints since 1818. I honestly don't know why my mother pulled them out of the attic last year and put them in here as if it were a *Nicolas Toussaint Charlet*. It's ghastly."

She turned toward him, astounded and impressed he even knew the works of Charlet. Few did. "Try not to be so hard on yourself. It isn't that bad."

"*Liar.* When my mother moves out into her own home next week, so do the paintings." He gestured toward the open doors. "Allow me to show you the rest of the house. Perhaps the uh...cigar room would be more to your liking? 'Tis far better than smoking in an enclosed carriage, wouldn't you say?" His tone went dry.

That had been him in the window, after all. She winced. "You must be appalled knowing I smoke."

He widened his stance. "Appalled? No. There really isn't much in this world that surprises me anymore. I have a brother and eighteen cousins. It's all been done." He flexed each hand. "The *ton*, however, won't be quite as understanding. Which means you'll have to stop smoking."

It was a good thing they weren't getting married. "I can assure you, I was well past the gates and out of everyone's sight when I did it."

He shifted from boot to boot. "You shouldn't be smoking, Clementine. *At all.*"

She paused. He called her Clementine. As if he'd always called her Clementine. Her throat tightened knowing she was going to hurt him. God. How was she going to... She needed a cheroot. Badly. She could feel her fingers twitching from need. "If you don't mind, could you please escort me to the cigar room? The one you mentioned? I haven't smoked all morning and am absolutely beside myself."

His mouth went tight. "Didn't you already smoke one in the carriage?"

"Yes, but I didn't get a chance to finish it." She fingered her reticule. "It won't take long. It's not like a cigar. Cheroots are rolled small. A few puffs and they're gone."

He hesitated.

"Please?" she added in the sweetest tone she could muster. "I desperately need one."

He sighed. Turning, he grudgingly extended his hand to the open door.

She almost smiled knowing that a domineering, six foot well-muscled man was capable of succumbing to a mere pleading tone. This man truly had Beelzebub in one hand and an angel in the other. "Thank you, Banfield." She sashayed out into the corridor and glanced back at him. "I appreciate your understanding."

He strode out after her, his eyes skimming the backside of her gown as if he were suddenly aware she had a backside. "I didn't say I understood, dearest. In my opinion, smoking is a disgusting habit."

Oh, no. The man went from calling her Clementine to dearest in two short breaths. She only prayed he didn't fall on his knee and announce his love next.

He now held her gaze. "Instead of smoking, why not lick ashes out of the hearth?"

Trying to tap away the tension between them, she said, "I've tried. It doesn't taste the same."

He jerked to a halt. "You had better be teasing me."

She sighed. "Oh, do calm down. I was. Have you no sense of humor?"

His brows came together. "I am fully capable of humor, but when you say things in that overly serious tone it's very difficult to know the difference. Next time smile or quirk a brow or something. You're too damn serious."

Sadly, she'd always been serious in nature. She couldn't help it. She hadn't exactly been raised by comedians. Her father had been ridiculously driven and dry and her mother had been more of a funeral director with wild screaming monkeys attached to each shoulder.

"Genteel ladies here in London don't smoke," Banfield added. "Which means...we'll have to do something about this." He continued down the corridor. "The best way to get rid of a bad habit is to get rid of whatever is causing the habit. You will therefore hand over whatever cheroots you have after you finish this one. I'll take the whole casing or whatever you have in your reticule."

Oh, now *that* was going too far. "Forgive me, but everything in my reticule belongs to me, Banfield. Not you."

He glanced back at her, his smoldering brown eyes intently holding her gaze. "I am about to be your husband. I therefore have the right to confiscate whatever I want. Especially if I feel it's in your best interest."

The way he said it made her feel as if he was about to do far more than take away her cheroots. "Why not take the shoes from my feet while you're at it?"

"Your shoes aren't the problem, Clementine." Putting his hands into his pockets, he casually resumed walking. "Whilst I'm permitting you to indulge in smoking this once, out of common courtesy, you need to understand that people here in London will judge you for it and it's my duty to protect your good name. I only hope you aren't too attached to the idea of smoking."

She was. She tried to quit smoking many times, as she knew it wasn't something respectable women did, but had quickly discovered it wasn't all that simple. She loved it too much. Much like her father loved his cognac too much. Her own weakness made her more forgiving of his. "I smoke every day. I genuinely enjoy it."

"And I genuinely enjoy drinking brandy, but I can also function without it."

A gasp escaped her. "How dare you insinuate I also drink?" She wasn't her father.

He lifted a brow. "As my mother says, a well-bred lady should always strive for perfection. And begging your pardon, but smoking does not define perfection."

"Begging *your* pardon, but if perfection defined me, I'd be a nun living in Madrid."

He swung toward her, the heat of his massive body startling her into leaning back. "Don't disrespect my opinion. I'm giving you a privilege few get. Because no one ever gets the chance to smoke in this house. No one. Not even my guests."

"Then why even have a cigar room?" she drawled, angling toward him to prove she wasn't in the least bit intimidated. She accidentally bumped him with her arm and winced. "Sorry."

He glanced at the arm she had bumped and edged closer. "I didn't build the cigar room into the house. My grandfather did." He straightened, his brown eyes playfully sparking. "Our first argument. How utterly charming. How quaint."

Her throat tightened. "We aren't arguing."

He quirked a brow. "You mean you're arguing with me about arguing?"

She pinched her lips. He thought he was so clever.

He slowly grinned, the edges of his eyes crinkling. "Do I get a kiss for being clever? Or are you going to make this poor man wait until his wedding night?"

Something told her he wasn't going to take her ending their engagement well.

LESSON FOUR

What happens to a man who finds himself facing

a woman who represents everything he is not?

-The School of Gallantry

D erek closed the door leading into the domed cigar room to ensure no smoke escaped into the corridor lest the footmen come running thinking there was a fire. After all, no one had lit a cigar in the house since 1823.

Letting out an exasperated breath, he turned to Clementine. He couldn't believe she had covered her entire mouth with both hands when he tried to kiss her. He had checked his breath. It wasn't that. Hell, he'd strategically eaten a piece of candy and given her one for a reason.

Their wedding night was going to be rough. For both of them.

He eyed her.

She had already set aside her beaded reticule and lit her cheroot as if showcasing her every right. Depositing the extinguished match into the ash pan on the marble side table, she glanced around the Turkish-styled blue and gold room. The fullness of her chartreuse morning gown that emphasized generous hips that had nothing to do with her corset, followed her sweeping movements.

She regally seated herself in one of the cane chairs directly before him, holding up the lit cheroot between two bare fingers. "The poor ash pan on the side table doesn't even appear to have been used. When was the last time anyone actually smoked in this room?"

He tried not to notice that the lace on her bodice was unusually high for a morning gown. Only the base of her throat and an expensive-looking emerald and gold necklace was showing. Despite the overly modest cut of her attire, the well-fitted material of her gown still couldn't hide the sizeable breasts stuffed into her corset. She was flat no more. It was amazing what a few years could do to a woman's body.

"Did you wander off to another land?" she prodded.

Yes. Tit land. "I uh..." He cleared his throat. "Never mind. It's not like you would want to hear what goes on in my mind." She'd probably panic. "My father was actually the last person to make use of this room. He was in here almost every night, smoking his jolly heart away. When he died, so did the custom. I don't smoke. I personally never cared for it." He was quiet for a moment.

Her features notably softened. "You miss him, don't you?"

His throat tightened. "Yes. He was a great man."

"I hear many stories about him. My father was incredibly fond of your father and speaks of him as if he were a brother." Her full lips encased the end of the cheroot, her blue eyes watching him intently. She slowly pulled it away, letting a small ring of white smoke rise from those lips and glide toward him.

He lowered his chin. He'd never seen anyone control smoke like that before. It was like watching a dragon entertain itself with its own breath. "You seem well versed in the art of smoking. I sincerely hope you're better versed in running a household."

She took in another puff of smoke, still watching him. "Why not sit down, Banfield? This is going to take a while and you and I need to talk."

"Now, now, there is no need to say everything to each other in the first five minutes. I say we take our time." He grabbed another cane chair and set it directly before her, allowing enough distance for her skirts. Heaven forbid he step on those again. Pushing aside his coat tails with a hand, he sat. "Might I ask what father would allow his own daughter to smoke as if she were a man? In my opinion, he ought to be hanged."

She sighed. "Please don't insult my father. He did the best he could. I was the one who had to raise him. And I think I did rather well given the circumstance."

What an odd thing to say. "Since when do daughters raise their fathers?"

She averted her gaze and shrugged. "When Mama died, he struggled quite a bit. More than I thought he would. Although they always argued, they were still oddly close and the first few weeks after she died, all he could do was sit in her room with a hand on the pillow she used to sleep on." A glazed look of despair overtook her face. "Even as a child, I felt sorry for him. I always did. He reminded me of a wounded pup."

She made it sound as if she had spent her entire life playing mother to a man incapable of being a father. It sank his soul. Derek softened his voice. "Do you want to talk about it?"

Her startled gaze met his. "Why would I want to do that?"

He held her gaze. "Because I would hope you can talk to me about anything. Just like we always did in our letters."

She hesitated. "Whilst I appreciate your concern, Banfield, I don't want you judging my father. You're already judging me merely because I smoke."

He snorted. "That is because smoking isn't very common amongst women here in England. You do know that, yes?"

"Nothing about my life is or ever was common. I've been smoking for years. So don't think you're protecting me. You aren't."

He lowered his chin. "*Years*? As in how many? Since birth? Or recently?"

She rolled her eyes. "Since I was eighteen. It was my way of bonding with my father. He always had a cheroot in his hand and what girl doesn't want to be like her father? Especially when she has no one else in her life but an overly stern governess? He was never a bad father, he simply endured a lot and wasn't ever capable of..." Her voice trailed off. She lowered her gaze. "I really don't want to talk about this. Can we talk about something else?"

He decided not to prod. In time, she'd tell him everything he wanted to know about her. They had their entire marriage for that. "Of course. What would you like to talk about?"

"Us."

The way she said it made him feel stupidly weak in the knees. "What about us?"

Her cheeks flushed. "Well...after you tried to kiss me in the receiving room, I...it made me realize we needed to discuss a few things."

Oh, now this he had to hear. He shifted toward her in his seat, setting his hands on his knees. "Go on. I'm listening." He paused and added, "Intently."

She averted her gaze, her flush fading to subtle pink. "Aside from your over-enthusiastic nature toward me, you've still been kind." She stared at nothing in particular. "I notice kindness. I wasn't around it very much. My father was loving, but my mother and my governess were both incredibly judgmental. They claimed I was too somber, too forward and stubborn in nature to ever be molded into what society defined desirable in a lady. My mother died before I could prove her wrong, but my governess was surprised when my father had announced our engagement back in '23. The woman started treating me with more respect, merely because I was going to be a lady, regardless of what she thought. So in many ways I have you to thank. It made the years tolerable. Not necessarily perfect but tolerable."

It was like peering into the world she had been trapped in all these years. A world he had only imagined. He'd always thought her curt ways was an extension of all the money she was worth. Not anything she had endured. It was humbling. "I didn't know that about you."

"There is a lot you don't know, Banfield." She drew in some smoke before letting it out through full parted lips.

God did he ever want to make those lips whisper his name with the same longing and reverence he'd felt for her all these years. "In private, call me Derek. And if you don't like the idea of calling me Derek, feel free to call me any other endearment you like. Make it worth your while and mine."

She smirked. "Oh, now, don't encourage me. Or you'll end up with a name like Adonis."

That sounded like an insult, not an endearment. "And what is that supposed to mean?"

"Women probably find you very attractive. Don't they?"

He supposed some did. Well...no...many did. He knew he was attractive. Certainly far more attractive than most of these lanky, buck-teethed, over-bred men walking around London. And various widows, in particular, always feigned to call on his mother, when, in fact, they were trying to call on him. Of course, he never acted on it. Setting aside his devotion to Clementine, acting on every woman's interest only led to the pox. One of his own friends from his days back at Eton had come down with bed-related diseases after shagging well over thirty women. It wasn't pretty.

He shrugged. "What can I say? Most of the men here in London make me look good. I'm young, my teeth are straight, and my biceps bulge in the proper direction."

She pursed her lips. "I'm so glad to hear you aren't *completely* conceit-ed. I was beginning to wonder."

It was like worshipping stone. Her regal, cool façade was the same and never changed. He only ever remembered it changing once. When he'd sent her into a panic after he'd used his mouth to take the candy stuck to her glove. "I suppose all that really matters is that you find me attractive. Which I know you do. Hell, when we first met, I took your breath away. You had trouble breathing around me, didn't you?"

Her pale face slowly flushed.

He grinned, watching that flush. "A woman only ever blushes when she realizes she can't hide the truth." He adjusted his coat, trying not to boast too much and gestured toward her gown. "Since we're on the subject, allow me to say you've become *incredibly* ravishing. Though I will admit that your...uh...décolletage is rather disappointing. It gives me nothing to look at. I'm assuming that you're entertaining American fashion, because even the most respectable women here in London show more cleavage." He cleared his throat and pushed on. "And since you wouldn't let me kiss you, and we still have a few hours ahead of us, do you think you could..." He whistled and pretended to tug the air downward.

Her eyes widened. "Are you insinuating that I lower my décolletage?"

"Just by a touch. I'm not asking to see nipples."

She gasped and rigidly pointed at him with her cheroot, causing a few ashes to scatter. "You haven't changed *a bit*. All that talk in your letters about being a refined gentleman, indeed. You're still the same seventeen-year-old trying to lure me into the library to do things."

He smirked. "You make it sound like such a bad thing."

"And you make it sound like it's a normal thing."

"You're flattered by my advances and you damn well know it." He pointed at her half-finished cheroot. "Are you done? I want to show you the rest of the house." He caught her gaze. "How about I show you my bedchamber and its rooms next? Are you wanting to see it? We can sneak over."

She pressed a hand against her throat. "No, I don't...I'm not—" She winced and quickly brought her cheroot to her lips, dragging in a breath and letting it out. Twice. "You and I have quite a bit to discuss, Derek. So if you don't mind, I plan to smoke at least one more. I need to."

The little devil. "Absolutely not. I'm being incredibly generous by allowing this much. Smoking not only bloody stinks everything up, but ruins the wallpaper. You should have seen this room before it was redone. It was disgusting. The layer of soot from my father's cigars on the ceiling were almost a quarter of an inch thick. Which is why...the one you are smoking is your last. In fact, I want you to hand over whatever you have in your reticule right now." He held out his hand and wagged his fingers toward her. "Be a dear. Your husband commands it."

"Commands it?" Her features turned incredibly serious. "You obviously think I am yours to command, and I am informing you, my lord, that you are very mistaken."

He shifted his jaw. This woman was dangerous. She acted like a wide-eyed prim and proper miss, but at heart, she only followed her own orders. Leaning forward and toward her, he announced, "You are *not* smoking another one in my presence."

She fingered her cheroot. "I wouldn't worry about my smoking if I were you. You and I have other things to talk about." Her voice was decisive and firm.

He fell back against the seat. It was obvious he needed to stop pushing and start impressing. Because he wasn't all push. He had some give. "Fine. How about we take this outside the cigar room? Because I actually wanted to show you the music room. I had this rather brilliant idea, when we were talking earlier, as to what we should do with it. No one makes use of it anymore, and given that you love to paint and that my mother is moving out, we should turn it into your own personal gallery. A place where you can paint and have your own space. There is more than enough room in there to display at least several dozen paintings on the walls alone. What do you think? Is that something that would please you? Do you want to go see it?"

She was quiet for a moment. She closed her eyes, then opened them. Her voice softened. "That is very kind of you, Derek, but I would rather we stay in here and talk." She glanced around. "I don't see a clock. How much time do we have?"

It was obvious she was counting down to the minute of when her father would return. Was he really that boring? Digging into his waistcoat pocket, he yanked at the fob and pulled out the gold watch attached to it. He glanced at the instrument. "It's after two o'clock. Which means we still have a few hours." He tucked the watch back into his pocket.

"I see." She was quiet for a moment then blurted, "Might I ask how your brother is?"

His stomach dropped at the mention of Andrew. He honestly didn't know how his brother was fairing. His mother, who visited his brother every week, offered only superficial information. Like what Andrew was wearing and what they had for supper. "I imagine he is well."

She paused. "You imagine? Don't you know? I thought you and he were close."

He shrugged. "We are, but it's complicated." For all he knew his brother had already married his birch mistress but was keeping it a secret so their mother wouldn't find out. "We had a falling out. A bad one. He and I always have our arguments, as brothers do, but it usually rolls away in minutes. And this...I haven't seen him in almost two months." It hurt.

"I'm sorry." She tilted her head of pinned black curls and quietly observed him. "I remember him always writing. Did he ever publish a book?"

"One. But given its violent content, no publisher on Paternoster Row was willing to touch it. So he hired a printer and published it himself. Only it turned out to be far more expensive than he anticipated."

"Is it any good? Did you read it?"

Derek cringed. His brother, God love him, wrote books no human ought to read. Just like Derek's own paintings that needed to be incinerated from existence for lack of creativity and talent, so did his brother's books. The Banfields were known for their good-looks, wit, and charms, but not their artistic talents. No one could be good at everything. "In all honesty, and I never had the heart to tell him, the book isn't any good. He used to write romantic books that were quite decent but after his horrid luck with women, he started slathering blood into it. It's stupid and violent. Lopped heads everywhere with no real purpose other than to showcase blood."

She lowered her cheroot to the arm of the chair, her dark arched brows going up. "People's tastes in reading varies. He might have an audience he simply hasn't found."

He snorted. "Yes, well, his audience is probably hiding in prison or in hell, because in my opinion, the content was created to entertain savage men bordering on insanity. I couldn't finish it."

She sat up and took another long breath of smoke before letting it drift from her lips. "Oh, now I *have* to read it. What is the title? I'll buy a copy later today. I have some shopping to do and will be about anyway."

He pointed. "I am *not* telling you the title or the name he is writing under. I wouldn't be much of a gentleman if I allowed you to read a book slathered with more gore than one finds in a mortuary after a city riot. Hell, I couldn't sleep for a week after I read it. A week. And I'm a man. You would faint and break a bracelet or an earring or something."

Her lips parted. "Break a..." She averted her gaze and stiffly rose. "Yes. I...thank you for gallantly pointing out that my sex is too weak to consume anything worthy of a man. I needed to be reminded of that." Walking over to the ash pan, she extinguished the small tip of what remained of her tobacco and sighed. "Derek, I think it's time we admit that you and I have never been well-suited. You have incredibly strong opinions toward everything, as do I, and I am only referring to the simplest of our conversations which have thus far only included books and smoking. We haven't even gotten around to weightier topics. Such as children or...life. We simply don't have anything in common. We never did."

He sat up. "What do you mean?" He swiped the tips of his fingers against his chin, trying not to get agitated. "I disagree with you on a few random subjects and all of a sudden we're not well-suited?" He set his hands on his knees. "I can assure you, heiress, on our wedding night, you won't have *any* complaints."

Her eyes flashed imperiously, but as always, the rest of her façade remained cool and calm. "I don't appreciate you teasing me, Derek. I'm being very serious. And I am asking you to be serious for once." Her blue eyes returned once again to its full composure. "We deserve better than what our parents wanted for us. We deserve to take paths that serve who we are as people so we may honor our character and in turn, our lives."

Why did he sense their conversation had suddenly veered into a dark forest with cackling goblins? "So what are you insinuating? Exactly?"

She sighed. "Wouldn't you have wanted the sort of life you could create and mold on your own? One you'd be able to better understand because the choices you made were your own? As opposed to the choices our parents agreed on and pushed us into when we were mere youths?"

What the hell was this? It was as if she was trying to brush aside what they shared. "I am creating the life I want. Having strong opposing opinions within a marriage is necessary to create anything worth holding onto. If we agree on everything, what would we be teaching each other and our children? Absolutely nothing. We'd be bored three minutes into the marriage."

Her brows flickered. "You clearly don't understand. What I'm saying is...wouldn't you have wanted to choose the bride you were going to marry?"

"I did choose you."

She stared. "You did not."

"I most certainly did." His entire body was obnoxiously warm just thinking about it. "Did our first meeting not prove that? Hell, I wanted you well before I even knew we were engaged. Are you telling me that doesn't count for anything in your eyes?"

Her cheeks flushed. "Derek, I'm asking that you please listen to what I'm about to say."

That tone was flat. Uncompromising. He didn't like it. At all.

She averted her gaze. "I almost didn't come to England. I almost went to Persia with a friend, but I didn't think it was fair to disappear into the night without telling you about it in person. Not after everything we shared and all the letters we exchanged." She hesitated. "I came to London to break off our engagement and announce that I am leaving to Persia and I hope you will understand and accept it."

His gaze snapped to her in disbelief, those words pummeling him through the chest like a newly sharpened saber. It was as if he had been sending all of himself into a void for seven years. He'd always thought, given the ten weeks they spent together in their youth and the countless genuine letters they had exchanged over the years that she had grown to feel *something* for him. Only it was obvious she didn't feel *anything* for him.

He felt like heaving up his chair and smashing it into mere splinters at the nearest wall. The only thing that kept him from actually doing it was the fact that the chair belonged to his grandmother. "Are you telling me there is someone else? Is that why you're going to Persia?" Bloody hell, he couldn't breathe. Why couldn't he breathe? "Are you physically involved with another man? Is that what you're saying?"

She pursed her lips, clearly offended. "I don't do kisses, Derek. I'm a respectable lady."

A respectable lady who had betrayed his heart. He'd dedicated seven years to the idea of her and them. *Seven.* She was all he'd ever known and all he'd ever wanted to know and she was going to—

He curled his hands into fists to keep himself from altogether standing up into her face and roaring. "The contracts are all signed, Clementine. My mother sent out over three hundred goddamn invitations weeks ago. The wedding takes place in six days. *Six.* What the hell are you doing waiting until six days before the wedding to tell me we're not well suited?"

She was quiet.

Did she honestly think she could do this to him? After pulling the wagon along for seven whole years? "I'm sorry to say you're already mine. This is done. I signed my name on the line. Eight different times."

Her gaze cooled but her façade, as always remained the same. Regal. "Don't you dare to speak to me as if I were an object you signed for."

He narrowed his gaze, his pulse thundering. "Begging your pardon, Miss Grey, but an object stays wherever I put it. And obviously, I can't say that about you, can I?"

She angled toward him. "Neither of our parents had a right to make such a life-altering decision for us. This wasn't the path either of us would have ever taken. Do you not see that?"

He stared in a quaking attempt to stay calm. "I only see a woman making excuses to be with someone else. So who is he? Some goddamn American boy from your Broadway Society?"

She sighed. "It isn't what you think. He is my dearest and closest friend."

"*Really?* And this so-called *friend* is now taking you to Persia for the rest of your life? Is that how he sold all of this to you? Are you really that naïve? Or do you also think I'm stupid?"

She gave him a withering look. "Not all men require a woman to lower their décolletage and offer up a kiss. He is a very respectable man. In fact, he is royalty. And to a select few who are privileged enough to stand in his presence, he is known as Prince Nasser."

Oh now, shite. How was he to compete with that? He gripped the sides of the chair until his fingers pulsed. He tried to keep his voice polite but it stayed rough. "So how the devil did you meet this prince? While you were traveling abroad? While you were— Christ, that certainly explains why it took so goddamn long for you to answer any of the letters I sent to you week after week. Because you and your special *friend* were too busy—"

"There is no need to invoke the devil, Christ *and* God in one breath, Derek. Now keep your voice calm."

"It is calm," he rasped, barely able to contain it. "Am I yelling at you? No. I'm not. I want to, and in my opinion I have every right to, but I'm not. Now how the devil did you meet this man? I have the right to know more about him and whatever the hell this is. Don't you think?"

She sighed. "I met him this past October. He had travelled from Persia to New York to visit certain members of Congress who were hosting a charity event I attended with my father. We shared many mutual interests and became close friends. My father welcomed all of his visits given his revered name. I've never been to Persia, so when he invited me to go with him, I agreed. I was supposed to leave with him straight out of New York without my father knowing, but I told him I couldn't go without seeing you one last time."

His throat tightened. "How kind of you."

She hesitated as if struggling with what she was about to say. "I'm not doing this to hurt you." Her voice wavered. "In fact, I'm doing this to ensure I *don't* hurt you."

Like that made any sense.

He couldn't understand it. Some pompous prince showed up into her life for a few weeks and she fell madly in love. Whilst he, Derek, showed up into her life and had been in it since 1823, practically kneeling at every turn and writing love letters Shakespeare couldn't pull off, and she *still* couldn't bring herself to love him?

A knife-like jealousy not only fully twisted his gut, but ripped it. He hardened his voice. "I'd sooner duel him in Hyde Park and get arrested for it than let some royal prick take you to Persia. You tell him that."

Her startled gaze met his. "Cease. I could have disappeared into the night without you ever knowing where I went, but I didn't. I am giving you the honor of knowing that I genuinely respect you and that every

letter I ever wrote to you was, in fact, genuine in its nature and response."

As if that made him feel any better. He felt stupid knowing how he'd
always carried her letters with him in his coat pocket, and how he'd read
them whilst lounging in his own bed late at night, thinking of better
things to come.

He set his shoulders against the chair. "So you feel *nothing* for me?"

Her cheeks flushed. "That isn't entirely true."

"You're running off with another man. That, to me, is true."

"He is my friend."

Damn her. Did she really expect him to believe that? "Right. So why
the hell wouldn't you let me kiss you if this man is, in fact, your...*friend*?
A friend wouldn't mind."

She swung back to the marble side table and shifted the ash pan with
a finger, lowering her gaze. "I didn't mean to offend you."

"You're announcing your devotion to another man six days before
our wedding. It's hard not to be offended."

She shifted the ash pan with her finger again and bit her lip. Dragging her reticule off the marble side table, she turned toward him. "One
of several truths I couldn't put into writing is this: you require an heir
and I simply would not be able to give you one."

He almost fell out of his chair. "What do you mean you wouldn't be
able to?"

She brought her reticule tightly against herself, pressing her fingers
into it. "I am not opposed to whatever physical relations happen between men and women. In fact, I have always been curious about it, but
that doesn't change the fact that I don't want children. I don't. Not ever.
And Nasser, being my friend, doesn't expect any from me."

He slowly rose from his chair. This kept getting worse. "Is that what
he told you?"

She lifted her chin. "I'm not getting pregnant. 'Tis obvious you are a man of high passions and will expect children, especially given your title. I cannot and will not give them to you."

Mother of God. "How the devil do you know this Nasser will keep his word to you? How do you know he won't force himself on you in the middle of the night?"

Her expression remained still. "He and I share an understanding few ever will."

An understanding he clearly wasn't worthy of. He wanted to walk out of the room and hit every wall in the corridor knowing this was happening to him. "So you expect me to accept this? You expect me to entrust you to another man merely because—"

"Derek, please." She averted her gaze. "You already signed all of the contracts. My father must fulfill his side of the agreement given this is a breach of promise. It was yet another reason as to why I came out and waited to tell you. So you could sign everything and get the money."

He set his shoulders, refusing to appear rattled. "So you're buying me."

A soft breath escaped her. "Try to understand that I never had the kind of life you did. There was very little laughter in my home. I was never taught how to be a good wife or a good mother and I refuse to subject a child to feeling a devotion for me merely because I gave birth to it. I know myself, Derek. I know what I would and wouldn't be capable of. Any form of affection is not in my nature and it would be cruel of me to subject you *and* a child to it. I have no doubt you will be an exemplary father. I also know you'll be an excellent husband. But not to me."

He swallowed back the ache in his chest unable to believe what she was saying.

"Surely there must be someone else you could share your life with," she prodded. "Haven't you ever wanted to…kiss someone else? Anyone else?"

He tugged at his collar, almost wanting to rip it off to keep it from agitating him. Only one. Lady Beatrice, who had been a dazzling debutante of nineteen back in 1822, a few months before he'd met Clementine. He had pined for his pretty neighbor for a full year before she astounded him one evening at a party his mother was hosting by grabbing him by the lapels of his coat when he was walking past an alcove and forcing him into an open-mouthed kiss in the shadows of his own house. It wasn't quite as exciting as he had imagined it would be mostly because Lady Beatrice then proceeded to cry, claiming she was set to marry a very old man of sixty-two. It made him feel used but it also made him feel sorry enough for her to offer up more than a few more passionate and heavy-handed kisses that included the touching of her breasts and thighs. She ended up marrying the old marquis a few months later, which ended their brief, quick kissing association.

"You're awfully quiet," Clementine added. "Do you mean to say there were that many? Or so few?"

He glared. "Don't bloody insult me. I've only ever kissed two women in my goddamn life." Lady Beatrice and a prostitute. Neither of them as memorable as he wanted it to be.

Her eyes widened. "You've already impregnated *two* women?" she rasped.

He pulled in his chin. "No. Of course not. What are you—"

Those blue eyes flared. "You admitted to kissing two women. *Two.* I'm not ignorant, Derek. I know full well that kissing a woman on the mouth impregnates her."

He paused, realizing she was serious. She clearly knew *nothing* about relations between men and women. Which meant...she hadn't been debauched by this Nasser. She hadn't been touched.

A half of a breath escaped him. In some way she was still his. "Kissing doesn't actually lead to children, Clementine." He held her gaze. "Pregnancy happens through other means."

She froze and then averted her own gaze. "I knew that." Her tone indicated otherwise.

She was truly an enigma. She was so sheltered in one aspect of her thinking yet overly hardened in another. He sighed. "There is no need to be ashamed about what you don't know. Given the way society reacts to any form of physical affection, I thought the same when I was younger." When he was eight. Until a stallion mounted a mare in the field and he ran to the gamekeeper about it, demanding the man save the mare. The gamekeeper laughed and sat him down on the nearest fence and explained every single last detail of copulation using two dirt-crusted hands. Derek had avoided his parents for an entire week knowing they were getting naked.

He knew it was his duty to say it. He owed her and them to say it. Because she needed to know what this Nasser might do to her if she allowed herself to run off with him. "When a man is ready to impregnate a woman, or pleasure himself, which also leads to children, all of her clothes come off along with his own. That is how it starts."

She stared. "And why on earth would the clothing need to come off?"

This was about to get awkward. "What I am about to say may keep you from ever being alone with a man again. Do you still want me to say it?"

She eyed him. "Keep it to ten words."

He lowered his chin. "I would need at least a hundred for you to fully understand."

She edged back, her breaths uneven. "If you can't keep it to ten, Derek, I would rather we end this conversation."

Sensing she was about to dart out the door, he inwardly groaned. How did one explain sex to a wide-eyed virgin? One didn't explain it. One did it. And he certainly didn't want to use his hands the way the gamekeeper had, waggling fingers into a hole. "Fine. I'll..." He huffed out a breath and glanced up toward the ceiling in a stupid attempt to focus. "Give me a moment." He counted out what needed to be said several times and then finally decided on, "Our clothes come off and my lower half penetrates you." There. That was ten.

Her cheeks colored. She glanced at the flap of his trousers and snapped her gaze back to his. "What do you mean your…lower half penetrates me? Penetrates what?"

He cleared his throat twice knowing she had just looked at the flap of his trousers. "The uh…the delicate area between your thighs that produces your monthly menses. I would…push in."

"*Push in?*" Her hands jumped to her skirts as if she were intent on protecting it. "Do you mean it hurts in the same manner a menses does? Or worse?"

He huffed out a breath. "I'm afraid I wouldn't know the measure of a woman's pain, but given it involves penetration, the first time is probably anything but—"

She snapped up a hand. "I would rather you not say anymore. I'm not comfortable with this conversation." She angled away, still holding onto her skirts. "Perhaps one of these two women you've already kissed would consider marrying you and enduring your…*penetration.*" She said it disapprovingly. As if him kissing two women was worse than her leaving him for another man.

He stared at her, anger biting into every breath he took. "The first one I kissed was well before you ever came into my life. The second one I kissed *and* penetrated was only a few months ago because I was trying to get some goddamn experience." He tried to keep himself and his words calm, but couldn't. "Am I really that worthless in your eyes? That you aren't even willing to give me a chance after I waited seven years for you? How could you use some pathetic excuse of not wanting children merely to—"

"It isn't pathetic, Derek. Nor is it an excuse. I've always known I would never marry or have children. Long before I met you. I started hiding away money my father gave me when I was ten. I wanted to ensure that by the time I was older, I'd have enough to go out into the world and be independent. I've saved over ten thousand since and had planned to talk to you as I am now before walking out into the world on my own. Nasser simply provided me a better way of addressing the situation. Because in time, despite the amount I have saved, I would have eventually depleted my funds. And aside from my painting, I really have no other talents that would allow me to survive on my own."

He swiped his face and sat down in his chair, unable to stand. She had to go and tell him all of this six days before the wedding. He was going to be publicly humiliated and everyone in London would whisper about the fact that even after seven years of betrothal, he couldn't win her. "I'm going to speak to your father about this. Perhaps he'll be able to make me understand why you think you'd be better off with someone else. Because I have no idea what to make of any of this. It doesn't make any sense. You want to be independent but you're going off with a man?"

Clementine's eyes widened. She hurried toward him, dragged her chair over to his and sat, leaning close enough for that citrus-like bergamot scent to make him breathe in. "Please don't announce any of this right now until I talk to him myself. My father would only blame himself. And he already blames himself for so many things after the way my mother— It's why he drinks. It's why he—"

She froze as if realizing she said something she shouldn't have.

His mind reeled and everything that had ever come into question about her father snapped into place and into focus. He always remembered the scent of cognac on that man. Always. Even years ago. It lingered in the air like cologne. And just yesterday, in less than a half hour during their contract negotiations, Mr. Grey had finished a full decanter of brandy. A full one. It astounded Derek. Any other man would have staggered after consuming a whole decanter of brandy. But Mr. Grey merrily carried on with their conversation and the contracts with a smile. The man's words hadn't even slurred. "Are you telling me your father is a drunk?"

A breath escaped her. She squeezed her eyes. "Please don't...don't tell anyone. Everyone would lose respect for him." She reopened her eyes, tears glistening within them. "He doesn't drink as much as he used to. He falters, like all men do, and goes back to it from time to time, but he has learned to stand on his own. Which is why I'm ready to leave. I know he'll be able to survive without me."

By God. The poor thing had been raised by a drunk. A drunk worth over eighteen million dollars. No wonder she was overly serious and untrusting. He softened his tone so she knew he was on her side. "Did he ever physically hurt you? Did he ever—"

"No." She shook her head. "He would never. He loves me. When he drinks, he is silly and overly jolly. Which is why he does it. It makes him feel happy and invincible." She touched a hand to his arm with the tips of her fingers. "I knew you wouldn't take this well. Which is why I came out to tell you in person. I felt like I owed you this much. We share a history and we wrote each other a lot of meaningful letters."

He tried to even his breathing, sensing he could either let her go or he could fight for her in the only way he knew how. "There are guaranteed ways not to get pregnant. If that is what you want, I'll ensure it. And maybe over time, I...you will change your mind and give us children."

Her startled gaze met his. "You would give up your right to children for me?"

He swallowed. Could he really marry a woman who was too broken to give him children? His life would turn into a lie. He'd always wanted children and had already written a list of names for them to choose from.

He lowered his gaze to her small hand that still fingered the wool of his coat. His chest tightened. "The wedding is set for next week. People will be at the church waiting."

"I know. And I'm sorry. I simply...I...I can't. It wouldn't be fair to you."

She and those overly serious blue eyes were confessing to being too broken to be part of his life. He'd first come to love her those many years ago because she'd come into his life when he desperately needed someone to cling to, someone who could see his pain and understand it and let him feel it without judgment. She was all he'd ever known and wanted to know. But maybe, just as his brother had accused, the comfort of that certain knowledge made him pompous, unworthy and lazy. Regardless of that one time he stupidly tried to surprise her with a visit by going to New York only to find out she was in Spain.

God knew, he hadn't even learned to properly bed a woman, because he'd kept telling himself over the years he was saving the entire experience for her. If not for one smirking gamekeeper and one bored whore he'd went to in desperation, he'd know as little as Clementine did about what went on between a man and a woman. And yet, here he thought he could command her and speak to her about sex, marriage, family, love, passion, all the things he thought he wanted—nay, deserved—from life. He had earned nothing. Not a thing. Certainly not her.

He slowly dragged a hand over to hers. He felt the room sway knowing what he needed to do. "Is this what you want? To go to Persia with this man instead?"

She dug her fingers into his arm. "Try to understand it's best for us."

It was like realizing his life had never been golden. A suffocating sensation tightened his throat. "Do you trust this Nasser to his word? Do you trust that he will honor and protect you in the way you want?"

"Yes. He has proven his worth. You needn't worry in that."

Jealousy bit into him knowing another man was taking what he had always thought was his and only his. It was childish of him to even think it but...it wasn't fair.

She gently laid her head against his shoulder, the softness of her bundled hair brushing his face. "I will miss our letters. I never told you but I always slept with them."

His jaw tightened as tears burned his eyes. Having her head tucked against his shoulder and admitting to having slept with his letters whispered of so many possibilities he wished he was capable of cradling. He set a quaking hand against the side of her soft hair, fingering its softness. "I hope you'll be happy." He meant it.

She lifted her head, moving away from his hand. "Derek?"

"Yes?"

"You're an amazing man. I want you to know that. It's why I came out."

His breath hitched. He turned his head and paused, realizing how close she was. Their shoulders were touching. Their faces were only inches apart. He searched those stunning and trusting blue eyes that held his. The ones he thought would always be his.

Drifting his hand up toward her face, he brushed the smooth warmth of her skin.

She stilled.

He leaned in closer and whispered, "If I'm so amazing, why do you refuse to be mine?"

Her chest rose and fell. "Because you deserve more than what I have to offer. Even if I did try to make this work, I know that in the end, I would only disappoint you and myself."

She genuinely seemed to believe what she was saying. He could see it in her face and in her eyes. "Clementine. How can you say that?" He traced his hand down toward her exposed throat and felt his pulse throb against his own ears knowing he was touching her. He brushed the tips of his fingers against the softness of her skin. "We could be happy together if you will it," he murmured. "I know we could. I adore you. Don't you feel the same about me?"

She brought her hand up, her hand visibly trembling and grazed her finger across his jaw line. "Don't make this anymore difficult," she whispered back. "Please."

He swayed against that hand, his heart almost skidding up to his head. It was like being seventeen again and letting his mind and body be consumed with senseless yearning. Every half-breath he took was tinged with her perfume, making him yearn for her all the more. He lowered his gaze to her full lips, every nuance of his soul wanting to prove to her that if there was any man capable of dispelling her fears, it was he.

He set his forehead against hers, struggling not to give in to what he wanted. To what he had always wanted. Her. "Give me one night in your arms and I'll let you go."

She edged away, her eyes widening. "Derek, I just told you—"

"No child will come of it. I swear. One night and I'll let you go. I'll stand before London without regret knowing I held you in my arms. Please. I need something from you other than good-bye. You can't leave me like this. Not after years of...you can't..."

"I understand." Her fingers stilled against his face. "Can you guarantee no child would come of it? If I allowed for it, could you swear to it upon all you are and I know you to be?"

His heart thundered, sensing she was about to give in. "Upon my life and honor, I swear to it. I vow." He held her gaze. "Come to me. Come to me at night and then I will let you go." He reached out and watched his own hands skim up her shoulders and up to her soft face. "Haven't you ever thought of having me in your arms?" Gently nudging her chin upward, so her full lips were positioned just below his own, he edged in, mentally willing her to be his the moment their mouths touched.

A knock came to the door. "Derek?" His mother called out in an exasperated tone from the other side. "Are you in the cigar room?" The knob rattled and the door opened.

They jumped away from each other and scrambled up from their seats, turning.

Derek staggered in an effort to even his breathing.

Lady Banfield casually walked in, her chartreuse morning gown rustling. She paused, her playful dark eyes veering toward Miss Grey. Her nose wrinkled. "Egad. I smell cigars." She glanced toward the ash pan which held the telling remains of Clementine's cheroot. She snapped her gaze toward each of them, her eyes widening. "Are you both in here smoking?"

Clementine winced.

Shite. He had to do something. Because God love his mother, she was a terrible gossip. She told everyone more than they needed to know. Be it the vicar or the neighbor.

Derek cleared his throat and did what any gentleman would do. "I desperately needed a cheroot and didn't want to leave Miss Grey unattended. She was very gracious about it. I wish to apologize for my lack of judgment."

Clementine swung toward him. "Your lack of—"

"I owe you an apology, Miss Grey." He gave Clementine a firm, pointed look. "I should have never disrespected you. I thought myself to be a greater gentleman than that. Do you forgive me?"

Clementine gaped.

Lady Banfield strode toward him and stared him down, her pinned graying brown hair practically quivering. "I'm appalled, Derek." She paused. "Since when do you smoke?"

He'd never been a good liar, but for Clementine's sake, he did his best to keep his tone even and his stare firm. "Since Andrew and I stopped speaking to each other."

Lady Banfield's strained features softened. She sighed. "The fact that you're smoking concerns me. I don't know what you and Andrew argued about, for neither of you are willing to tell me about it, but I want you to put an end to it. The boy is living in self-imposed squalor and refuses any assistance I have repeatedly tried to give. When I last visited, there weren't even any chairs for me to sit on. I'm at a loss as to what he thinks he is doing. He tells me nothing."

Anger rippled down his spine at what his brother was putting them both through. He wasn't particularly fond of his mother after she kept his father's illness from him, but she was still his mother. "I don't feel sorry for him at all. His blatant disrespect toward both of us is no longer one I wish to reward. This is not what family does to each other and it's time he grows up. If he needs coal for the bucket, he knows where I am."

Lady Banfield's brown eyes pleaded. "You can't leave this to fester, Derek. Your father would have wanted this resolved."

There were many things his father would have wanted. Things Andrew had refused to honor after the man's death. Like how his father would have wanted to see Andrew in the military and rise through the ranks as opposed to being a mere novelist. Like how his father would have wanted to see Andrew associating with men and women who would make him a better man as opposed to associating with men and women who made him into a rebel without a purpose.

Derek shook his head. "I'm sorry, Mother, but I cannot continue to reward him when he acts like an imbecile. If he cannot open the door when I knock on it, how is that my fault?"

Clementine veered closer. She touched his arm. "Derek?"

He stilled at the unexpected touch and lowered his gaze to hers. "What?"

Her blue eyes softened. "You have more than proven that you are kind and compassionate and willing to listen, even when a person may not be worthy of it. Gift that to your brother. Especially if you know he is financially struggling."

He shifted his jaw, angling toward her. It damn well riled him knowing that she thought she could have any say about him or his life when she didn't even want to be a part of it. "I have not disappointed him. He has disappointed me. I didn't turn him away. He turned me away. And it reminds all too much of someone else I know." He held her gaze.

Clementine hesitated and dragged her hand back.

The silence around them pulsed.

Lady Banfield let out a soft breath. "I sent your brother an invitation to the wedding, insisting that he come. It is my hope he will."

How absolutely fucking fitting. His brother would arrive at the church on Monday to find him without the very bride his brother claimed was all his without having to try.

His mother turned toward Clementine and paused, her dark eyes softening. "Look at you. So perfect and darling." She beamed. "At long last, I have a daughter of my own." Whisking toward her, Lady Banfield held out a gloved hand. "I apologize for not being here when you first arrived. I left one of the events early in an attempt to make amends for it."

Clementine swept forward, her hand grasping his mother's outstretched hand in mutual greeting. "I am so honored you would leave an event merely for me. You really shouldn't have."

Lady Banfield let out a pert laugh, shaking their clasped hands together. "With grandchildren on the horizon, I would leave *any* event for you."

Derek cringed at the mention of grandchildren.

Clementine's stare appeared to be plastered.

Lady Banfield took Clementine's arm into her own, patting her hand. "We should introduce you to the housekeeper and our chef at once. The duties that will face you as the new lady of the house will be staggering. Banfield, I am afraid, is far too popular for his own good and has too many acquaintances, which will mean countless events and nothing but work, work, work. Come along. The sooner we introduce you to your duties, the sooner I can forgo mine." His mother paused and gave Derek a long pointed look from over her shoulder. "We will leave my son to finish smoking on his own. I'm afraid his antics just lost him the right to see you for the rest of this day. Hopefully, that will teach him to never smoke in your presence again."

Trying to be a good man in the name of a woman was a bitch.

Clementine glanced back at him as she and Lady Banfield made their way out the door.

Derek held up a quick hand to her, silently informing her to play along.

When they were gone, and their voices were a mere sound one had to strain for, he shifted his jaw, turned, and trudged over to the ash pan where Clementine's nub of a cheroot had been meticulously extinguished in the center of the small bronze pan. He stared at it and almost touched the rolled end where her lips had been. He pulled on the calling bell hard so the footman could clean it up before he did exactly that.

The quick sound of running steps made him pause and glance up.

To his surprise, Clementine rushed into the room, her cheeks flushed.

He stared as she bustled over to him.

Coming to a halt before him, she hesitated, as if struggling to admit to something, and then grabbed his face and kissed his cheek hard.

He staggered, his very skin feeling sparks.

She released him. "I have thought about you and us. Send me a missive as to how I am to come. Then after our night, I will go. I trust you to let me go. It's the only reason why I'm doing this. Because I trust you." She nodded, turned and hurried back out, disappearing as quickly as she had come.

A shaky breath escaped him as he grazed his fingers across his shaven cheek where her mouth had been. He couldn't believe it. She admitted to having thought of him and wanting him. But if that were true, why was she leaving him?

It made no sense.

But then again, she never had made any sense. She was very much a beautiful fairy one came across in a forest, whose existence one always refused to believe in, but upon seeing its wings had to embrace it without being allowed to ever ask it any questions.

In some way, he knew his father had wronged him. His jolly and overly optimistic father had raised him on a grand scheme to believe that life and the world was anything and everything he wanted it to be. And that when a good man laughed and smiled and made the most of life by giving his heart and soul to what he believed in, good things unfolded. Especially when one passionately fought for what one wanted most.

But not everything could be fought for. How did one fight to change a woman's heart if it had remained stoically the same for seven years? What more was he, as a man, to do? Bleed through his knees waiting for another seven years to pass?

One night in her arms was clearly all he could hope for.

As opposed to the countless nights he had always imagined.

Up until that moment, he had imagined long snowy nights spent in the quiet country making passionate love to her before the hearth and then drowsily waking up to find their children piling into the room. He had imagined that his brother would come out during the winter with his own wife and children in tow and together, they would all gather into open sleighs, bundled in furs and ride through fields toward a frozen pond so their children could skate.

It was tragic. Because getting over three million bank notes shoved into his right hand was completely worthless if it couldn't buy him the one thing he'd always wanted most: her.

LESSON FIVE

Pleasure can fool the mind

Into thinking happiness is at hand.

-The School of Gallantry

Thursday, a breath after midnight

If Derek was the flame, then she most certainly was the moth. But unlike all moths, Clementine had no wings left to burn, for she had long removed them and locked them away into a box not even she was permitted to touch. Selfish though it was to go to him, cradle him and then leave him, this was her one and only chance of ever truly knowing what, if anything, could have been possible between them.

Because once she followed Nasser to the throne, her life would be exactly what she had always wanted it to be: free of any and all choking emotions that always turned even the most civilized of people into simple-minded savages unable to control their own minds, their own bodies and their own breath.

Tightening her hold on her moonstone cashmere shawl, given the chill of the April air that pushed its way into the old estate house, Clementine quietly followed the footman down the vast candlelit corridor. The silence of the night and the falling rain beyond the windows was amplified by the clicking of her slippers and the rustling of her primrose evening gown. A tall, broad shouldered figure dressed in a long green-velvet night robe lingered at the far end, intently waiting, his husky features blurred by the shadows.

Pausing before him, her heart jolted realizing his hair was down, barely brushing his muscled shoulders. The golden light of the candles within the corridor illuminated the contours of his lean, smoothly shaven face and glinted across the thick strands of his wavy brown hair, which fell around his face. It was a face that had always haunted her in her youth and a face that was haunting her now. A part of her didn't want to let him go.

She quietly noted the naked smoothness of his broad muscled chest where the open neckline of the robe veered down to the belt on his narrow waist that held everything in place. It was obvious he was naked beneath that robe.

Her own fear of passion, which she had clung to since she was old enough to understand it, urged her to turn and run. But her mind whispered that this one night of passion was far better than eighteen thousand, two hundred and fifty nights of passion she wouldn't be able to control. Which was what fifty years of marriage amounted to.

His gaze skimmed her appearance. "Thank you, Wallis. You may leave. Please don't mention this to my mother."

The footman inclined his head and quickly departed, disappearing around a corner.

Derek's brown eyes softened. "You came." He said it as if it were a blessing.

Her stomach flipped. She wished she could control the way his voice and his eyes made her feel. She wished she could control how he had always made *her* feel. Because that is what truly scared her. Her inability to control what she knew beat within her. The very thing she didn't want to trust. "My father is off on the town somewhere," she quickly offered. "So it was rather easy for me to slip away. Heaven only knows where he is. He didn't tell me where he was going, although I imagine he is off trying to meet women or...I still had to get past Mrs. Langley, seeing her room is adjoined to mine. Fortunately, she sleeps rather heavily, so it was easy. Hopefully, she won't wake up." That was pathetic. She was babbling.

Searching her face, he smiled. "Don't be nervous. How long do you have? Can you stay until morning?"

It was like they were discussing dinner plans, not her ruination. "I have to be back well before morning. My father and I always have breakfast together. Earlier than most. At seven."

He half-nodded. Intently holding her gaze, his large frame stepped toward her.

She braced herself for having her clothes ripped off right there in the corridor.

He gripped her gloved hand and tugging her close to his body, touched his bare hand to the back of her waist, guiding her through the open door of his bedchamber. He closed the door behind them with the back of his heel and released her waist and hand, turning the key in the door. "Remove your shawl, bonnet, and gloves. I want to show you something." He strode past, toward the other side of the room, his robe flowing around his muscled body.

She was genuinely surprised as to how everything was unfolding. Not at all what she imagined. Knowing how eager and hot-blooded he was, she rather thought he'd get straight to stripping her down to her silk stockings and shoving candies into her mouth.

She paused.

A massive hearth across from his mahogany four-poster bed had a cheerful fire blazing, warming the large bedchamber while casting shadows and light with the movement of its flames. Countless lit candles set in various silver candelabras were scattered around the room, whispering of a man who enjoyed being surrounded by light.

He paused before an easel that had a white canvas placed onto it. Set beside the easel was a small walnut table with several inlaid wooden boxes filled to the rim with oil paints in small glass bottles and a large jar of mineral spirits. Everything was angled into the far corner of the room, clearly planned.

He wagged a finger. "I pulled out all of my old paints and my easel from the attic. I checked the oils and they're still good. I was hoping you could paint something for me."

A breath escaped her at the unexpected request. She removed her shawl, her gloves and bonnet, and draped them all onto the bed in an organized manner, the idea of painting something for him making her feel more at ease.

Gathering her skirts from around her slippered feet, she walked toward him. She edged in beside him, grazing a hand across the large blank canvas. "What would you like me to paint?"

His husky features stilled, his skin visibly flushed. "Us naked. In an embrace."

Her hand drifted away from the canvas. Why was she not surprised? "Before or after we...?"

He searched her face. "After. You can't very well paint what you don't know." He shifted his jaw and edged his entire body closer.

Spiced ginger nipped the air, warning her of what was about to come.

Her face grew unbearably hot knowing exactly what he wanted. After some intricate prodding, Mrs. Langley had *finally* gotten around to telling her what really went on between men and women. And it only made her more apprehensive. Because it was very involved.

Quickly turning, Clementine faced the canvas, giving him her back in an attempt to remain as blank as that canvas. "I was finally told more about what happens between men and women. Aside from what we discussed."

His large hand slid down the sleeve of her arm, shifting the material of her gown. He now lingered from behind, the heat of his body penetrating hers as he pressed himself closer.

She closed her eyes and swallowed, listening to the rush of her own pulse. She touched his hand, stilling it against her arm and gripped it tight. She was fine. She would be fine.

The warmth of his masculine lips softly touched the exposed skin of her neck. Gently. As if to assure her that she was still very much in control.

Her pulse hitched. She swayed as his lips delicately wandered across the curve of her exposed neck, prodding her into a secret world she didn't expect.

His tongue slid across her exposed shoulder, nudging away the lace around the trim of her gown as both of his hands slid down and around her waist. He gripped and bundled the material of her gown while still sliding his tongue back and forth, delicately tracing and teasing her skin.

Her head rolled back as the heat of his mouth and tongue overtook her ability to think. She finally knew what it was like to turn all of his fire-ridden words into reality. It was strangely beautiful. Far more beautiful than she ever expected.

The tip of his tongue slowly probed and traced and teased as his hands slid down to her corseted waist. Gripping her sides from behind, he ground his hips into her backside. His lower half was already rigid. She could feel his erection pushing through his robe and into her gown.

He sucked on her throat hard, taking skin in between his teeth.

She gasped, an astounding sensation rippling down the length of her entire body. It was too much. Everything about him was too much. He made her want to kneel to not only his passions but her own. The ones she had always tried to bury in fear of them turning her into something she didn't want to be.

He dragged and rubbed his lower half against her even more, his breaths fanning her throat as he sucked her throat harder. She felt his hand stiffly jerk his erection a few times, bumping her backside as he groaned against her skin. His hands trailed their way up her back, digging into the fabric as if he had every intention of shredding it with his palms. He edged back and quickly unpinned and unlaced the material of her gown, his fingers pulling and tugging and stretching the satin away from her body with an intensity and fever that made her stagger. He worked his way, down, down through the lacings.

Her chest rose and fell in an effort to breathe knowing he was undressing her as if she were a doll. Her eyes snapped open at the thought. The blank white canvas mocked her, telling her nothing of what was about to happen next or what she was or wasn't supposed to feel. All she knew was what she had always known whenever around him: she was too overwhelmed. Wasn't that exactly what passion did? Erase one's ability to breathe and think until the person became nothing but an animal reacting to its environment?

Turning toward him, she dragged in several breaths in a desperate effort to ease the unbearable sensation of being overwhelmed. "I can't breathe."

His rugged features stilled with need. "You're not the only one."

That didn't lessen her panic. "I need to get used to this. Can we take this slower?"

His chest rose and fell. His erection protruded against the velvet fabric of his robe, angling toward her. He raked his hair back and said hoarsely, "Go sit on the bed and give me a moment."

Right. Moving around him and that erection that was still nudging his robe outward, she hurried to the bed, knowing her legs weren't going to hold her up for much longer. She quickly seated herself on the side of its edge, feeling the back of her dress flop open. She cringed and yanked up the sleeves of her gown that was slipping off her shoulder.

"Mrs. Langley told me a gentleman always starts with kissing a lady on the lips. But you didn't. You went to undressing me. Is that normal?"

He winced and puffed out a breath. "Nothing about this situation is normal." He swiped his face and crossed the room, his bare feet peering out from beneath his long robe. Lingering for a moment, he sat beside her, causing the mattress to tilt her toward him. His eyes trailed down to her breasts and stared. Snapping his gaze back to her face, he said, "Your décolletage is barely above your nipples. It's making it difficult for me to think."

She nervously folded her hands. "It was one of the few evening gowns I have that display more. I wore it because I knew it would please you."

A tremor touched his lips. "What I said to you earlier was stupid. You're beautiful no matter what you wear."

A shiver of awareness traced its way down her spine. There was no turning away from this or him now. She was here. This was a moment she was taking for herself knowing Persia still waited. Nasser had already sent her a missive to call on him. "No babe."

"I told you I would see to that. Upon my word."

She nodded and tried to focus, knowing that they only had a few hours. She dug her fingers into the silk of her gown in an attempt to calm her over-stimulated senses. "I think I'm ready."

He scooted closer, his large shoulder grazing hers. "Are you asking me to start?"

Heat flowed to the side of the shoulder he was touching and the tantalizing mixture of his hair tonic and soap floated toward her. She turned her head and glanced up at him, trying not to panic. "Mrs. Langley told me there would be blood. Copious and copious amounts of blood. No matter what we did."

He rumbled out a laugh, his eyes brightening. "Mrs. Langley exaggerates. Or every woman would be dead."

She rolled her eyes in exasperation. "I don't know why I listen to that woman," she muttered. "Her husband has been dead for twenty years. She probably forgot everything."

"Probably." His grin faded into a faint smile before altogether stilling into a level of intense seriousness. He tucked the length of his freed hair behind his ears. "How about we keep the first few minutes between us simple. While I still have control over myself and this situation. How about we just..." He heatedly glanced down at her, his shaven face lingering above hers. "Kiss."

The heat of those smoldering brown eyes could have convinced her to do anything.

She half-nodded, silently affirming she was more than ready.

Nothing mattered in that moment. All that mattered was that she was ready and willing to give herself a breath of what they might have shared had she been born under a different star. A star that had always warned her of dangerous things to come.

****

Her rose water perfume tinged the air of every breath he took. It was too much.

He edged in closer. Slow. Very slow. So as not to startle her.

She searched his face, let out a shaky breath, and closed her eyes, her features stilling with a trust he'd only dreamed of. Tilting her chin upward, she puckered her full lips out like a fish in desperate need of water.

It was adorable. He skimmed his fingers around her shoulder, wanting so desperately to remember this moment. He lowered his head to hers, trying to steady his breathing and grazed his lips against hers.

Everything tipped. Everything pulsed. And then everything went perfectly still.

Her lips stayed stiffly puckered but her body tilted toward him, ready and willing.

He possessively dragged his arms around her, yanking her softness closer and felt her loosened gown fall over his hands. Closing his eyes, he parted her lips with his own, holding her so tightly against his rigid body, he felt like he'd break. His tongue slipped into her mouth and erotically grazed her tongue and teeth. Wanting all of it, he heatedly deepened the kiss, unable to go slow and tipped her back in his arms.

She grabbed him by the face with both hands, yanking herself away.

His eyes snapped open, as his chest heaved in disbelief that it was already over.

She stared up at him, her breaths uneven. "That wasn't a kiss."

He coughed out a startled laugh. "What do you mean, it wasn't a—"

"It wasn't a kiss," she repeated, clearly abashed. "Are you saying people kiss like this?"

And she thought his candy was strong? Ha. "I can't speak for all people, but any man who doesn't use his tongue to kiss a woman ought to be hanged." His fingers dug into the stiffness of her corset as he attempted to drag her back toward himself. "I went fast. I can go slower if you want."

Her hand popped up between them as she pressed it against his forehead to keep him from leaning in. "Your tongue is not going in my mouth again. That was downright animalistic."

He released her in exasperation. "Clementine, we haven't even gotten to the animalistic part." Jesus. Something told him this night was going to be a complete disaster. And why wouldn't it be? He was asking a 'non-affectionate' virgin who didn't want to be a mother to have sex with him. Not really the most brilliant of plans. He swiped his mouth, trying to control the erratic beat of his heart. "Would you rather we not do this? Because your hand pushing my forehead away isn't really much of a compliment."

She winced and flopped her hand down to her side. "I'm sorry. I am willing. I just...it felt like my heart was about to get pushed out of my chest."

He quirked a brow. "My tongue wasn't *that* far down your throat."

She puckered her lips. "What were you trying to do with your tongue? Clean my teeth?"

He choked on a laugh. "No, I wasn't— That's how we're *supposed* to kiss. Are you telling me you didn't enjoy it?"

Her flush spread down toward the rounds of her breasts. "No. It wasn't that, I...I guess I imagined kisses to be quick, is all. Like a butterfly landing and taking off again."

This woman was too much. "I'm not a street vendor waiting to move on to the next person, dearest." He leaned in. "We don't have to kiss if you don't want to. I'm fine with that. Would you rather I get to undressing you instead?"

She hesitated and then nodded. "Did you need me to stand?"

Damn. He honestly didn't know what to make of her or this. She was like a doll asking to be positioned because it wasn't capable of positioning itself. He searched her face. "Why did you really come to me?" he asked, trying to understand. "Why are you doing this? Why are you giving yourself to me only to leave me?"

She lowered her gaze and after a long moment whispered back, "Because I always wanted to know what it would be like to be yours."

His breath hitched. "But you are mine."

She closed her eyes. "Please don't do this. I don't expect you to understand."

Which meant she didn't want him to understand.

But maybe...

He slowly splayed his fingers across the cool, smooth fabric of her evening gown, his heart pounding. He swallowed against the tightness working his throat, sensing that the possibility of them came down to this in her eyes. If he could breathe enough fire across that cool façade of ice, maybe she'd melt and stay. Maybe. "I want you to look at me."

Her eyes opened, revealing blue eyes that were the only thing to ever express what brewed within her thoughts and heart.

"Tonight we belong to each other. And don't you ever forget that." His fingers moved into her black, pinned, silken tresses. He removed the pins randomly tucked in her hair, and tossed them one by one, letting them tinker to the floor. Her long, thick bundled hair eventually fell down past her corseted waist and full gown.

Her soulful, blue eyes continued to quietly watch him.

Removing the last of the pins, he asked, "What are you thinking?"

"I'm surprised that you started with my hair."

He smirked. "Leave off. I'm trying to surprise us both."

"I'm not complaining," she softly chided.

God, was she ever darling. He honestly didn't know how he was going to let her go after their night. After waiting years. How was he going to keep his promise of letting her go given how long he'd wanted her and this? His chest tightened.

When there were no more pins to remove, he skimmed his hands down the length of those soft, smooth tresses, letting it frame her flushed oval face. A breath escaped him. This is what he would always remember about her. *This.* Not her nudity he had yet to see and had always imagined at stupid seventeen, but this. Her hair down around her face making her look like a young woman about to run into the fields free. Free. Very much like she wanted to be. All that was missing was her ability to laugh and smile.

It was the only thing about her he would ever change.

He drew in a ragged breath and edged it out as he dragged his hands up the sleeves of her arms in an effort to his keep himself from altogether ripping the fabric. It was agonizing and painful to keep his desire at a standstill. Because he wanted to rip into her and consume all of her in one tongue-burning swallow. Then do it again and again until it was time for her to go.

But one didn't rip into spun sugar. Not unless one wanted a mess on their hands.

Her bare hand hesitantly touched his knee. "You don't have to go slow anymore," she informed him.

That single touch and those words sent a searing heat right to the core. His cock hardened beneath his robe. "Clementine," he rasped, fighting his need, his want. "I'm going to try not to scare you. All right?"

She half-nodded, her eyes never once leaving his.

The level of trust she was holding out made his very soul stagger.

His hands rounded toward the back of her slim shoulders, his fingers hooking into her open gown. He dragged the fabric away from her shoulders and slipped her pale arms from out of the bell sleeves, exposing an ivory chemise and a rose-colored corset that showcased the fullness of pushed up, tightly constrained breasts that made him let out a breath. "Damn."

She stilled, her chest visibly rising and falling. "Is something wrong?"

He didn't know how the hell he was going to take this slow. "The fact that you're bloody leaving me is wrong." He lowered his head and his lips to the rounds of those breasts and dragged his mouth against their warmth and softness, the faint scent of soap making him close his eyes and groan in disbelief. She was so damn soft and perfect. Everything he imagined and more. His hands curved around the still hidden fullness of her breasts as he opened his eyes. He slid his rigid tongue down her throat and shoulder and made his way down the length of her body, yanking her gown down past her waist hard. "I need you to get up."

She slid off the bed and stood, letting the weight of the gown fall to the floor until she stood only in her chemise, corset, stockings, and slippers.

"Kick off your slippers," he commanded still sitting on the edge of the bed.

She did. They fell into the fabric of the bundled gown.

He patted the space beside him. "Now lay down so I can untie your corset strings."

She averted her gaze and came back onto the bed with each knee, raising her chemise past shapely legs and thighs. She slowly lowered herself onto the bed with a silent trust that made his own throat burn. Her black hair cascaded around her shoulders as she laid herself belly flat against the bed, her cheek resting on the linens. Her hands trailed up slowly across the expanse of the mattress around her leaving ripples in the linen, as if she were openly reveling in the smooth feel of the fabric draping the bed.

He swallowed, realizing something.

This wasn't a virginal woman who feared him and his dastardly advances in the typical sense. This was a woman who had laid herself half-nude, waiting to be touched and pleasured. So why was she refusing to stay? What was keeping her from him?

She glanced back at him from over slim shoulder, still laying on her stomach and captured his gaze. "Aren't you supposed to undress?"

He *loved* this woman. He frantically undid his belt and shrugged off his robe, letting it fall off the bed. Naked, he straddled the backside of her thighs and yanked at the corset strings, loosening them as fast as his hands could move. It took him eighteen heavy breaths (yes, he was counting) before he pried it free from her body and tossed it.

He rolled her over, tugged her chemise up the length of her body and over her head. Whipping it aside, he exposed all of her. "Jesus." He ran his hands across the naked, white smooth expanse beneath him that felt like newly ironed silk with the heat still clinging to it. Seeing the plump fullness of her breasts, dark nipples, her smooth stomach, wide hips and the curling hair between her thighs, blurred his passion into savage need.

His breath hitched in his throat. There was no going slow. Not after waiting seven years.

He captured her mouth with his own and heatedly parted her lips with his moving tongue, her scent, her warmth, her softness surrounding him until he could barely breathe. He possessively cupped her full breasts, pushing her hard nipples against his open palms.

She stiffened beneath him, her hands still laying at her sides, but slowly used her tongue to return his kisses as if she were genuinely trying to enjoy whatever he was doing. He deepened their kiss and blindly grabbed each of her arms and brought them up and around himself. Her hands stayed around his shoulders, where he left them, and even though they didn't tighten around him as he'd hoped, they stayed.

He shifted his naked body against hers and ground his stiff cock into her thighs, the friction bringing a chest-tightening awareness to every inch of it that made him groan. Breaking their kiss, he lowered himself down the length of her body, his fingers trailing down that smooth, endless, glorious skin.

He was about to spread her legs, when he froze, noticing several thick, whitened scars on her stomach and legs. Ones he didn't notice earlier. Maybe because of the fact that he'd been too delirious. A tight knot seized his gut as he slid his finger on the largest that extended from the outside of her thigh to the inside just below her hip. He captured her gaze. "What happened?"

She covered her breasts with her hands and shifted beneath him, as if only now realizing she was naked. She looked down to where he pointed. "I tried crawling through a window that had been smashed when the house caught fire three years ago," she awkwardly whispered. "It cut through the fabric of my robe. It was when those men broke into our home at night back in New York after the election. I wrote to you about it."

His eyes widened. "You didn't tell me you were hurt or that the house caught fire. You only told me the men had all been arrested before any real damage was done."

She shrugged and tried to use the linens to cover herself. "What would my telling you that I was hurt have done? Healed it?" She eyed him. "I can assure you, I survived. I smashed a few vases against their skulls when the pistol was out of bullets and my father went for an ax. My only regret is that I never learned how to properly aim." She said it matter-of-factly. All while laying naked beneath him.

Goddamn her for continuing to devour pieces of his heart like hard candy.

Whoever thought the blue-eyed girl he'd sent into a breathing panic by removing a piece of candy from her glove could shoot from a pistol and smash vases over the heads of other men. It almost didn't make any sense.

He gently kissed each small scar. "I'm sorry I wasn't there to protect you. I should have been. We should have been together all these years. Not apart."

She watched him from where she laid, all shyness and uncertainty fading.

He dragged the tip of his tongue toward the area he knew would make her forget any pain she ever thought she knew. He parted her thighs and lowering his head, slid his tongue across that hidden velvet nub.

She stiffened and gasped, her knees locking his head and tongue into place.

There was no need to take her slow. He wanted her to damn well remember what it was like to scream at high speed. He sucked and flicked, flicked and sucked, lapping faster.

She gasped again, her body quaking beneath him.

"Think of having this every night," he whispered against her moist opening.

Her hands jumped to his head and pressed him harder, as if demanding he go faster.

He obliged, dragging and dragging his tongue against that hardened nub. He sucked, licked and circled it. Sucked, licked and circled it, waiting to feel her shatter.

She cried out, "I feel like screaming. I feel like—"

NIGHT OF PLEASURE | 125

"Do it," he said. He licked faster.

She bucked against him and shuddered, crying out, "Derek!"

It was stunning hearing his name being shouted out by that lush, American accent. It made him feel like he'd finally won. For it was the first time she had ever raised her voice beyond a respectable level.

When she stilled, he lifted his head and smugly licked his lips. "How was that?"

Her breasts heaved and her eyes were closed. "Unreal."

"Good. We're not done yet." His hand slid down toward the curve of her wide hip and toward her smooth stomach until his fingers found the soft curls between her legs. He uncovered that small nub again and rubbed his fingers between now very wet folds.

She moaned, her thighs quivering in response as she curled up against him. "Noooo. It's too much."

"Don't you dare argue. There can never be too much." Knowing her senses were still reveling from fading pleasure, he slowly inserted his finger into that opening, trying to stretch her and ready her for his length. She winced.

"Shhhh," he soothed as he stretched her out more and more, his fingers growing slick from moisture.

She winced again.

Removing his finger, he positioned himself between her thighs, setting the tip of his cock at her opening. "Relax," he whispered, his lips dipping against the softness of her outstretched neck. "It should be a touch easier now." He held himself up with one arm above her, gripped his cock firmly, and slowly pushed it into the mouth of her womb. Her heat and wetness swallowed his erection as he pushed himself deeper into her. He edged in and continued to stretch the walls of her womb with his length until he couldn't push any deeper and his hips were ground into hers.

She stilled against receiving him completely.

The feel of her virginal tightness squeezed him into a delirious state of ecstasy. "You're almost too tight," he rasped. "If I move, I'll burst."

"Don't burst," she hoarsely retorted. "Don't. I know what that means. Keep it in. Or I'm kicking you off."

He was too delirious to laugh. He sucked in a breath to steady his thrumming body and mind and tried not to give into wanting to thrust. "Don't kick me off, darling. I'll behave. I promise." Holding himself perfectly still within that tightness, he bent his head toward her and kissed her forehead, the bridge of her nose, and mouth. "I don't want you to be in any pain."

"I appreciate that." She let out a shaky breath. "It pinched quite a bit. It hurt."

He kissed her mouth again. "I'm sorry. Tell me when you're ready for me to move."

She said nothing. Only stared up at him.

He had to get her to do something other than lay there. "Wrap your arms around me," he offered. "That will help."

She hesitated and wrapped her arms around his neck, her full breasts jiggling.

He swallowed and stared down at her, his arm and body tensing. "Can I move?"

She shook her head, tightening her hold around his neck. "No. Don't. I'm not ready."

He groaned, her moist warmth holding his cock tightly. "I'm going to die."

"Well, now you know how it feels to be penetrated."

He bit back a laugh. "You aren't being very nice."

"I can say the same thing about you. Mrs. Langley never said anything about size."

"I'll take that to mean you're impressed," he breathed.

She pressed her lips together but said nothing more.

He dipped his head and licked her lips. "Can I move now?"

She still shook her head, scattering black hair onto her shoulders and throat. "No."

He shifted his jaw and held her gaze, breathing harder. "I'm going to have to move sometime, you know. I was hoping it would be...soon."

She hesitated. "How long will it take once you start moving?"

Jesus. It was like they had just taken up a painting project and she had things to do. "Clementine, I really don't know how long I'll take." His voice was ragged. "But the longer you make me wait, the longer it will be."

Her fingers skimmed his shoulders as she lowered her gaze to his chest. "Go on then."

It wasn't the sexiest of invitations, but he'd take whatever he could get. He covered her mouth completely with his and started to move inside of her, sending rippling sensations through his core. He eased the length of his cock in and out of her, slowly at first. Cupping one of her breasts and circling his thumb around the hardened nipple, he moaned breathlessly into her mouth. Pressing his mouth harder against hers, he started to thrust hard. And then harder.

He groaned into her mouth, his body responding with quicker, sharper thrusts. If he never made love again after this, he knew he could live with that. Because he knew he'd never find a woman who mentally and physically challenged him into wanting more. He gasped as his core grew tighter against each solid movement he made within her.

She wrapped her legs further around him, sliding her hands down the length of his back until she planted them onto his buttocks and stilled her hands.

Her unexpected exploration of his body made him want to spill.

She peered up at him with pinched lips, searching his face.

Realizing she was only watching him and not at all physically responding, he paused, his breaths ragged. "Are you not feeling any of this?"

She shook her head. "No. I liked your tongue better."

That certainly made his cock proud. "Oh, hell. We can't have that." He repositioned himself against her and stuck his own finger between where his cock reached and where her nub was. He hadn't been hitting it. At all. He was such a moron. Thank the Lord he'd gone to a prostitute or all of this would have dashed right over his head. "Sorry."

He pulled her up and kneeled between her thighs, still holding onto her hips and slowly started pushing himself in and out of her, ensuring this time he hit it. He pressed and pushed, rolling his hips into her.

Her lips parted. She closed her eyes, rolling her own hips against his.

Now that was more like it. He gave her a steadier rhythm to match, trying to get her as close to climax before he hit his own. They pushed and pushed into each other until they were both gulping for air. She gasped as he jerked in and out of her again and again and again, each thrust growing more savage in need. Holding her tighter, he challenged her to ever let him go after this. He pounded into her.

She cried out, his fingers fisting the linens beneath her.

His slick, urgent thrusts continued until she finally stilled and he himself had reached the highest level of mind-reeling sensations his body could take. He scrambled to pull out, falling away from her body and shuddered, releasing everything he'd ever felt in his entire life.

He threw back his head as his entire body convulsed and let his seed pulse out of him onto the linens around them. It was an overabundance of seed he didn't realize he could ever spurt out. It felt wrong to spill outside of her. Because he knew he was meant to give her children. They were *meant* to be more than this.

With that thought, he collapsed against her and tugged her softness against him tight, setting her hands against his now damp skin. He clung to her, his deep, heavy breathing eventually returning to normal.

He brushed back her long, black hair away from her face, scattering it back over her bare shoulder and planted a lingering kiss on her forehead. "I don't know how I'm going to let you go. I can't. I can't—"

"You promised," she murmured up at him without the slightest hesitation.

It was as if what they shared hadn't moved her but had been a random night of pleasure. It might have been good enough for when he was seventeen but not for a man who was heading toward thirty. He swallowed. He never imagined himself alone.

Shifting his jaw, he grabbed her face and kissed her, fully knowing that regardless of whether they were ever together after tonight, he was handing over not just his heart but his entire soul to her. It was such a deranged feeling knowing he had given himself completely to someone who wasn't capable of giving herself at all.

When she didn't return his kiss, merely waited for him to finish, he tore away from that mouth and fell back against the pillow.

She set her chin against his chest.

Maybe if he walked down that aisle, maybe if he waited at the altar dressed in his finest, she would realize after what they shared tonight she would be making a mistake. "This doesn't need to be final. I'll still be at the church the day of the wedding. I'll wait an hour before I announce the end of our union before those in attendance. In case you change your mind."

She was quiet for a moment. "No. I won't make the decision of taking away your right to have children or exposing myself to the possibility of— Please don't do this before London. Don't— I won't be there."

He tightened his hold. "It makes no difference to me where or how I do this. The result is the same. You intend to walk out of my life."

She closed her eyes. "Don't do this. Please. You promised."

"Did I?"

She set her cheek against his chest. "Mend the rift between you and your brother. You will need him. And given the way your mother speaks of his struggles, he probably needs you more."

He squeezed his eyes shut. She was giving him walking orders. She was letting him go. Without giving him a chance to show her the sort of husband and father he could be. "I'll mend the rift," he murmured. "You needn't worry in that."

"He is the only sibling you have, Derek. Cherish it."

What did she know about cherishing? She couldn't even cradle what he was laying out before her very eyes. The room grew quiet and all he could hear was his own breath and hers. Though he wanted to believe there would be more heavenly nights like this between them, this was it. No more letters. No more dreaming. No more wondering. No more yearning.

This was where their story ended.

LESSON SIX

Look into the future. What do you see?

Love and bonny kisses? Or the roaring of a deadly sea?

-The School of Gallantry

The candles still glowed but within another hour, she knew they would wane. Long after his breaths had settled into an even rhythm that announced he had well-exhausted himself and fallen asleep after he pleasured them both a total of three times over the course of five hours, Clementine carefully slipped out of his arms.

He didn't move. His eyes remained closed and those masculine lips remained slightly parted. The sheets of the smooth linen had been pulled up barely to his waist, exposing the muscled contours of his large, lean body.

He was so beautiful. She had always thought so. Since the moment they first met.

She lingered beside the bed for a long moment, watching him sleep. She watched that broad chest rise and fall, remembering the way it felt against her hands. Now she knew what was possible between a man and a woman. It wasn't as fearsome as she had always imagined. But then she knew that was because it was Derek she had submitted herself to. Who knew what sort of malicious things went on between men and women around the world behind closed doors?

She only hoped that in time, Derek would forgive her.

She had already forgiven herself. After all, she knew his worth. She had always known his worth and it had always outweighed her own. This laughing, playful Adonis deserved a world she would never be able to offer him. Unlike other females, she didn't laugh. She didn't flirt. She didn't sashay into a room with a whirl, looking for things to play with next. Her sense of humor was nonexistent and pathetic.

Her eyes burned. Everything about her was pathetic. And a man like Derek, her beautiful Derek, deserved so much more.

Turning, she quietly gathered up her chemise, slipping it over her naked body. A very sore body. Glancing back at him, she pattered over to the easel and gently started laying out all the paints, mentally picking out the colors she needed. Her hands moved and arranged and mixed and flowed with the one world she always whole-heartedly submitted to: painting moments of life.

She didn't focus on what she was leaving.

She focused on what they had shared.

What she loved about painting was replicating the world around her and adding whatever color and light she pleased, molding it into the way she wanted it to be. Not what it necessarily was. She wandered over to the mirror and perused herself and her features, lifting her chemise high enough to expose her legs. Holding onto her own image in her head, she veered back over to the canvas. Dipping the tip of the largest brush she could find into black paint, she started moving the brush effortlessly across the canvas, the sound of the brush creating a rhythm in her mind as her gaze followed the lines and curves of what she saw.

Painting was the only time she ever felt in complete control of not only the world around her but her own breath. It was like seeing the stars for the first time whilst laying out on an open field with the breeze floating around her. And knowing that she was re-creating a stunning moment she would remember for the rest of her life, she painted and painted and refused to stop the brush until it was all over the canvas where it belonged.

****

Sunlight glimmered beneath his closed lids making him open his eyes and squint. Realizing he was alone in bed, Derek scrambled to sit up, his heart pounding. Her clothes were gone. She was gone. It was as if she had never been.

She had left without saying good-bye. Without—

Gritting his teeth, he grabbed up the pillow she had been sleeping on and whipped it off the bed, not wanting the scent of her anywhere near him. Seven goddamn of his years gone in a breath. "Fuck."

Swiping his face that was in need of his daily shave, he pushed himself off the bed and standing naked beside it, stared at the linens, images of his body pushing into hers making it difficult for him to breathe. For all he knew she was going to submit herself next to this friend in Persia.

The very thought made him jump forward, savagely grip the linens and rip them off the bed. He mindlessly tugged everything off the mattress, stripping everything in between ragged breaths. Anything and everything that had touched her body. He flung it all into a large pile on the floor and even grabbed up all of the pillows and flung them all onto the linens.

He had three million now.

He could afford new linens.

Letting out uneven breaths, he swung toward the back of the easel that faced him. The easel he had set up for her. She hadn't even taken the time to gift him the one thing he had asked of her. A moment of their embrace.

Ready to grab the canvas and throw it across the room, he stalked toward it and then jerked to a halt. The small table beside the easel and the floor around the easel were countless small bottles of paints pulled out from his wooden boxes. They had all been scattered. The wooden pallet was dabbed with various oil paints, colors smearing into one another from use and the jar of mineral spirits he had left out was murky and clouded. Eight different brushes sat in it.

His breath hitched as he quickly rounded the easel, making sure he didn't step on anything that was laid out on the floor. As the canvas came into view, with the morning light angling in from the lattice window, he paused, his lips parting.

It was so life-like and so evocative it startled him.

On a linen covered four-posted bed, with a red velvet curtain bundled and draped off to the side of it, lay his Clementine naked in his arms, her hair beautifully spilled over the side in a wave of black silk that gleamed like real tresses in candlelight. Her nudity was covered by his own nudity, the linens tangling and rippling around their legs and waists. Their faces were dipped close to each other, barely a wisp away from a kiss, their lips delicately parted and about to join. Their eyes were half-closed, their expressions both romantic and soft.

It was so good Michelangelo most certainly would have wept. Or altogether take himself in hand and pleasured himself.

Derek brought a shaky hand to his lips and plastered his entire palm hard against his mouth in an effort to remain standing. He was never going to love another woman again.

LESSON SEVEN

When a heart is forced to beat to a rhythm it never set,

it begins to learn the true meaning of why it should fret.

-The School of Gallantry

Saturday afternoon

When a gentleman beautifully proved his golden worth to a lady by defending her honor before his own mother whilst assuring her that she was free to walk away from a seven year engagement, even after a shared night, it was up to that lady to prove her own worth in the only way she knew how. Even if it meant leaving her ruffled chaperone, Mrs. Langley, in the safety of the carriage so she could walk into a bachelor-infested townhouse that smelled like ale had been burnt on the stove.

Or at least Clementine *hoped* it was ale that had been burnt on the stove.

A muffled thump, along with several pronounced thuds, vibrated the painted walls, echoing its way from upstairs to the wooden floorboards beneath her slippered feet. Clementine swung toward the wooden narrow staircase, the sash on her bonnet swaying. The brass chandelier above her head quaked with each solid thud. Several of the melted stubs of wax threatened to tilt out of their narrow sconces.

It was like someone was trying to dismantle the house.

Tightening her hold on her beaded reticule, she glanced up toward the buxom female servant who was hurriedly coming back down the stairs after having delivered her card.

"Is everything as it should be?" Clementine asked the woman.

The young brunette came to a halt on the landing, letting out a melodious laugh that showcased surprisingly beautiful teeth. "Nothing is ever as it should be in this house." The maid ushered Clementine toward a small receiving room off to the side. "You and that gorgeous gown of yours ought to wait right in there. I'm afraid Mr. Holbrook isn't about, but Lord Brayton, after receiving your card, insisted on seeing you. Consider yourself lucky. He never sees anyone. Not even from his own family."

Oh, dear. "I didn't realize there was anyone else living with Mr. Holbrook."

"Oh, now, everyone right down to the butcher knows the two share living quarters due to their lack of finances. It's sad, really. Two men from well-to-do families and nothing to show for it."

Clementine stared at the young woman, abashed. "You really shouldn't belittle the circumstance of the very men who hire you."

The maid pulled in her chin, her green eyes brightening as she set a roughened but dainty hand against the apron of her grey wool ensemble. "Oh, I'm not the rude sort, I dare say. I was raised better." She puckered her lips, clearly not sorry. "But Mr. Holbrook owes me money, Miss Grey, and Lord Brayton thinks himself cheeky, so between the two, I have no trouble saying it. *At all.*" The woman sighed, dropping her hand. "His lordship will be down shortly. I apologize for the lack of formality, which a lady like yourself is no doubt accustomed to, but I'm the only remaining servant. I have a boy, you see, so every decision I make is for him. He rather likes it here."

The maid edged in, the scent of scones and cinnamon teasing the air, and lowered her voice. "Now if you'll excuse me, Miss Grey, I've got a long list of duties that include cleaning up all the trays. These men are messier than my six-year-old. Good day." The maid patted her food-spattered white cap back into place and hurried past. She heaved up a large wooden tray from a dilapidated side table that was piled with chipped, dirty dishes, then clumped down the darkened corridor and disappeared around a corner.

The ticking of a slanted hall clock now pierced the deafening silence.

Her father would have grabbed her hard by the ear if he knew what she was up to. From all of his riled commentaries, she knew that Derek's younger brother was involved with incredibly disreputable individuals and wasn't known for being a gentleman himself. Which meant she had exactly forty-five minutes to deliver her letter, swing over to a random shop to buy something and get back to the hotel with her chaperone before her father returned from his afternoon ride.

Taking in a calming breath, she eased it out and made her way into the small receiving room. When she reached the middle of the narrow room, she paused.

The green curtains hanging around the row of windows had been drawn tight, shutting out the day's remaining light as if the lone servant had never gotten around to opening them. Which was no surprise. Several lit candles sat on sconces, illuminating the darkened atmosphere.

She lingered, pitying what Derek's mother said she would find. There were no chairs or sofas or tables, merely one painting depicting a battle scene and a large well-worn leather trunk that had been set on the floor, its lid flipped back. It was filled with swords and daggers.

Curiosity getting the best of her, she wandered to the trunk. Several large moon-shaped curved blades with silver casings were assorted side by side, clearly arranged by size. Her lips parted in astonishment. They looked Arabian and were carved with various symbols she'd seen on Prince Nasser's own ceremonial sword.

"They're from Persia," a deep voice rumbled from behind her.

She jumped and spun toward the doorway.

A very large, very broad-shouldered man loomed, dressed in the most unconventional attire of only a waistcoat, shirt, matching trousers, and boots. No cravat and no coat. The commanding stance he held and furrowed brow made him look all the more intimidating.

Ice-blue eyes pierced the distance between them, emphasizing a long jagged scar that menacingly traced its way from the left side of his ear to the bottom of his unshaven jaw. "Good afternoon," he rumbled, skimming her appearance. "I'm Lord Brayton."

He wasn't like any aristocrat she'd ever seen. He looked rough. And she highly doubted that sizable scar had been delivered at a dinner table with a butter knife. "Good afternoon. I'm Miss Grey."

"You most certainly are. 'Tis a most unexpected and...pleasant surprise."

Her brows came together. "Pardon?"

"I have heard so much about you." He stepped into the room, shrinking the already small room with his presence. "Allow me to provide more light." He strode toward the drawn curtains on the other side of the room.

Clementine turned, her eyes pinned to his massive body. And she thought Derek was blessed. She cringed as his backside came into clear view. It was rather startling seeing a man strut about without a coat. The way his waistcoat sat just above his waist was scandalous. As were his tightly fitted black wool trousers, which were kept taut and straight with the foot straps he'd buttoned beneath large black leather boots.

He paused before the window and whipped the faded green velvet curtains apart in one swift motion. Soft, gray morning light poured into the room as the blurred movements of the street outside were displayed through the glass panes. He turned and strode back toward her, drawing steadily closer.

She eyed the door and its distance to measure an escape if it was necessary.

Fortunately, his massive body stopped a respectable few feet away, enabling her to breathe well enough to stay. "How do you do, my lord?" she managed.

"Very well, thank you." His dark brows came together, emphasizing the curved scar on his face. He folded his arms across his chest, the broad outline of his shoulders straining the fabric of his linen shirt and black waistcoat. "I would ask you to sit, Miss Grey, but I'm afraid Holbrook sold most of the furniture."

"There is no need to apologize. Standing will be satisfactory, thank you."

He eyed her. "After hearing so much about you, I didn't expect you to be so..." He paused and stared her down for a moment. "Pretty," he concluded, dropping his arms down to his sides.

Apparently, Andrew had confided things he shouldn't have. And now this man thought he had a right to comment. "No gentleman ought to comment on a woman's appearance." She pointed at him. "I'm not entirely alone. My chaperone is waiting outside for me. So don't you dare think you can waltz right into me with an advance."

He smirked. "Thank you for the warning, Miss Grey. I'll do my best to, uh...control myself around you." Weighing her with a critical squint, he took another step toward her, closing the distance between them. "Is there a reason why you're calling? Do you require assistance of some sort?"

"Assistance? No." She peddled back and scrambled to open her reticule by tugging and loosening the braided cord. "I'm here to deliver a letter." She pulled out the neatly sealed ivory parchment she had written and hesitated, noticing that he was observing her rather intently. Fully extending her arm, she held it out as far from herself as possible with the tips of her gloved fingers to ensure he didn't have to step any closer than was necessary. "Would you please give this to Mr. Holbrook?"

He glanced at it but didn't take it. "What is this about?"

"A plea that he show more respect to his brother. Can you please give this to him?" She still held it out by the tips of her fingers, praying she wouldn't have to go near him.

"Do you expect me to cross the room for it, Miss Grey?" he asked. "Surely, I'm not that intimidating, am I?"

She winced. Closing the distance between them, she walked up to Lord Brayton and sheepishly held out the letter toward his massive, scarred hand. A hand that appeared to have sustained more blade-related wounds.

He slipped it from her hand and tucked the letter into his waistcoat pocket. "I'll ensure he gets your letter. He should be back within a few hours."

A breath escaped her. "Thank you." Her brows came together, curiosity getting the best of her. "You wouldn't happen to know what their argument was about, would you?"

He shrugged. "Holbrook wouldn't say. Which means it was personal. Things certainly haven't been easy for that boy. The girl he wanted to marry rejected his offer of matrimony, leaving him in a financial quandary given he'd been overseeing all of her bills. I tried to assist him, but he prefers prison as opposed to hanging his pride. And then there is the business of his livelihood. Or lack thereof. He only sold fifteen books in the past twelve weeks." He cleared his throat. "I bought all fifteen and handed them out to people on the street. He doesn't know it."

Something told her she could trust this man to far more than a letter.

Since Andrew wasn't about, she considered calling again at a later time, but preferred to do it this way as it wouldn't require an explanation. She quickly dug into her reticule, pulling out the thick roll of bank notes she had saved up since she was ten.

She held it out. "I am entrusting this to you, Lord Brayton. Please see to it Mr. Holbrook gets it. Feel free to take out a thousand for yourself for delivering it. There is certainly enough for you to do that."

He searched her face, his features softening. "The man is fortunate you care enough about his struggles."

She held it further out. "It is his brother I care for. I am merely hoping this will help."

Reaching out a hand, he took the wad of bank notes of ten thousand and glanced at it, letting out a whistle. "I have no doubt it will. I will ensure he gets every penny of it."

A breath escaped her. "Thank you." She fidgeted. "Please tell him I would have preferred to give it to him in person but I'm leaving London in the next few days."

He stuffed the banknotes into his pocket. "Are you? That isn't what I heard." He grabbed her face hard. "Come here. I have a message for you."

She winced against the roughness of his hands and panicked, trying to shove at him. "What are you—"

He kissed her on the forehead, startling her.

The familiar musky and sweet scent of *davana ittar* on his large hands, which she knew only belonged to Persian nobles, overwhelmed her. He smelled like Nasser.

She scrambled back in disbelief, her fingers swiping at the moist area on her forehead. Nasser had officially infiltrated every last corner of her life by sending over-muscled men with titles to kiss her. What next? "Why is a grown man working for the Persian crown living with Banfield's brother?" she demanded.

Lord Brayton's blue eyes held hers. "You and I are like family. There is no need to panic. His Royal Highness simply asked that I investigate Banfield so he might better understand how to approach terminating your engagement. Unfortunately...there has been a change of plans since you and he last spoke in New York."

Dread seized her, wondering what Nasser had been doing all along behind his red velvet curtain. "Setting aside that I am not by any means pleased with His Royal Highness for treating Lord Banfield as if he were a criminal in need of investigation, what exactly do you mean there has been a change of plans?"

He set a scarred hand to his chest. "His Royal Highness wishes to announce that you will be marrying Lord Banfield, after all."

Her eyes widened. "*What?*" She almost staggered. "What happened to the original plan?"

"It was tossed. He isn't pleased with you. In fact, he is miffed."

She stiffened. "Why? What did I do?"

"He expects you to call on him at once."

This didn't bode well. Was it because of the night she gave to Derek? Oh God. "I cannot call on him. My father would be on to us within a breath and Lord Banfield and all of London would know of it in less than fifteen minutes. These Brits gossip like old women trapped together in a windowless room."

"His Royal Highness will not tolerate disobedience," he coolly offered. "To disobey him, in his eyes, is treason."

To Nasser everything was treason. "Pardon me for throwing a fit, but how is my marrying Lord Banfield going to allow me to leave the country? I would legally become the property of the very man I am trying to leave. By law, Lord Banfield would have the right to send constables after me." And a part of her knew if given the chance, he would.

His ice-blue eyes darkened with emotion. "Have you told Lord Banfield of the agreement you and His Royal Highness made? Have you betrayed what you swore to protect?"

She huffed out an exasperated breath. "No. Of course not. He knows nothing. No one does. Not even my father. I would never betray him. *Ever.*"

Those tense features softened. "Good. His Royal Highness wishes to see you at once. You have permission to call on him anytime. In fact, I suggest you call on him in the next hour. His schedule is fairly light to-day."

She felt a groan of frustration grip the back of her throat. One would think dealing with a prince would be more of an honor, not a curse. "I am not meeting him in broad daylight. This isn't Boston and I have no tea. Unless he and I are leaving London promptly afterward, I am not calling on him."

"Don't agitate him, Miss Grey. He isn't always as charming as he ap-pears." Lord Brayton stepped back. "His Royal Highness wishes to ex-tend an invitation to buy your wedding gown. From his understanding, you never bought one." He turned and strode away.

Her eyes widened. She gathered her skirts and frantically followed him out into the foyer. "I don't understand any of this. He said nothing in his missive to me about— Did he tell you why he changed his mind? Because I haven't betrayed him. I haven't—"

He came to a halt and glanced at her from over his massive shoulder. "Is someone waiting for you?"

She paused. "Yes. My chaperone is waiting outside in the carriage. Why?"

"I suggest you leave at once. Your visit has lasted too long and I have things to do."

"But—"

"But what? It's incredibly simple, Miss Grey. His Royal Highness commands that you go to your own wedding."

She floundered between panic and uncertainty. "But I...but...go? And then what?"

"You marry Lord Banfield and live happily ever after. What else?"

It would be a mess if she stayed. It would be a mess if she tried. There was no doubt it would end in her smashing the last of who she had al-ways fought to be: reserved, calm, and collected. "But Nasser knows how I—"

"His Royal Highness believes it would bring dark spirits into all of our lives if you left Lord Banfield and went to Persia."

Dark spirits? What— This wasn't happening. This was supposed to be her way out. This was supposed to be—

She was beginning to wish she had never slipped into that alcove where she happened upon an overly serious, tall dark figure in ceremonial attire who asked her one very simple question in an alluring foreign accent: "*If you were a man, azizam, and had complete control over an entire country, what would you command from that country?*"

It was the beginning of a twisted friendship that had led to the ultimate bargain between a man who was a lover of men and a reserved woman whose greatest fear was loving a man she had fallen in love with through a bunch of stupid letters. "He can't do this to me. He can't—"

"He just did." Lord Brayton reached into his pocket and snapped out a calling card. "If you have any complaints about the new arrangement, take them up with His Royal Highness."

She snatched the card away and sighed. It would seem she was going to have to call on Nasser in broad daylight after all.

There was a scraping of metal against the floorboard and the pattering of feet. "*Brayton?*" a young boy's voice echoed from atop the stairs. "Can I play with this?" A dark haired boy held a saber so massive, he was physically tilted to one side in an effort to keep its weight off the floor. His wool trouser-clad leg was barely inches from the thick side of the sharp blade that dangled.

Startled, she snapped out a gloved hand toward the boy standing at the top of the stairs. "Don't move. Don't— Your leg— Lord Brayton, *do something!*"

Lord Brayton sighed. "Pardon me for a moment." He jogged up the stairs, shaking the floorboards she was standing on, leaned down and gently removed the saber from the boy's small hand. "Never touch these unless I'm around," he gruffly pointed out. "Or your mother will use every last one of these blades against me. Is that what you want? Do you want me to die?"

That freckled nose scrunched itself. "No."

"Good," Lord Brayton returned. "I appreciate that."

The boy's features brightened. "Can I play with the smaller daggers instead?"

Dearest Lord. She didn't know anything about children, but she knew this wasn't right.

Lord Brayton tsked. "I already asked about it. Your mother said no."

"She *would* give me the mitten. I never get to have any fun. Not *ever*." The boy paused. Seeing Clementine, he perked and jogged down the stairs toward her, landing with a big hop and a thud before her. He craned his head back to look up at her, his dark hair falling back and away from his forehead. "My name is Jacob. But I ask that you call me Mr. Jacob. I'm a gentleman, you know."

She hesitated and politely offered, "How do you do, Mr. Jacob? My name is Miss Grey."

"*Miss Grey?*" He grinned, exposing three missing teeth. "You don't look grey to me."

That actually made her smile. "Why, thank you, Mr. Jacob. I appreciate that."

He lowered his small chin, perusing her gown. "Jumping crickets. I've never seen anything so nice." Reaching out a small hand, he slid a hand over the fabric, then brought over the second hand, his lips parting. "Mama would like this dress." He paused and glanced up at her. "Can I buy it off you for a shilling? Her birthday is next week."

Oh, dear heavens. If only the boy knew it had cost her forty pounds.

She lowered herself to the floor, her gown bundling around her as she searched his bright and eager features. His teeth were missing in three different places and for some ungodly reason she momentarily imagined what it would be like if she and Derek had a boy. He'd be just as bright eyed and full of mischief. Like his father. And she had no doubt

Derek would be giving the boy his own tin of spiced candy to carry around.

Her throat tightened. "If you give me a shilling, Mr. Jacob, I'll ensure she gets a new dress. A far better one than what I'm wearing."

He blinked. "A far better one?"

"A *far* better one," she assured him.

His eyes widened. He swung away, hopping up and down on scuffed boots as he pointed at her and addressed Lord Brayton. "She needs a shilling! Give the woman a shilling. *A shilling!* Before she changes her mind!"

Clementine set a gloved hand to her cheek and slowly shook her head. Were children really this adorable? Why had she never noticed that before? She paused. Maybe because she had actually never been around any children. Ever. Not even as a girl. She hadn't even played with any. With the amount of traveling she always did for her father's political events, she had only ever been in the company of adults.

Lord Brayton heaved out a breath and dug into his waistcoat pocket. "I don't have a shilling, Jacob, but I do have a guinea. *Here.*" He tossed a coin from above stairs.

The boy popped out both hands and scrambled in an effort to catch it but it tinkered and rolled past his reach. He booted his way over to it with pumping arms and swiped it up. Hustling back over, he triumphantly held it out to her between two fingers. "It's a guinea. And a full guinea amounts to exactly twenty-one shillings. I know my math. So please send my mother twenty-one pretty dresses. And maybe even a bonnet."

A startled laugh escaped her. "Even a bonnet, you say?" she drawled.

He paused, still holding out the coin. "I'm not being funny. If the bonnet is too expensive, don't include it. But she needs dresses. Pretty ones. Not the ones she has."

Now she knew what it was like when others chided her for not having a sense of humor. She gently took the coin from his hand. "Thank you for your timely and generous payment, Mr. Jacob." She sighed, her smile fading. Now she was going to have to add this to her list of things to do before leaving London. "What is your mother's name?"

"Miss Leona Olivia Webster."

She paused. Miss? That meant the woman had the boy out of...wedlock. Her heart squeezed knowing the hardship the two must have endured. Now she knew she had to help. "I will take your mother's name to the Nightingale at once. Have you ever heard of it?"

"Isn't that a bird?"

"Yes. But this a very special bird. From what I am told by Lady Banfield, it's a very exclusive shop on Regent Street that very few people have access to. It is said the French gentleman, Monsieur Luc Chevalier, who heads the shop is related to the same woman who had once made all of Marie Antoinette's clothes."

Those eyes widened. "The queen who lost her head during the revolution?"

"The very one. Have your mother go there and give her name. Tell her when she gives her name, she will have as many dresses on credit at the shop as she wants. After all, why limit her to a mere twenty-one? She must have however many she needs. Yes?"

He laughed. "Yes, yes, yes!" He kissed her on each cheek leaving sloppy, wet marks that made her cringe. He jumped up and down, flailing his arms and leaning left to right and right to left again. "She will have the most wonderful birthday yet! All thanks to my guinea!" He skipped down the corridor and back again, his face flushing in excitement.

Clementine slowly rose to her full height again, smoothing her skirts around herself and felt an unexpected sadness grip her. One she had never allowed herself to feel. Because she would never know this. She would never know the skipping of feet or flushed cheeks or excited voices. Not unless she...knelt to giving herself and Derek a chance.

Jacob clumped up the stairs, stair by stair, up toward Lord Brayton. Jumping onto the landing with swinging arms, he pointed up at the towering man standing beside him and said, "I owe you another guinea. I'll pay you when I become a chimney sweeper."

Lord Brayton smirked. "I heard that one before." Grabbing hold of the child's head, he pushed him toward the corridor. "Now go and read some books."

"The ones in your room?" the boy asked. "With the pictures of bubbies?"

Lord Brayton paused. "No. The ones in *your* room. With the pictures of gardens and animals."

"Gardens and animals? I'm six, Brayton. Not *two*." The boy huffed out a breath and grudgingly stomped out of sight.

Lord Brayton whirled the saber as if to test its weight and then stabbed the long end of the blade into the wooden floorboards, using the floor itself as a holding place for the blade. He cleared his throat and casually thumbed toward the direction the boy had disappeared. "He isn't mine," he rumbled out.

She stared up at him disapprovingly. "Thank goodness for that. A boy of his age should never touch a sword that size or be referring to books with *bubbies*. Where is his mother?"

His demeanor cooled all the more. "Where she should be. In the kitchen." He inclined his head. "It was a pleasure." He disappeared around a corner.

She glanced in exasperation at the calling card she had been given. The expensive gold lettering on the ivory cardstock revealed the number 14 on Park Lane. She sighed. It was time to call on the Persian devil with whom she had clearly made one too many bargains.

****

The double mahogany doors leading into the lavish private quarters of His Royal Highness were swept open by two dark-skinned men dressed in identical flowing emerald-green garbs bound by thick, red sashes around their waists.

To her surprise, a very pretty silver-haired woman sashayed toward her, a long string of expensive pearls swaying against a sizable bosom hidden beneath a lavish morning gown that rustled with the sway of her corseted hips. The woman formally inclined her head, sending the small feathers within her pinned hair waving. "*Bonjour.*" She flirtatiously smiled in the way a woman did when harboring a naughty secret and pertly whisked her way out into the corridor and out of sight.

It would seem Nasser was trying to make a new name for himself.

Without waiting to be formally announced by the wigged butler in livery, Clementine swept in, her slippered heels clicking against the gleaming white marble. A line of servants departed the large receiving room and the doors she entered through finally closed, leaving her to address the prince alone.

She veered toward a long-legged young man of olive skin. He was dressed in formal black, save his red silk cravat and red embroidered waistcoat, and was leisurely stretched out on a green velvet chaise with a book angled open just below his square shaven jaw. His black hair was meticulously swept back with tonic, making it look like smooth glass. His features were sharp and incredibly manly. One would never know by looking at him or interacting with him that he was a lover of men. Of course, she knew he had to play the manly role very well. A whisper of who he really was would annihilate his chances to take the throne.

Set beside his chaise where he lounged was a decanter of brandy, grapes, and a half-eaten browning banana that had been angled onto a silver tray.

She came to a halt beside his chaise and coolly glanced down at him. "You must find yourself amusing. All of a sudden you think you're Cupid?"

Still intently reading an Arabian leather-bound book, with his dark brows drawn together, he said in a heavy accent, "I am Persian, *azizam.*

Not Roman. If you are going to toss gods at me, please reference *Tammuz* instead. Otherwise, you are insulting me and my culture."

She rolled her eyes. "Might I ask who this Lord Brayton is and why in heaven's name a man of his size is living with Banfield's brother?"

He kept reading for a few moments. "His name is Dalir."

"Dalir? You mean it isn't Lord Brayton?"

"To his people he is known as Lord Brayton. But to me, he was reborn when he came under my protection. He has been serving me and the Persian crown since I was sixteen." He kept reading. "He was not at all pleased when I gave him the assignment to come to England. He did not want to return to his old way of life, but he was the only one with British heritage who could come into London without anyone suspecting I was sending him."

"You sent a *spy*? Are we at war now? Is that what you're saying?"

"No. Not at all. I sent him into London ahead of me to investigate what I was getting into. A man does not seize another man's woman without knowing what his rival is capable of. That would be ignorant on my part." He glanced up at her. "Did you find my Dalir dashing? Did you like him?"

"Like him?" she echoed. "He has more muscles than tact."

"Leave him be. You know nothing about him." He turned a page and kept casually reading. After a long moment, he asked, "Did you miss your prince? Or are you here to be a woman and scold?"

She sighed. "What is this business of you commanding me to stay in London and marry Lord Banfield? Given all that you know about me, you cannot possibly—"

"Forgive me, but are you a good-looking man and do you own a crown?"

His sense of humor was as non-existent as hers. "I thought we were friends."

"Yes, I thought so, too. And then you disappointed me." He lowered the book onto his chest, resting it against his embroidered red waistcoat.

Piercing black eyes of immeasurable depth met hers. "Why did you not tell me Lord Banfield was in love with you?"

She flushed and felt the room shrink. It would seem *everyone* knew about Derek's affection for her. Not that he had ever been particularly quiet about it. Derek had more or less asked her to marry him within five minutes of them knowing each other. "It's complicated."

"Complicated." His masculine lips pursed. "Does this mean you love him, as well? Did you also omit *that* complication?"

She inwardly winced. "Why are you— You have no right digging into what he and I share. This is between him and me."

He rigidly pointed at her. "*No.* You involved me and therefore it is now between all three of us." He sat up, slapping his book shut and tossed the book onto the chaise beside him, the large ruby on his gold ring glinting against his finger. "When it comes to matters of the heart, we Persians dare not disrespect its strength or its honor. In our culture, love begins with God himself. It is known to our people as *tawhîd.* If a woman violates the sanctity of love by hurting the man she claims to loves, she is violating God himself."

Lovely. She was officially Satan in his eyes. "So what are you saying? That I get three lashes on the back for this?"

He glared. "Do not forget who you are addressing. In my country, when someone lies to the crown, they get more than lashes. Their heads are removed from their bodies with a saber the size of tiger." Grabbing her by the waist, he yanked her down hard onto his lap and adjusted her skirts around them, smoothing the fabric. The musky sweet scent of *davana ittar* surrounded her. He tucked his chin against her shoulder. "I am not happy with you, *azizam.* You lied to me. You told me you were forced into the arrangement and that you and he had nothing in common and would only make each other miserable. That is why I offered my assistance. To prevent you from being miserable. That was our agreement. But Dalir informed me that there is a far greater bond between you and this man that goes beyond the arrangement. This Lord

Banfield apparently has been writing you love letters since you were fourteen. And that *you* have responded to every single one of his love letters."

She groaned. "This isn't fair. You have no understanding of—"

"If you think life is fair, allow me to show you the door," he bit out. "Dalir investigated *everything*. Why? Because I never go into anything blind, azizam. Not even when I trust the person whose hand I shake. A man of my ranking and power would be stupid to do so. I have already entrusted far more into your hands than I have ever allowed myself to trust anyone. And how do you reward me? By telling me lies. Apparently this Lord Banfield and his brother are good men and come from a loving family. A far better family than I could ever hope to offer you. Because unlike my mother and brothers and sisters, my father is a cold and wicked man. Your very breath would freeze in his presence. Knowing all this, why are you asking that I take you to Persia and destroy a good man who loves you? I wish to understand."

A soft breath escaped her, remembering the anguish in Derek's face and brown eyes when she had announced the end of their union. It still hurt. It still— "Please don't do this."

He adjusted his chin harder against her shoulder. "You worry about becoming your mother, but you are still hurting this Lord Banfield. As such, you are becoming your mother whether you wish to be or not. Do you not understand that, *azizam*? If you love him, and he loves you, you cannot hurt him like this. Are you truly that cruel?"

She closed her eyes and laid her head against Nasser's, wishing she could make everything inside her own mind disappear. The shouts. The breaking of glass. The words of hate. The words of hate that still lived within her. "He deserves more than what I have living within me. He sees the world in a beautiful golden light I've never been able to touch. Even when we were younger, he had this-this...*incredible* quality and tone and playfulness I never had. He has always been Adonis and I am...*Bubona*. The goddess of unsmiling cattle."

He gripped her arms and gently rattled her against himself. "No more Roman references. My ears are burning."

"I knew I shouldn't have come to London," she confided brokenly. "I knew I shouldn't have thought I could face him and then leave him. You should have seen him. He was so angry and so hurt and..." Tears burned her eyes. "I hurt him. And then when he asked me for a night, I...I couldn't tell him no."

He traced a hand up the sleeve of her gown and fingered a misplaced lock within her pinned hair. "You cannot go with me. If I take you to Persia and make you a princess in the hopes of protecting my own name before my father and my people, I foresee bad karma. Leaving things unsaid and love unresolved leads people down very dark paths. No one knows this more than I. His suffering will follow you, and I cannot allow for it. I have heard nothing but good things about this man. He is good to his brother and his mother and his cousins and anyone else who comes to him for assistance. And you mean to make him kneel in his own pain in your honor? How is that fair? Given that I know what you feel for him, and what I know of him, you must marry him, *azizam*. It is the right thing to do." He nuzzled her cheek. "Your heart is far more beautiful than you think. You are simply too blinded by your own doubts to see it."

Her breath seemed to solidify in her throat. Marrying Derek was the easy part. She wanted to cling to his arms. She wanted to cling to his heart. She wanted to lay beside him on pillows and trace his lips with her fingers and know what it would be like to be his. But there was more to love than that. Happy times always brought out the best in people. But bad times...they brought out the worst. And it was the worst she feared. For she knew about the darkness hidden within her. A darkness not even her paints could brush over. "I'm still going with you to Persia. I'm still—"

He snorted. "You are *not* going to Persia. You either marry him or I will personally deliver you to him right now. You decide. Sadly, this royal door has closed. Which means…you only have one door left to walk through. The one you fear walking through."

Her heart pounded. Oh, God. She didn't even have her money. All of the money she had been saving and saving and saving since she was ten-years-old was gone. She had given it all away to Andrew because she thought—

She closed her eyes in disbelief and dragged in deep uneven breaths, over and over and over, trying desperately to calm the whirling in her head knowing Derek was going to be waiting at the altar. No matter what she decided.

"If you keep breathing like that, your lungs will rip," Nasser chided.

They already had. She opened her eyes.

What was she doing? Never mind that she had run out of choices.

She couldn't leave Derek at the altar.

She couldn't publicly humiliate him.

Not after everything they had shared.

She swallowed and lowered her gaze to her hands lying limply on her lap. Maybe he would bring out the best in her. Not the worst. Maybe what they had shared would be stronger than the passions she feared. Tears burned her eyes. "He will ask questions."

"You must answer them."

She shook her head and kept shaking it. "If I tell him about how I grew up, he'll start comparing me to my mother. He'll start—"

"Your pride has no place in this. If he truly loves you, he will understand and help you. Now are you going to marry him? Or do I have to get Dalir involved?"

"If I do marry him, what becomes of you? What about your name?"

He smoothed her skirts. "Our association will be enough to start me on a new path. Maybe you and I can go riding together in public for all to see. A little gossip between the pages of a British newspaper that would mention my name alongside that of a beautiful married woman would quickly find its way to my father. It would please him as he is forever complaining to me about my lack of interest in women." He eyed her. "Is your Lord Banfield the jealous sort? Could we make use of him?"

She gasped. "You are *not* going to torture poor Banfield. I have tortured him well enough, don't you think?"

"We would not torture him long," he chided. "Maybe a week or two. Enough to get the newspapers involved."

She elbowed him hard. "You mean to marry me off to him and *then* ruin me? What sort of friend are you?"

"I am merely teasing." He grabbed at her elbow, tightening his hold. "Tell me more about this Lord Banfield, *azizam*. I'm curious. Dalir is overly dry and never tells me what I want to know. Is he handsome?"

She bit her lip, dreamily remembering Derek sleeping naked. "Beyond."

"*Beyond?*" He dropped his voice low. "Dalir tells me he wears his hair long. Like a woman. To make him pretty. I like that. Is that true?"

She rolled her eyes. "He wears a *queue*. It's not what you think. It used to be fashionable in Western society." She paused and added, "Forty years ago. I don't know why he wears it. I personally think he should cut it."

"Do not make him cut it. Keep him pretty." He eyed the doors and quieted his voice. "How big are his hands? Large enough to do things?"

She elbowed him again in exasperation. "Cease. He is *mine*. Not yours. Mine."

"Oho. Suddenly the man she wanted to leave behind is no longer mine but hers." He smirked and kissed her cheek. "We must find a gown worthy of you and make him stumble at seeing you."

Derek most certainly would stumble given he still hadn't cancelled the wedding or announced the end of their union to her father or the public. It was as if he was challenging her to meet him at the altar. A panic of uncertainty rose within her. "What if everything I believe about myself is true? What if I cannot control my emotions and I hurt him?"

He tsked. "You will not. Cease doubting. Have faith in yourself."

He had become the older brother that had never been born. "I can't believe I'm doing this. I can't believe...I...I'm so nervous."

He grinned, his eyes crinkling. "Good. That means you are doing the right thing." His grin slowly faded, his husky features turning somber. He squeezed her back. "I have been taking private lessons on how to be more comfortable around women and have progressed very well. While I am in London these next few weeks, you must help me. You must make everyone think I am a virile man. Perhaps you can introduce me to women in your new circle? With you now getting married, I must convince one of these aristocratic British women to be *my* princess."

She pointed at him. "Do *not* be a rake about this. If you do intend to marry, she had better know what she is getting into and that your love is for men. You had better be honest with her."

He quirked a brow. "As you were with me?"

She eyed him. "Do as I say but never do as I do. I'm an American. Remember?"

He smirked and poked her cheek again. "Yes, *madâr*. You most certainly are."

****

Bustling back toward the direction of her waiting carriage, just as the sun began to fade from the late afternoon sky, Clementine jerked to a halt, her eyes widening.

Her father flicked his cheroot onto the pavement, crushing it with his boot and widened his stance, staring her down. "Mrs. Langley sent a footman over to the hotel to inform me what you were up to. I immediately rode out, sent her away and am taking over."

An exasperated breath escaped her. She forgot who was getting paid by whom.

Mr. Grey wagged his finger toward her. "You. Come here. We are going for a long walk through the park."

She cringed, feeling as if she were six again. "Yes, Papa."

He swung toward the direction of Hyde Park, which was just across the cobbled street. He held out the crook of his arm, waiting.

She grudgingly walked toward him and slipped her arm into his.

Glancing both ways for oncoming carriages, he hurried them across the street. The late afternoon breeze rustled her skirts and the ribbons of her bonnet as she tightened her hold on her father's arm.

"Are you leaving him at the altar to be humiliated?" he asked. "Is that the plan?"

She peered up at him, her throat tightening. "No. I...I decided against it."

"So you were going to leave him?" he pressed.

"Yes."

"And when were you going to tell me?"

She inwardly winced. "I was going to write you a letter and ask you to see me in Persia."

His voice hardened. "Is that all you think I'm worth?"

"It was stupid, I know, but I knew you wouldn't take it well."

His gaze was trained firmly on the path leading them into the quietest section of the park. "I would have never insisted on this marriage if I didn't believe it was going to make you happy. Especially after what I went through with your mother. I knew his father for over seventeen years. He was a great man. He saw the world in a way few do: he saw opportunity when there was none. I'll never forget how I met George. The same night he and his wife were robbed outside of Paris, while that woman cried, he knelt before her, holding both of her hands and sang her a ballad in the hopes of getting her to smile as if they weren't in a smoky tavern full of drunken strangers in a helpless situation. That was how I found them. Her hair a mess and he was trying to make her smile, brushing her hair from her face. It made me stop and ask them if they needed assistance. What those two had shared was...I don't know how to say it...enchanting. It was how I imagined my life being with my future wife. Before I married your mother and..." His voice trailed off.

Tears stung her eyes as she set her other hand against her father's arm. "You never told me any of this."

He cleared his throat. "I'm rather sorry I didn't. After everything you and I have been through, I sometimes forget there is still a lot unsaid between us. Simply know that Banfield comes from a good family. Not the crazy one your mother came from."

She swallowed and trained her own gaze ahead of them, remembering the way Derek had cradled her head against his chest as if it was all he had ever wanted. "Yes. I know."

"If you know, Tine, then why the blazes are you still associating with Nasser? I am *astounded* that he followed you out all the way into London. What is this? What is going on? I am demanding you be honest with me. Are you and he romantically involved?"

She groaned. "Noooo. Men and women are perfectly capable of being friends, Papa. That is all he and I are to each other. Friends."

"*Friends?* And what is this Nasser offering that Banfield can't? Explain this to me."

A shaky breath escaped her. "It's different with Banfield. He...he isn't interested in being my friend."

He glanced over at her. "And how do you know that?"

Oh, if she could count out the ways. "Being around him is like being in Paris. Do you not remember how the men there would publicly whistle at women and use the head of their canes to lift the back of their skirts in passing? That is exactly how I feel whenever I'm around him. Our conversations always return to him whistling and wanting to lift my skirt. Always."

His laughter rippled through the air. "I think you told me far more than I needed to know about you and him."

"But that is *exactly* how it feels being around him," she insisted. "You've read every one of his letters. It has always been his intent to make me blush. He knows nothing of sharing in a conversation that doesn't involve me blushing."

"There is nothing wrong with blushing, Tine."

"Yes, well, when it's all a girl is doing, it gets rather...*exhausting*. And it bothers me given what I feel for him."

He paused, his shoulder purposefully bumping into her own. "Oh, well, now. This is news to me. What do you feel for him? Tell your father."

She almost swung at the air for letting that one out. "Nothing. I'm babbling right now."

"Of course you are," he chided. "Why would you admit to feeling anything for him? You've never even been able to tell your own father that you like him."

"I'm simply not that sort of girl, Papa. I've never been."

"You and I both know that, but does Banfield know it?"

A breath escaped her. This was all so twisted. "No. He doesn't."

"You see? You need to allow him to see another side of you, Tine. Or he may think you don't feel any devotion for him at all."

"Another side of me? And what side are you referring to? I'm not at all interesting or exciting, Papa. I don't even have a sense of humor. He says things sometimes and all I can do is stare. Do you know how awkward that is?"

He was quiet for a moment. "Maybe you don't share his sense of humor, but you did help your father away from the sideboard. And you don't cower when men break into the house. In fact, with over a dozen paper curlers in your hair, you ran for a pistol you didn't even know how to use. To me...that is interesting."

She snorted. "You're making me sound pathetic."

His voice became firm. "Show him the girl who isn't afraid to share more of who she really is. If you want friendship from him, make an effort to take it."

Now there was an idea. She could physically wrestle Derek down to the ground in the hopes of gaining his... *friendship*. She quickened their steps, trying to push out some of the building angst within her. "So you really think he and I could be friends? Real friends? Despite the fact that he only sees my lips?"

He brought them to a halt. "Banfield is not unreasonable in nature. He will see whatever you want him to. The question is: what do you want him to see? The girl who wants to leave him at the altar because she can't admit to liking him? Or the girl who I'm talking to right now?"

For a man who had been shackled to a miserable marriage and couldn't give himself advice, he certainly knew how to give it to others. She squeezed his arm and chided, "You can be so smart sometimes."

He smirked. "Only sometimes?"

She gently rattled his arm. "Must you really leave after the wedding, Papa? I'm not dashing off anywhere. So why should you? Can't you live here in London? New York is dreadfully boring. More importantly, if you stay here in London, you'll be able to travel quicker to the places you always have to go to. Meaning Spain and France."

He eyed her. "Are you inviting me to stay for grandchildren? Because I *will* quit politics for that. But only if you guarantee it."

She bit her tongue knowing she wasn't quite ready for that. It was unnerving as it was knowing she was marrying a man whom she adored but who only ever seemed to notice her breasts. "Let me think about it."

LESSON EIGHT

Just when you think you know everything, you do not.

-The School of Gallantry

Two days later – St. Paul's Cathedral

Excited whispers floated all around as Derek silently strode down the long aisle, heading to the altar where the bishop in his ceremonial robes and domed cap waited.

As per his instructions, every wooden pew and every marble pillar in the grand cathedral had been meticulously decorated with wreaths of white blossoms, pale pink roses, and forget-me-nots. They sweetly perfumed the muggy air around him, mingling with the sultry scent of melting bees-wax.

Countless candles lit the marble altar, making everything appear golden.

It was everything he had ever wanted in a wedding. The red carpet at his booted feet. Too many candles to count. Violins playing from the pulpit. An abundance of eager faces belonging to his friends and family that included every last one of his cousins and their children.

But it all blurred into superficial nothingness. Because it wasn't real.

Within the hour, everyone in London would know the truth.

That he had walked down the aisle knowing she wouldn't come.

He arrived at the altar, which brought all of the violins to a final lull in honor of the official commencement. He half-turned as he had been earlier instructed by the bishop to do and waited. The bright sun sparkled in through the rows of stain glass above, highlighting portions of the altar with a rainbow of muted colors. Minutes ticked by and only the occasional whispers and coughs of people in the pews interrupted the silence.

Derek eyed the large double doors at the end of the altar, his pulse drumming. He knew she wasn't going to walk through that door, but a part of him still stupidly hoped she would. After what she painted, he couldn't imagine that she could just walk away from an image like that.

Setting his trembling hands behind his back, he swallowed and waited.

He mentally counted out another minute and another minute and twenty others. One could say he had the patience of God because he was standing in a church. The restless conversations and whispers of people shifting in their pews and glancing toward the closed doors became more of a pronounced rumble. People were staring at him. Many of them already offering up silent horrified apologies.

Letting out a slow breath, he decided not to wait the full hour. He turned to the bishop and finally said in a strained tone, "My Lord Bishop, I wish to—"

The doors opened.

An excited murmur overtook the crowd.

Derek swung toward those open doors and dragged in an astounded breath.

His pulse roared to life and he almost staggered.

She came. She— He couldn't believe it.

Dressed in a stunning lace lilac gown, Clementine calmly and regally walked down the aisle toward him, one gloved hand resting on her father's bent forearm and the other gloved hand holding a bouquet of orchids. A yellow silk bonnet decorated with silk flowers was poised atop bountiful pinned black curls, a short veil draped over its rim in true French fashion. Although there was still quite a distance between them, he could faintly see her flushed, pretty face through the thin, white veil beaded with pearls.

He paused, realizing she wasn't even looking at him.

Her eyes swept from one side of the pews to the other as if she were intently looking for someone of more importance. She even slowed her steps to allow herself to better look.

Tightening his jaw, he mentally willed her to meet his gaze. If only once. If only to make this moment feel the way he needed it to. To make this moment real.

Her lips tightened through the swaying veil as she continued to peruse pew after pew, letting her head pertly go left and right.

Who the hell was she looking for?

His chest tightened. What if...what if the prince showed up and objected to their vows? What if this had been planned? What if she was about to humiliate him before all of London in the name of a prince who owned an entire country?

His nostrils flared in an effort to stay calm as he mentally chanted to himself to remain at the altar. Because the odds were not with either of them. There were three hundred and twenty-two people in the cathedral, not including the bishop, the musicians, or altar boys. If he walked out now, or reacted to anything he shouldn't, every single person in London would know about it within less than forty-five minutes.

Clementine arrived at the altar, still glancing toward the closest pews. Mr. Grey cleared his throat, bringing attention to the fact she wasn't turning as expected.

She winced and faced her father to allow him to lift the veil.

Derek shifted his jaw and eyed the pews. There was nothing out of the ordinary about the people around them. Most of them were people he knew. One of his older female cousins, Mrs. Gangley, waved excitedly toward him over the bonnet of his mother who tilted herself away and glared at her for being so rude.

He counterfeited a smile for them and returned his gaze to Clementine. "Looking for someone?" he coolly asked.

She glanced toward the crowd again, clearly astounded. "I simply didn't expect there to be *this* many people. This isn't a wedding, this is a circus."

He coughed out a rough laugh. Shite. Leave it to Clementine to surprise him every single time. Now he felt like an arse instead of glorying in what he had: her. "You're marrying a very popular man," he chided.

"Obviously. I hate to say it but you're marrying a very unpopular woman."

He grinned. "Not in my opinion."

As the bishop commenced the ceremony and droned on and on about their duties and God and faith, Derek found he was no longer listening to words but reveling in all that was Clementine. This was going to be his life. He would spend day after day with a woman who would surprise him and make him feel special in those moments when he needed it most.

The main doors suddenly opened and a figure strode down the aisle toward them.

The bishop paused and whispers ensued.

Clementine turned and her lips parted. "Heavens above. It's…"

Derek veered his gaze toward the figure, half-dreading he was about to kill a Persian prince in church. He froze, realizing that striding down the aisle toward them was none other than Andrew who wore a dapper morning coat and matching trousers announcing he was ready to attend a wedding. There was even a small flower tucked into the upper buttonhole of his coat. His wavy dark hair was fashionably brushed back with tonic and his face—

Derek felt his breath cut off. The left side of his brother's entire face was lacerated with scabs, one eye swollen and his jaw bruising. Jesus. His throat tightened in emotion. "Andrew." He frantically stepped toward him. "Your face. Are you—"

"I'm fine." Andrew came to a halt before him at the altar. He met his gaze for a moment and then brokenly offered, "I gave up writing and took up boxing. It uh...pays better." His roughened features twisted. "I know I'm not fit to stand here, but I...I needed to be here."

Swallowing hard, Derek stepped toward him and grabbed him hard, tugging him into an embrace. He hissed out a breath. He hadn't lost his brother. He was here and he was all right. Face aside, he was all right. "You have no idea what this means to me. Father may not be here, but you are. And that is all I need."

His brother squeezed him back in turn. "I'm sorry. You were right. About me. About everything. I just wasn't ready to listen."

He hadn't seen his brother cry since their father died. It was too much. "Shhh." He cradled that head, his eyes burning. "Shhh. It's all right. I'm here for you. You know that. You've always known that."

With a hard sniff, Andrew pulled away and nodded. He scrubbed his good eye and cleared his throat. "Forgive me for being late. The streets were something awful. Full of traffic. The footmen are waving sticks at people to get away from the carriages." Andrew glanced over at Clementine and smiled, despite the bruising and swelling and cuts to his face. Quickly approaching her, he grabbed her gloved hand and kissed it, holding his lips to her hand for a long moment before releasing it and straightening. "I cannot thank you enough for your generosity and assistance at a time I needed it most. And I agree with everything you wrote. My brother is the greatest man I will ever have the privilege to know. I've taken him for granted. I guess we both have." Andrew stepped back.

Her features twisted in anguish.

Derek's breath hitched, realizing she had gone to her brother about...him. He snapped his gaze to hers and managed, "Do you really think I'm a great man?"

She peered up at him, fingering the bouquet. "Why do you think I'm standing here?"

By God. The girl who had once wiped away his tears had come to wipe them away again when he least expected it. He wanted to grab her and kiss her and smother her with every emotion he'd ever held within.

Only they were in a church and the violins had stopped and people were staring.

"God love you," he rasped. "God love you for astounding me."

Her blue eyes searched his face, tears rimming them.

"I love you even though you never laugh or smile," he added.

A sob escaped her.

Sweet meadows, it was like holding her heart. Not caring that the world was watching, he stepped toward her and cradled her face. "Don't cry," he whispered.

She sobbed harder. "You shouldn't have been here waiting. Not for me. You shouldn't have—"

"Shhhh." He tightened his hold on her face, forcing her to look up at him. "Shhh. It's all right. Why do you think I came? That painting you left behind gave me hope."

Uneven breaths escaped her. "I...I want that hope. I need that hope."

"And it is yours. It was always yours."

The Bishop cleared his throat. "Might we proceed, my lord? So that God may bless this union?"

It was as if the doves had been released on cue for he felt like a man about to marry a woman on the brink of change. "Yes, Bishop," he announced, still holding Clementine's gaze out of fear that he was dreaming. "I ask that you bless this union."

****

Early Evening - The Banfield House decorated in all its garland glory in honor of the Celebratory Masked Ball

Whisking through the crowds, with her view of the world limited to the round slits of her Venetian mask, Clementine excitedly searched for Derek's tall figure garbed in black and gold.

For the first time in her life, she felt like the world had more than mere potential. It held magic. All because of one person: Derek. He had stood at the altar before all of London without even knowing if she would come. He hadn't given up on her or them. It was something she would cherish for the rest of her days and she prayed what they shared would bloom into everything she imagined and more.

"*Cousin!*" a masked female exclaimed, rushing toward her while tugging along a young masked boy who stumbled to keep up with the woman. "Do wait!"

Clementine turned, realizing the woman was referring to her.

The tall blond, whose features were hidden beneath a peacock mask, came to a halt before her and with bright blue eyes announced, "You have an admirer." Grabbing the arm of the young boy who wore a carnival paper mask, she set him between them. "This is Mister Edward Peddler. The youngest male in Lord Banfield's extensive family. He has been watching you from a distance and wondering if you would grace him with a dance. I promised him I would ensure it."

Clementine lowered her chin to better see a boy whose smooth face and height indicated the boy was about twelve. He barely reached her shoulder. It was adorable. "Of course. A minuet is set to begin, Mr. Peddler. Can you manage?"

The boy's lips, which were visible beneath his mask, parted as large blue eyes stared up at her. "I don't dance very well."

Clementine leaned down toward him. "Good. Because I don't either." She held out her gloved hand to the boy.

He grabbed her hand and glanced up at her. "I rather like your accent."

She bit back a smile. "Thank you, Mr. Peddler." Walking him to the line of masked dancers, she settled them into place and positioned them.

He gripped her hand and stared directly at her bosom where his head was leveled. "Welcome to the family," he offered, still staring at her bosom.

He most certainly was related to Derek. "I'm up here, Mr. Peddler."

The boy veered his gaze upward. "Welcome to the family," he said again.

"Thank you." When the violins commenced, cueing all dancers, she moved them in the direction everyone flowed.

He scrambled to keep up, his half-boots barely managing to keep their distance from the hem of her skirts. He stumbled against her. "I'm so sorry!"

She tightened her hold to keep him balanced and kept them moving to the rhythm of the music, pushing him in the direction he needed to go. "Don't apologize. All I ask is that you try to lead. Because right now, I'm leading you."

He glanced down at his feet and glanced up. "I can't see past my mask very well."

"Then push it up onto your head."

"I can do that?"

"Of course. You're a guest *and* family."

"I am, aren't I?" He released her waist to push up his mask onto his head and tripped mid-step, spilling to the ground with a thud.

Coming to a halt to prevent herself from tumbling over him as he lay flat in the middle of the dance floor, the couple dancing behind them, bumped into her hard, jarring her into also spilling forward and over the boy. "Oh!" Rolling to the side, she sat up against her bundling skirts in an attempt to scramble over to her little dance partner who was still laying sprawled like a starfish out on a beach. "Dearest heaven, are you all right?"

People rounded them and stopped.

The boy rolled onto his back and sat up, groaning. "I told you I couldn't dance." He tugged down his mask over his face. "Don't look at me. I'm a disgrace."

She laughed and no longer caring that she was sitting on the middle of the dance floor, she used her slippered feet to nudge his own booted feet to the left and right. "Look. We are still dancing. And quite beautifully, I might add."

He eyed their moving feet and then giggled. "I made you fall."

"No, actually, the couple behind us made me fall," she pointed out.

Muscled legs in well-fitted black trousers and polished boots suddenly came into view. "That was by far the best minuet ever danced," a familiar male voice drawled.

Clementine's gaze veered up the length of those legs up past a black evening coat and gold embroidered waistcoat and white cravat, up toward the black velvet mask tied around Derek's eyes and nose. Her stomach flipped as Derek grinned and held out a gloved hand. "I leave you for ten minutes and you're already getting into trouble?"

She rolled her eyes. "Can you imagine what would have happened if you left me for fifteen?" She grabbed his hand, letting him pull her up onto her feet. "Be a gentleman and help poor Mr. Peddler, will you?" She tidied her skirts around herself.

The boy scrambled onto his feet himself. "I'm going to go find a corner to hide in for the rest of my life."

Derek rounded Clementine, reached down and adjusted the boy's mask. "My first dance looked a lot like yours. It gets better with practice. I promise." He leaned in and covering his mouth with the back of his hand whispered something to the boy. He then pulled out his tin of candies and held it out to him.

The boy grinned, grabbed the tin and shoved it into his own pocket. "Thank you, my lord! I'll be sure to try it." He then darted from sight, pushing through the masses.

Clementine veered over to Derek and tapped his arm. "Dare I even ask?"

He grabbed her hand, tugging her close and strode them off the dance floor. "I told him the best way to impress women is to offer them ginger candy. Not dances."

Clementine playfully hit his arm. "Hardly good advice."

"So says the woman who almost left me at the altar." He brought them to a halt and waved over one of the passing footmen who held a silver tray of champagne glasses. "Are you up to playing a game I used to play when I was his age?" He grabbed two glasses off the tray and turned toward her.

She eyed the glasses. Why did she have a feeling Derek was looking to get them into trouble? "What sort of game?"

"Whoever can balance this glass the longest on the palm of their hand wins."

"Wins what?"

He stared. "Nothing. You simply win. It's a game."

She bit back a smile, sensing that he really wanted to play. It was like finding the playmate she never had as a child. It was...charming. "All right. I can play that." She carefully took the glass from his hand, trying not to spill it. "Maybe we should drink a little before we...?"

"And ruin the ultimate challenge? *Never.*" He stepped back, glancing around himself to ensure he had room and holding up his palm, carefully set his glass onto it. Despite a slight tremor of the champagne within the glass, it stayed. He grinned. "One. Two. Three. Four. Five. Six. Seven. Eight. Nine—" The glass tilted and tumbled to the side, spraying champagne as glass shattered.

She cringed.

He popped up both hands into the air. "Nine!" he yelled out. "I dare my wife to beat nine! Let everyone in masks know of it!"

People gathered around them, laughing.

She had never been one to willingly play games, even as a child, for she considered most of them pointless, but she had to admit, pointless games led to something more meaningful. Getting to know a person through simple and mindless entertainment.

This was going to be fun. Clementine sipped the champagne, eyeing Derek. "I've never played before, so permit me to cheat."

He groaned. "That isn't fair. Stop drinking the game!"

She tsked. "You always set the rules whenever we played your games back in '23, so permit me to set this one." She took a few more sips, lowering the level of champagne to about half and then daintily set it on her gloved hand, trying to balance it. It stayed. She couldn't believe it. "One. Two. Three. Four. Five—" The glass tilted and tumbled to the side, spraying champagne as glass shattered.

She scrambled back and then yelled, "Six, seven, eight, nine and ten! Ten! Let it be known to all in the room that I won! I made it to ten!" Yes. She had a sense of humor.

Men and women clapped and laughed.

Derek lowered his chin and smirked. "I'm asking for a second opinion on that win."

She pointed at him. "I'd be more than happy to do it again."

He jumped over the broken glass. Skidding next to her, he leaned in. He hesitated then said in a soft, genuine tone, "How is your night so far?"

Knowing people were watching them, she shyly offered, "Absolutely wonderful. How is your night?"

"Even better than yours." He stepped back and gestured toward the dance floor. "Might I interest you in a tamer version of the minuet that won't involve you landing on the floor? For it would be an honor to dance with my wife." He paused and eyed her. "Do you know that I have waited seven long years to call you my wife?"

Her heart squeezed and in that moment, Clementine realized this was her life-long companion. Not the one who had forever tried to seduce her and frisk her, but the one who simply wanted to adore her and share a life with her. It was a beautiful feeling. One she had been waiting to feel.

Taking his arm, she said, "Thank you for waiting seven years."

He captured her gaze and lingered. "Say that again."

It was like he needed assurance after everything she had put him through. She tightened her hold on his arm and offered, "Thank you for waiting seven years."

He smiled. "You are most welcome."

LESSON NINE

Are you ready to admit that you have a problem?

-The School of Gallantry

Later that evening, well past midnight

Her father hadn't touched a single finger of liquor or champagne all night. Without her even having to ask him to. It made her remember why she had always loved her father. Because when it mattered most, he was always willing to prove the strength of his heart. A heart that had been beaten out of his chest so many times. And even though he normally never danced, he danced with not only Derek's mother but every woman wanting a dance partner.

She knew he was dancing out of happiness.

The world had become so achingly lovely. After she had danced all night with Derek, who laughed and grinned in a way that made her glimpse that crazy boy of seventeen, they became silly and snatched flutes of champagne from passing trays and dared each other to balance the filled glasses on their palms. They ended up spilling it every time and smashing more than a few glasses. It was stupid but fun.

Not that there were any more glasses to break or any guests left to get stupid with.

Even her father, Lady Banfield, and Andrew had departed for the night.

"No more wine for any of you!" a woman sternly scolded. "You ought to be *ashamed*. Between the four of you, I believe you've emptied every last bottle in this house. Now come along!"

Muffled giggles escaped a group of four young women as they stumbled and bustled by with their chaperone in tow, their feathered peacock masks wagging and only revealing their bright playful eyes.

"Congratulations, cousin dearest!" one of them called, flopping a gloved wrist. "Thank you for all the...*wine!*" They burst into uncontrollable giggles.

Derek hadn't been lying when he said he had a lot of family. She thought she had met every last one. Fortunately, merriment aside, none of them had gotten into any fights. "Good night," she called back as her gaze turned to the departing flock of colorful skirts, her view of the world limited to the round slits of her own Venetian mask.

She lowered her gloved hand, realizing there was no one left in the ballroom but footmen and servants tending to the scraping of wax on the floors and the gathering of silver trays filled with leftover champagne. She pushed up her mask and glanced around. "Derek?"

The servants kept scraping and gathering in silence.

It was eerie. The whole house had gone quiet.

Gathering her skirts, she made her way out toward the adjoining candle-lit corridor where shadows inked every corner. She could hear her own breaths. Where was he? She'd seen him about fifteen minutes ago. "Derek?"

A large hand caught her gloved hand and tugged her back toward the wall the person was leaning against. "What took you so long?"

Her heart popped. She bumped against his solid, muscled frame, pushing him into the wall. "What are you—"

"I had to see the last of our guests out the door." He grabbed her corseted waist with his other bare hand and molded her firmly to his body. "I practically threw them out." Although half his face was hidden, his sultry brown eyes captured hers through the slits of the black mask hugging his brow and nose. "We should retire," he said as his shaven jaw tightened. "Into bed. What do you think?"

Her heart pounded, knowing what he wanted. She couldn't focus knowing that her breasts were pressed against his waistcoat and chest. But she tried. She focused on what she wanted most for them: a real relationship. Something her parents never had. "The stars are out," she offered. "Do you want to go outside and talk?"

He tightened his hold even more, making her fully aware of every rigid muscle in his body. "I'm not interested in talking or looking at stars. I'm looking at a star right now."

She stared up at his visible lips, remembering all too well how her entire body had erupted by the command of his tongue. He wasn't making this easy. "I was hoping we could talk."

His mouth quirked. "After." His hand slid across the back of her gown, his fingers tracing the stitched pearls sewn into her moonstone evening gown. "Expect to be up all night," he whispered.

He bent over and yanked her up and into his arms, startling her. He effortlessly carried her up the stairs and then deposited her onto the landing before him.

His warm hand jumped to hers and tightened. Using his other hand, he stripped his mask and tossed it over the railing of the staircase below, causing his queue to come undone. His brown hair fell around his face and onto the top of his broad shoulders. He nuzzled her cheek. "I'm going to behave long enough for us to get into the room. I promise."

The heat of his mouth and stubbled jaw grazed her skin. In a half-daze, she desperately tried to piece together her own mind. "What were you like before I met you? Even crazier? Or more subdued?" It was a silly and unfocused question, but she was trying to get him to talk to her. About something. About anything.

He drew away, his large hand tightening around her fingers. "Are you trying to seduce me? Is that what this is?"

She let out an exasperated breath. "No. I'm trying to get to know you."

"We have our whole lives for that." He walked them down the length of the corridor, hand in hand, until he paused before a closed door. He pushed it open and lifting her hand high into the air, guided her inside with a graceful whirl as if they were once again on the dance floor.

She whirled to a halt on his command, her hand catching his broad shoulder.

He searched her face heatedly, his features tightening. "I want you naked."

She pinched her lips, her hand still resting on his shoulder. So much for them being friends. "Derek, don't you think maybe we should—"

"Get naked? Brilliant idea." He grinned, released her waist and stepped back, closing the door. "Take a quick look around, love. I ensured that the servants had everything in place before you retired. Let me know if there is anything else you need before the candles go out."

It was like talking to a dog that only saw the meat dangling from her hand. It was exhausting. Letting out a breath, she turned to what now was hers.

The fourteen sizable trunks that had been delivered earlier and stacked with her belongings were gone, leaving the palomino silk-walled room more open. Her gowns were all neatly hanging within the massive wardrobe on the far wall that had been left open. Her ribbons, cosmetics, curl papers and perfumes were all neatly laid out on the white marble of the ornate dressing table that had once belonged to his grandmother.

Her lips parted, realizing there was an easel angled into the far corner of the room. The painting of their night together had been set on it. She jerked toward him. "We really shouldn't leave that out."

He waggled his brows. "We'll only pull it out at night. We'll cover it during the day, of course, so as not to startle the servants." His smile faded. "Your talent is beyond anything I have ever seen, Clementine. *Ever.*"

She sensed he meant it. "Thank you."

"Of course. In my opinion, you deserve to have anything you paint hanging in the National Gallery."

She sighed. "If only I had been born a man."

He snorted. "Do not say that to the man you just married. I rather need you to be a woman or this night could get awkward."

She rolled her eyes, knowing they were back to his favorite subject. She grudgingly turned to see the rest of the room. The large mahogany four-poster bed with its countless rose silk pillows and matching linens loomed just a few feet away.

She eyed the side table beside it, pausing.

Realizing her music box wasn't out, she removed her evening gloves and walked toward the dressing table, tossing both gloves onto it. She carefully opened and closed each drawer. As each drawer revealed only her ribbons and a hairbrush and jewelry and sashes, her heart pounded at the realization her music box wasn't in any of the drawers at all.

Derek walked over to her. "What are you looking for?"

She slammed the last drawer closed. How was she going to sleep without it? "My music box."

"Allow me." He walked over to the side table, opened it and pulled out a large ornate wooden box inlaid with ivory. "I asked the servants to put it in the drawer beside your bed as opposed to setting it out. That way it wouldn't collect dust."

A breath escaped her. "Thank you." She hurried over and carefully took it from his hands. "My father gave it to me on my birthday when I was eight. I play it every night. It helps me sleep." She turned and lowering it onto the side table, centered it to ensure it was safe.

She smoothed her hands across its inlaid surface, its real history hidden within the wood.

She opened the lid, slid out the turning key tucked into its compartment beside the brass cylinder inside, and inserted it into the side of the box. Leaving the lid open for better sound, so that the pins of the comb could clink against the cylinder openly, she turned the key fifteen times, as she always did before going to bed, and let it chime the melodious tune of playful bells she'd known since she was eight. "There isn't another one like it in the world. The music was composed specifically for this one box by a Boston musician who was hired to play at certain events for the President of the United States."

A large hand slid down the sleeve of her arm. Derek lingered from behind, the heat of his body penetrating hers as he pressed himself closer. "Fascinating." His voice indicated otherwise.

Trying to get him to talk about anything was like trying to explain philanthropy to a man sitting in prison. "The masked ball was wonderful. Wasn't it?"

The warmth of his masculine lips softly touched the exposed skin of her neck. "Mm."

She swayed against the melody and his wandering lips that curved against her neck. "Your cousins...I...they were all very pleasant. How many do you have again?"

His tongue slid across her exposed shoulder, nudging away the lace around the trim of her gown as both of his hands slid down and around her waist. He gripped and bundled the material of her gown while still gliding his tongue back and forth, delicately tracing and teasing her skin. "I have a confession to make," he whispered.

Her head rolled back as the heat of his mouth and tongue overtook her ability to think. "And what would that be?" she whispered back.

"I don't want to talk about my cousins while I'm doing this." He turned her and grabbing her face, kissed her hard, his tongue finding its way into her mouth with a swiftness that almost made her choke.

She stiffened against that dominating mouth, everything between them feeling strangely different. Because there was no way out. If anything went wrong, if anything fell apart between them, she was trapped in this forever.

He broke away and in between heavy breaths said, "The next time I kiss you, heiress, I want you to make me feel like it's welcome. Kiss me back and put your arms around me, will you? Don't make me feel like I'm forcing myself on you."

She swallowed. "I'm sorry. I'm still getting used to—"

He turned her away and unpinned and unlaced the material of her gown, his fingers pulling and stretching the satin away from her body.

Her chest rose and fell in unsteady breaths knowing that they would be naked again.

The fabric of her gown and its petticoats fell away and onto the ground. He turned her back toward himself and dug his fingers into her hair, moving them through to loosen all of the pins without having to pluck them. Most rattled out against the force, tinkering to the floor around them as the weight of her hair fell onto her shoulders.

His rugged features stilled, his skin visibly flushed. "Much better." He lingered, the heat of those smoldering brown eyes luring her into giving them both pleasure.

Entertaining a conversation was clearly not what he had in mind. No surprise.

****

Derek grazed his lips against hers, feeling everything tip like it always did when he touched and kissed her. He pulled away again and held her gaze, needing to know the one thing that had haunted him all morning, afternoon and night. He stepped back, a slow breath easing out of his lungs. "I wanted to ask you something."

She paused as if surprised that he stepped away. She brightened. "Of course. Ask me anything."

If it was over, she would tell him it was. If there was one thing he knew about her was that she was almost too honest. Which he needed right now. "Did you end your association with Nasser? Does he know he is to never contact you or call on you again?"

Her fingers played with the satin of her exposed corset before she stripped the mask perched atop her head and tossed it, sending it fluttering to the floor. "Please don't ask me to end my association with him. In truth, he is the only friend I have."

Derek felt the blood drain from his head. He had already spent all of the days leading up to his own wedding thinking about her naked in another man's arms. And it ripped at his heart and his gut. She kept calling him a friend but Derek knew full well men and women only associated for one reason: the end result. "I can't— Why are you doing this to me? Why do you need to see him?"

She released a breath. "Nasser is my friend. He is also your friend. He—"

He grabbed her face hard and forced her to look up at him. "He almost took you away from me. How can he be my friend?" He held her gaze, willing her to feel the intensity of what he felt and repeat what he had said to her at the altar. "I love you, Clementine. You do know that, yes?"

Her features softened as she searched his face. "Yes."

"The night we shared brought you back to me. I know it did." He used his thumbs to brush the silken skin around her pretty eyes. Eyes he was so thankful to see again. "We have to protect what we have. Do you understand? You can't let another man come between us." He released her and stepped back. "Where is he staying? I need to go resolve this and talk to him. Tonight, if need be."

Her brows came together. "Derek, you have no need to be jealous."

He tried to keep his voice calm. "I want to talk to him."

"It's obvious you don't mean to talk. You clearly mean to swing at him."

He set his shoulders. "Do you blame me? Given you almost left me for him?"

"You don't understand the situation. *At all.*"

His chest rose and fell more heavily than he could control. "Damn right I don't. You still haven't told me about whatever arrangement you had with him. What the hell am I to think? What the hell am I to—"

"Don't you dare take that tone with me." Her lips thinned. "I didn't have to tell you about Nasser at all. But I did. I was honest with you about my association with him from the very first breath."

He edged in, his body pulsing. "Shall I extend my unending gratitude knowing you're capable of being honest about the fact that while you were engaged to me, you were involved with him?"

She stared up at him. "Nasser is like a brother to me. *A brother.* It isn't romantic in nature. It never was. Nor will it ever be. So cease thinking the worst. *Cease.*"

Derek found himself momentarily speechless. Stunned. He honestly didn't know what to make of this. He wanted to trust her, if only to keep his mind from falling apart, but his gut told him no woman would try to run off with another man in the name of wanting to be his sister.

After pushing out a few uneven breaths, he admitted, "I don't believe you."

Her eyes flashed. "And how is that my fault?"

He tried to shove aside his distrust, his anger and his jealousy in an attempt to understand. He tried. "What are you not telling me? Clementine, I can't understand you or this situation if you don't tell me. What happened between you and Nasser? Was it love? Was it more? Did you spend a night with him after you spent a night with me? *Tell me.*"

"I didn't spend a night with him."

"Then why do you feel the need to continue your association with him?"

"Because he and I are friends."

"Friends. I see. So what was the original agreement you and he had? I want you to tell me about it. Right now."

Her voice wavered. "I can't tell you."

Ice spread across his chest. "Can't? Or won't?"

"Please." Her lips trembled. "Don't do this."

This Nasser did something to her. He could see the panic and fear in her eyes. "I'm going to kill him," he rasped. "I'm going to kill him, because it's obvious he—"

"*Stop it,*" she choked out. "I'm devoted to you, Derek. I married you, didn't I? But I am also devoted to Nasser. He is the only real friend I have ever had in my life. The only real friend I—"

"Stop talking about him as if you and he share something more than we do. Because you can't be devoted to him *and* me. You can't—"

"Leave." She pointed a finger to the door, her body trembling. "You obviously don't know what is and isn't capable between men and women, and I don't like how you're making me feel. I don't like how you're assuming the worst while treating me like an object you can't even share a conversation with. Because this isn't what I want in a relationship, Derek. This isn't what I—" She clapped her hands over her ears and squeezed her eyes shut.

It was like watching a child who needed a reprieve from a thunderstorm.

He swallowed, knowing he was upsetting her. He softened his voice. "Clementine." He reached out for her, trying to gently drag her toward himself. "Come here. Let me—"

"*Don't.*" She scrambled back and away, searching his face. "I didn't ask you to touch me or coddle me, Derek. I asked you to leave. Because you're clearly not interested in talking to me as if I were a person."

He had to stay calm. He had to believe he meant more to her than this Nasser did. "It's obvious you aren't ready to talk about what you and he share. And I'm fine with that. I'll just..." He held out a hand, willing himself to trust her. "It's late. Come to bed."

She shook her head. "No. I'm not— You haven't earned it."

He dropped his hand. "Haven't— You're my wife."

"I see. And that makes you think you can bed me anytime you want?"

"Jesus, why am I suddenly the villain in this?" He let out a breath, trying to calm himself. "I am genuinely worried about you and this entire situation. It doesn't sit right with me. And until you explain it to me, you cannot expect me to let it go." He undid his cravat and stripped his coat, whipping it onto the bed. He unbuttoned his waistcoat, shrugging it from his shoulders and tossed it onto the bed, as well, yanking out his linen shirt from his trousers.

She eyed him. "What are you doing?"

"Getting ready for bed. What else? Hopefully, if we stare up at the ceiling long enough, you'll be able to tell me what the hell is going on. I have a right to know about the agreement you and this-this...*Nasser* had made. Don't you think?"

Her eyes became pools of appeal. "You cannot and will not insist on knowing something I cannot tell you. Nasser is heir to an entire country on the verge of another war. I vowed to protect him in the same way he vowed to protect me. Do you understand?"

He lowered his chin. "How can I understand? You haven't told me anything."

She snapped a finger toward the door. "*Leave.*"

"No." He yanked off his boots, sending each thumping to the hardwood floor. "And because I'm such a good *friend*, I'll keep my shirt and trousers on even though it's my wedding night. How is that?" Without sparing her a glance, he rounded the bed, whipped back the linen and climbed in, flopping himself back onto the pillow. He hit the pillow beside him. "Now get in. I expect your arms to be around me. Right now."

She narrowed her gaze. "Don't you dare rile me, Derek. Don't you dare."

"Or what?" He stubbornly held her gaze. "You're mine to protect and to love. Mine. Not Nasser's. *Mine.* And don't you ever bloody forget it. Now get into this bed before I put you in it."

"*Stop trying to control me and get the fuck out!*" she boomed in a thundering voice that exploded from the depths of everything that had ever been contained within her prim façade.

Derek was too astounded to do anything more than breathe. Aside from the fact he never thought her capable of raising her voice at all, he most certainly didn't think she even knew words like 'fuck' given she didn't even know what 'fuck' meant until a few days ago.

It was the first time that cool façade had ever given him so much...*intensity.*

If only she could apply it to him and his bed, they'd actually get somewhere. Staring her down, he hit the pillow again. Only harder. "If you 'fuck' me," he drawled, mimicking her earlier choice of words, "maybe I'll get the fuck out."

She hitched up her skirts to her knees, climbed onto the bed, picked up a pillow, and thwacked him with it. Hard. Hard. Hard. Hard.

He rumbled out a laugh and snapped a hand up against the pillow bouncing against his head. "Clementine— What— It's a pillow. If you plan on hurting me, I suggest you use a vase or something."

She thwacked him again and glared. "You think it's funny that you're riling me?! You think it's funny that you're—"

He rumbled out another laugh as the pillow kept bouncing off his head. "If your father could see this, he'd probably give me another three million."

She gasped, whipped aside the pillow, sending it across the room and fell back, a choked breath escaping her. She cradled her hands against her chest as if it hurt and let out a deep, aching sob that penetrated Derek's chest.

Jesus. Taking hold of her shoulders, he gently pushed her down onto her side of the bed and used his body to pin her in place against the mattress, both their breaths coming at each other hard.

He stared down at her as her unraveled black hair lay in waves across her shoulders and the pillow. He smoothed her face, brushing away tears. "Darling. Don't...what— I'm sorry. I didn't mean to— Please don't cry."

Her chest rose and fell heavily beneath him, her face, throat, and cleavage flushed. She swiped away her tears with trembling hands.

It was like he'd let a Siberian tiger out of its iron cage when he'd thought he'd been dealing with a mouse all along. "Don't cry," he murmured, still hanging over her and smoothing her unbound hair away from the sides of her face. "I'm here."

Her lips quivered as she intently searched his face, her chest still heavily rising and falling. "I knew it. I...I knew it."

He pinned her against the bed with the mass of his body, trying to understand. "What? What do you know?"

Those full lips parted as her entire face flushed to a deeper red. "Our marriage is already turning into a mess." Tears glistened in her eyes. "This is supposed to be a happy night. Not...not this."

His throat tightened. He had made her cry. On their wedding night. Not knowing what he should do, he did the first thing that came to mind. Something his father always did with his mother whenever she was upset or crying. "*My dearest dearest,*" he sang softly to her in a husky, soothing tone, "*who is so civil in her carriage, this song is sent to you to be happy in your marriage. Try before you cry, be merry and consenting, and above all thank the Lord that your husband is repenting.*"

Her expression stilled. "That was...beautiful."

He swallowed. He'd never sung for anyone before. "If it will keep you from crying, I'll...I'll sing all night."

A breath escaped her. To his surprise, her hands jumped to his face and yanked him down toward her lips hard. Her mouth fully molded against his as she forcefully nudged his lips apart and slid her tongue deep inside his mouth, moving and rolling her tongue against his.

He couldn't breathe knowing she was trying to seduce him.

It was so wrong for him to want it and to love it and to need it in that moment.

But he'd been waiting for her to seduce him since they first met.

He kissed her back, his cock hardening.

Her hands slid into his hair and fiercely gripped its length as if she were fighting a need she couldn't contain. Her velvet tongue pushed deeper and harder toward the back of his tongue. It moved against his as if she had been tonguing him all her life.

It was like the cool and calm Clementine he knew was no more. He was being introduced to the real thing. A woman with enough bite to remind him of every gingered candy he had ever swallowed.

His hands rigidly slid down her arms toward her full breasts as he worked his probing tongue harder against hers, willing her to feel and taste and want what he also wanted: passion. He feverishly used his tongue to graze her teeth and lips. He angled his head to gain better access to her mouth, pushing his tongue deeper and angled his head again, pressing harder.

He ground the rigid length of his cock, which was still buried in his trousers, against her bundled chemise and thighs, willing her to give him more than just her body, but also her soul. He kissed her harder, tugging down on her corset. His hands pushed out the softness of those breasts from her corset as he kept kissing and kissing her.

Seven years of unbridled fantasies were coming true.

They were more than husband and wife.

They were twisting their passions into each other.

He released her mouth, the moist taste of her lingering on his lips and opened his eyes. He slid down her body so his mouth could explore her exposed breasts whose nipples had hardened to rough peaks. "Clementine," he whispered. "When are you going to realize that you need me as much as I need you?" He sucked on her nipple hard, taking that peak in deep against his tongue and felt as if his body and his cock were going to burst.

She gasped and arched against him, her hands gripping his bare shoulders.

Knowing she was letting him do whatever he wanted with her body, he flicked his tongue against her other breast, his hands dragging and dragging across the softness of whatever skin of hers he could touch. Her neck, her shoulders, her arms, her hands. All his. Every inch of her. He shoved up her chemise exposing her lower half.

He lifted his hips to make room between them, still straddling her, and dragged her hands down toward the flap of his trousers, forcing her slim fingers to unbutton it.

Their chests heaved uncontrollably against each other as she freed him.

Heatedly holding her gaze, he molded her soft hands against the hard corded length of his cock and forced her palms and fingers to trail down and up. Slow at first. Then more and more determined. Muscle straining sensations rippled through his entire body as he let the rhythm of their breaths control the rhythm of his physical pleasure. He used her hands to jerk himself off faster, groaning in need.

Every rational thought from his head ceased to exist except for one: that she was his.

More and more overpowering sensations spiked through the length of his cock and up his chest, tightening his core until every muscle in his body tensed. He wanted to spurt all over her so that she understood that every inch of her belonged to him and only him. He dragged himself higher up her body and raised himself above her so his cock was positioned close to her fully exposed breasts.

Using her hands to stroke himself harder and faster, he tightened his jaw and pushed and rolled his hips against those hands, feeling his core going beyond what he could bear. "Watch me," he raggedly urged. "I did this to myself for years waiting for you. Years."

She stared up at him through parted lips reddened from his kisses. Her half-naked body and those large breasts shook with each jarring movement he forced her to make, taunting him into wanting to physically shatter.

Pushing back her hands, he shoved open her legs and positioning himself at her wet entrance thrust into her hard.

They both gasped.

He gripped her hair, winding silken strands around his fists and pounded and pounded into her hot tightness, seething out breath after breath as he pushed his cock closer to his own climax. Nothing in that moment mattered but releasing every emotion she had ever made him feel. No more chasing the untouchable. This was his and it was staying his.

Knowing he was about spill, he pulled out and kneeled over her.

He released a quaking breath that bucked his hips as he pumped himself with his own hand. He yelled as his cock spurted thick seed all over her breasts.

She startled.

He yelled out again, the last of his senses shuddering and dragged in uneven breaths, trying to regain control of his body and his mind. His chest heaved as he staggered and stared down at her and his now sated cock. They both continued to breathe hard.

He lowered himself back onto her half-naked body. Using the linens of the bed, he wiped his seed from the curve of her breasts.

She didn't move. She only silently eyed him as if waiting for the clean up to end.

He paused, realizing he'd only pleasured himself. He was such an idiot. He shifted against her and dragged his hand toward her gown. "Come here, love. Let me—"

"No." Her voice rose an octave. "I'm done. I'm sorry."

He gently pushed up her gown. "No, we're not done. Let me—"

Her hands came down hard against his own, hitting his wrists. "No. What I made us do was wrong. I wasn't thinking. I shouldn't have—"

"Clementine, it wasn't wrong. Getting seduced by you was rather nice for a change. Hell, I'd love to see more of it. I just—"

"Cover me. *Please!*"

He swallowed, nudged up her corset back over her breasts and pulled her chemise down. Holding her gaze, he kissed her exposed shoulder. Twice. "For God's sake, you can't keep doing this. Half the time, I don't even know what you want from. One moment you're using words I didn't think you knew and telling me to leave, and the next you're seducing me. You're acting crazy."

A shaky breath escaped her. "Maybe I am crazy."

He released her and rolled to his side of the bed, flopping himself back onto the pillow. He raked back his hair from his face and squeezed his eyes shut, letting his hands drop to his sides. Fuck. He'd said the wrong thing. He dragged in a ragged breath, trying to steady his mind and his body. "You're not crazy," he confided in an uneven tone. He puffed out a breath and re-opened his eyes, buttoning the flap on his trousers. "Clementine. I'm worried about you. You can't—"

"Understand that I can't even breathe or think around you," she rasped. "You keep pushing and pushing for me to be physical with you when I'm trying to create something more meaningful between us. And...I...I'm done for tonight. I need to be alone. *Please.*"

It was like no matter what he did, she refused to acknowledge that he was trying. How was he supposed to— He sat up and pushed off the bed, setting both feet onto the floor. From the moment they'd met, she'd been pushing him away. And there was only so much of it he could swallow. "I'll let you sleep because it looks like we're both done here." He walked across the room in four long strides. Opening the door, he stepped out and shut the door.

A shaky breath escaped him as he quietly set himself against the nearest wall in disbelief. A part of him waited for her to come out and tell him everything and that she didn't mean to throw him out. He waited.

He could hear her winding and winding and winding her music box in between sobs before padding her way back into bed. The golden candlelight that faintly fingered its way from beneath the door faded to black. The tinkering of music played on as she sobbed. The door remained closed.

He wanted to go in but knew she would only push him back out.

For the first time in his life, despite always having a firm sense of direction of knowing *exactly* what he needed to do, he didn't know what he was supposed to do. It was obvious she needed him but he was confused as to *what* she needed from him. Even worse, something muttered to him that this Nasser knew far more about her than he did.

Shoving himself away from the wall, he stalked down the corridor. They were married and she still wasn't his. They were married and she still— Unable to hold in the anger riling him, he veered toward a wall and punched it, jarring his knuckles and arm to the bone. For the first time since laying eyes on her he wondered if maybe, just maybe, he shouldn't have married her.

LESSON TEN

It isn't enough to want change.

One must lick it from corner to corner and swallow it.

-The School of Gallantry

The following morning

When deep fears became deep reality, it made a woman realize she had a problem that needed to be addressed. It was even more terrifying to know she was actually part of the problem. She had spoken to Derek and acted toward him as she had often heard and seen her own mother acting to her father. In riled passionate tones laced with harsh words and objects smashing hard against floors and walls at night, only to all end with a door slamming shut. A door she would linger outside of as a child in fear of the worst to come as muted, strangled moans and pants and groans drifted through the wood paneling. The governess would grab her and hurry her back to her room, coldly scolding her for not giving her parents their privacy.

She had sworn to never have their relationship.

She had always wanted more for herself.

She had always wanted honey on the moon.

Tears burned her eyes. She had never yelled at anyone before or raised her hand to anyone before. It wasn't in her nature to do so. Not after having grown up with a mother whose first reaction was to roar.

When she, Clementine, had thrown herself at Derek like an animal in the hopes of drowning out all the noise he was putting into her head, it made her realize she was only making it worse. Because no one knew more than she did that if passion wasn't properly controlled or guided, it destroyed everything.

She refused to re-live her childhood in adulthood. She *refused*.

So what path could she take now that she was married?

Only one. Ensuring that her marriage didn't fall apart.

Clementine carefully added a spoonful of sugar to her tea, feeling the tips of her fingers trembling in an effort to keep sugar from spilling outside the cup. The sound of her silver spoon clinking against the gold-rimmed porcelain sounded almost like a church gong at the breakfast table where she sat across from Derek. She set aside her spoon. She glanced toward him knowing he had waved away every last footman out of the room.

She expected him to say something.

He didn't. He still silently held the newspaper high enough to cover his face.

It was the only view she had of him in the last five minutes since he sat down at the table with her to have breakfast. He hadn't bothered with his plate of food or his coffee. Nor had he rustled with the newspaper to turn a new page. It was obvious he'd been staring at the same two pages for the past five minutes.

She knew he was waiting for her to start the conversation. And given she hardly slept, getting up on the half-hour to wind her music box throughout the night to ease her distress, she was done with choking on misery.

She lifted her teacup to her trembling lips, taking a calming warm sip and set it back down onto the saucer. It tipped and spilled, soaking the tablecloth. She winced and used her napkin to address the mess. She eyed Derek.

He continued to stubbornly hold up his newspaper.

Setting her empty cup back onto the saucer, she confided, "I'm sorry about last night. I was...I was overwhelmed."

His newspaper flopped down. "Is that what you call it?"

An exasperated breath escaped her. "You're very forceful and passionate in nature, Derek. It leaves very little room for us to get to know each other outside of your passions."

"Is that how you see it?" Without meeting her gaze, he folded the newspaper and set it aside onto the table beside his plate. His gruff features appeared all the more severe given he was not looking at her. He took up his fork, his gaze still lowered and turned it back and forth against his fingers. "So are you saying Nasser knows more about you than I do?"

Poor Derek. It was like he didn't understand what men and women *needed* to share. "Yes. He knows a lot about me. In fact, he and I talk about everything." Knowing he needed an explanation she wouldn't be able to offer him without betraying Nasser's secret, she quickly added, "I cannot speak for Nasser, given I am sworn to protect his name, but I will give you the name of a man who will be able to at least answer some of your questions. Go to him first and set aside your doubts. His name is Brayton."

His brown eyes snapped to her face. *"Brayton?* As in...Lord Brayton?" he echoed. "Doesn't he live with my brother?"

She nodded. "Yes. He was tasked to investigate your family for the Persian crown."

His eyes widened, reflecting the horror of knowing that a British aristocrat was working with the Persians and that it had treason slapped all over it. "Does my brother know he has been living with a spy?" he demanded.

"You needn't worry about Andrew's safety, Derek. The Persians have no reason to attack England. Not when they are dealing with Russia. And Nasser, although he revels in playing a fierce leader for his father, is far too kind in nature to ever bring harm to anyone."

Derek fisted the fork he was holding until his large knuckles went white.

Everything grew quiet. So quiet, she could hear herself breathing.

"You speak so highly of him." His cool tone indicated that he was struggling to keep his voice respectful. "Certainly more highly than me."

A breath escaped her. "No, Derek. That isn't true. For heaven's sake, he and I—"

"Forget it. I'm not looking to argue. I'm done with that." He tossed the fork onto the table and stood, his chair scraping the hardwood floor. "We aren't talking about him ever again. Because it's obvious he means more to you than I do."

Everything was falling apart. Just as she knew it would. She knew if she stayed and loved him, he would set fire to everything with his damnable passions. The sort of passions she had vowed to avoid all her life after choking on it since childhood.

Rounding the table, he veered in and lingered by her chair. He rugged features softened, as did his voice. "Clementine." His voice cracked. "What do you want from me? Tell me. So I can do it. I don't want to lose you."

He wanted to genuinely love her. She could see it in his face and his eyes. And that was more than enough for her to want to love him in turn.

She rose and lifted her gaze to his, her misery making it almost impossible for her to breathe. She turned toward him, her skirts brushing his trouser-clad thighs. "Derek, it isn't any one thing you must do. It's what we both must do. I'm transitioning into a new way of life I wasn't prepared for. And it's obvious you yourself are transitioning into a life you aren't prepared for. All I ask from you during our marriage is that you...please stop treating me like an object. Get to know me. Not as a woman but as a person."

He nudged her chin upward with the curve of his hand, his brown eyes intently searching her face. "How am I to know you as a person if you aren't even willing to tell me things? You told me last night there are things you can't tell me. Where does that leave us?"

She swallowed, knowing he was right. "And that is why I am sending you to Lord Brayton. Because the one secret you want is not mine to give."

He hesitated, his expression turning to anguish. "I see." He released her and stiffly stepped back. "I'm uh...I'm going to talk to Lord Brayton in the hopes he'll be able to answer some of my questions. Because although I want to trust you, right now...I don't." Without meeting her gaze, he rounded her and strode out of the room, his steady footfalls leading down the corridor announcing that addressing Lord Brayton was next.

Sometimes there was such a thing as a calm before the storm.

She had seen it too many times.

Her heart popped. She scrambled around her chair and the table and bustled toward the entrance of the breakfast room. Peering out, and noting he was gone, she dashed straight for the nearest footman so she could be ready to leave in time knowing there was only one way to prevent two men from hurting each other: getting between them.

*****

An hour later - 11 Berwick Street

Derek thudded the ceiling of his coach with a gloved fist, signaling it to stop when the hackney he'd followed all the way from his brother's quarters in an effort to talk to Lord Brayton, pulled to a halt in what appeared to be a quaint neighborhood of merchants.

Derek leaned toward the window.

On the other side of the street, a gruff-looking, well-muscled man who would have easily sent fear into a constable holding a pistol, hefted himself out of the hackney, those broad shoulders over-stretching his wool coat. Lord Brayton effortlessly landed onto the cobbled street just before the pavement leading toward a long row of townhouses. Tugging down a dark wool cap over his brow, he dragged up his coat collar, extending it high enough to hide what appeared to be a long jagged scar on the side of his face.

Derek paused in astonishment. Someone had clearly taken a blade to the man's face.

Lord Brayton trudged past one of the black iron fences that belonged to a whitewashed townhouse with shutters framing all of the large windows. Moments after twisting the bell, a butler opened the door, took his card, and let him inside, the door closing behind them.

Damn it. He knew he should have gotten to the man sooner.

Using the tips of his gloved fingers, Derek quickly angled his top hat forward as the footman opened the door to his carriage and unfolded the steps. Derek rose and without using the steps, landed onto the cobbled stone. "Return within a half hour. If I'm not outside, go down another street and come back in another fifteen minutes after that."

The footman inclined his head. "Yes, my lord."

Adjusting his morning coat, Derek crossed the street and stepped onto the pavement. He strode up the small set of stone stairs, toward the door Lord Brayton entered and paused. The polished brass numbers '11' beside the door glinted in the sunlight as he reached beneath it and twisted the bell.

He glanced behind him toward the narrow cobbled street, waiting.

The clattering of carriages and the occasional shouts of various vendors selling wares in the far distance floated in the late spring air that smelled, not of countless flowers in bloom, but rather, of acrid coal smoke from surrounding chimneys.

He turned back toward the door and twisted the bell again.

The door swung open.

A portly, gray-haired gent in well-ironed, dark blue livery observed him from beneath the thick, fuzzy tufts of his brows. "Do you have an appointment, sir?"

Derek cleared his throat. "Ah, no. Forgive me, but I don't. The name is Lord Banfield. I apologize for the intrusion." He gestured toward the foyer behind the man. "I would actually like to speak to the gentleman who just entered. It should only take a few minutes. Can I please step inside to speak with him? Because I would rather not do this in public."

The butler lowered his round chin onto his stiff collar before holding out a gloved hand. "Five pounds will see you into the foyer. And ten pounds will see you straight to the gentleman himself."

Derek shifted toward the man in disbelief. "Are you asking that I pay you to see him?'

The man sniffed. "Was I not clear in that, my lord?"

Something told him this wasn't the first time this man held out a crooked hand. "Where is your mistress, sir? I'm asking to speak to her regarding your outrageous behavior. Does she know you're soliciting money from her guests?"

Those thin lips retracted. "Judging by your tone, and that you have been watching this house and the gentleman who entered it from a carriage you were hiding in across the street, perhaps I ought to not only close the door but call for Scotland Yard. You don't appear to be friendly and I doubt your intentions are either."

The old man had been watching him. "I'm not looking to hurt him." Yet.

"Have you seen the size of the man? I doubt you would be able to."

Derek rolled his eyes. "Given you aren't worried for his safety, may I please speak to Lord Brayton? It's important."

The man's bushy brows popped up. "It would be rude of me to allow anyone to intrude on his appointment. You do realize that, my lord, yes?"

It was obvious where this was going. It's not like he was financially struggling. Far from it. He was officially worth three million and could probably buy his way into heaven. Derek unbuttoned his morning coat and pulled out his leather pocketbook. Flipping it open, he yanked out one of many bank notes he had: a fifty pound one. A month ago, he would have panicked at the idea of parting with so much money. Now? It was like handing over a shilling.

Derek held it out between gloved fingers.

Those eyes widened as the older man glanced up. "I will ensure you are given a glass of our best port to go along with your visit. Is there anything else you require?"

There was no doubt money was power. It was downright dangerous. "No need. I only require entrance." He still held out the bank note. "Now take the money."

The butler took the bank note. "Thank you. You are beyond generous, my lord, I...thank you." Tucking it frantically into his pocket, he pulled the door wide open and cleared his throat. "Shall I take your coat and top hat, my lord?"

Derek stepped into the foyer, removing his top hat. "No, thank you, sir. I'll hold onto my hat. I don't plan on staying long." He made a promise to himself and he was keeping it. Resolve and go. Not punch and go. Resolve and go.

The door closed, darkening the quiet foyer.

The sweet smell of mulled wine floated in the air and a clock chimed in the distance, somewhere upstairs, before clicking back into silence. The butler glanced toward the stairwell beyond, as if to ensure no one was coming, then sidled up to him and imparted in a low tone, "I will notify madame that you are here. Lord Brayton is in the parlor to the right. Whatever you do, I ask that you not rile him." With that, he strode past and hurried up the stairs.

If his brother was still sharing quarters with the man, how bloody dangerous could he be? Derek shifted his jaw and slowly made his way into the adjoining room and across the wooden inlaid floors of the parlor. He paused at finding Lord Brayton seated in a single gilded chair set in the middle of the receiving room.

Lord Brayton's ice blue eyes veered toward him.

Derek paused, realizing that the room was eerily devoid of carpets, side tables, lamps or anything else that might have made it look mildly welcoming. More disturbing was seeing four life-size, marble statues of well-muscled, nude men lining the section of the empty receiving room across from where Lord Brayton stoically sat.

They all seemed to be staring at him with cold intent waiting for him to make his move.

The calling bell rang in the distance.

Derek adjusted his coat and approached Lord Brayton, intent on saying what he needed to say so he could get out, because it was rather obvious based on the statues alone that this house was designated for things he didn't even want to know about. "I'm Holbrook's brother, Lord Banfield. We haven't formally met but I was hoping to have a quick word with you."

The man rose to his booted feet and straightened, his massive muscled framed looming to what appeared to be a full height of six feet and five inches. His dark brows came together, emphasizing the long jagged scar that ran from the left side of his ear to the bottom front of his jaw. "I know who you are. How did you know I was here?"

"I tried to wave you down earlier when you were getting into the hackney but you didn't hear me. So I followed you."

Brayton stepped toward him. "Is there a problem?"

Although the man was incredibly big and looked like he could chew lead bullets for breakfast, after the sleepless night Derek had, not even

Hercules was going to stop him from putting this to rest. He veered in close and imparted in a very cool tone, "I'm going to ask you some questions and you're going to answer them."

Those gruff features hardened. "You're incredibly bold to be coming up to my face like this. I point at a person and they die."

Derek leveled him with a hard stare. "If you think I'm intimidated by the fact you ate too much beef growing up, you ought to take your treasonous British arse back to Persia...*spy*."

Brayton stared. "Don't take your bedchamber problems out on me. I got my own."

Derek whipped his top hat aside, sending it rolling off to the side and fisted his right hand hard. It trembled from the effort he took to keep it from flying. He swore to himself, for Clementine's sake, he would try to understand this situation. He swore to it. "This isn't about my bedchamber problems. This is about my wife. My wife didn't grow up in a sheltered home like other ladies. As such, things affect her more greatly. Which means I have to protect her in a way not even her own father did."

"Nasser knows that."

What else did this Nasser know? "Does he also know I love her? Does he know that? Does the *fucking bastard* know that? Or do I need to introduce him to my own two fists?"

Those features darkened. "I don't take kindly to a mere civilian addressing the prince as if he were worthy of disdain."

Apparently, thunder was trying to send a storm. "A mere civilian? You're calling me, a viscount, a mere civilian? You're clearly standing in the wrong country, boyo. Setting aside what I think of this entire situation, herein is the problem I'm *really* having. Whenever I ask my own wife what her association is with Nasser, I get the same answer: *no* answer. In fact, she panics. Never mind that a part of me *is* jealous knowing she is devoted to a man I know nothing of, I'm actually more worried about her safety and state of mind than I am about losing her to another man."

Searching his face, Brayton said, "Her safety and peace of mind is assured. His Royal Highness is heir to the throne of Persia."

Derek rolled his eyes. "A royal bloodline hardly assures me of anything. Royalty is well known for greater perversions than your average honorable man. And I doubt he is honorable. An honorable man does not convince a young, engaged woman to join him in Persia. Nor does an honorable man violate a respectable woman by obligating her to keep secrets she can't even share with her own husband. What the hell does he want from her? Does he want her body? Her mind? Her soul? All three? *What?* Because I'm trying to understand."

"I cannot speak for what His Royal Highness wants."

"I'm asking you to help me understand my wife. Because she *needs* me. And I therefore need to understand this situation."

Brayton shifted his scarred jaw but remained indifferent. "If you do not understand your own wife, my lord, perhaps it is time to give her to someone who will."

What the hell was this? What did they want from her? Derek felt his breath burn in his throat. "She belongs to me. Do you understand? Not Nasser but *me.*"

Those ice blue eyes held his gaze. "If she belongs to you, then why are you standing here trying to convince me of it?"

Derek's nostrils flared. It was like a game. "I suggest you tell this Nasser, wherever the hell he is, he better not *ever* show his face to me. Or I will duel him and kill him."

Brayton stared. "You would have to go through me first."

Derek stared back. "How about now?"

"Don't make me laugh. Your cock is hanging over the wrong shoulder."

"I'm so glad you noticed its size. Are you jealous?"

A muscle ticked angrily in that jaw. "His Royal Highness intends to call on you in the next few days to discuss this entire situation and why he ultimately did not make *your* wife his wife, even though she pleaded to be with him up until a few days ago. Sadly, I think I understand the poor girl. You're like a dog chewing its own leg. Hell, I'd run, too."

Derek stepped back, feeling the very blood leave his own head. The beautiful girl he first met who had cradled him at his worst hour was no more. Everything she told him was a lie. She had planned to marry her so-called *friend* all along.

Brayton cleared his throat and thumbed toward the entrance. "You have a shadow."

A what? Derek swung toward the entrance and froze.

Clementine lingered, her silk pleated bonnet crookedly affixed on her head as if she barely had time to put it on. Her gloved fingers clutched her reticule as she stared at him. "There is more to it than what he just said."

Derek shifted his jaw, his body tensing. He always thought himself capable of forgiving her anything, but not this. Not lying to him and agreeing to belong to another. He could hardly breathe. "You lied to me. You told me to trust you. You told me to—"

"If you think you understand me and this situation, Derek, you're wrong. I never lied to you. I simply couldn't tell you what we agreed on. I couldn't—" Lowering her gaze, she opened her reticule and with trembling hands pulled out her silver casing of cheroots. "Dearest God, this whole situation is nothing short of a mess. Please just…just allow me to smoke something. So we can talk."

Stalking toward her he veered in and grabbed that silver casing and shoved it into his own pocket. "We're done talking."

She reached into his pocket. "Stop acting like this. I want my cheroots, Derek."

He jumped away, keeping her from getting them. "Why? So you could stick it in your mouth and keep lying to me?" He stepped back in and breathed out, "You can have your Nasser, Clementine. Because I'm about to tell you something that may surprise you: I don't want you. In fact, we're getting a divorce." He stalked around her and out into the corridor.

She scrambled in front of him, keeping him from leaving. Her features twisted. "Derek, you can't— I...we're married."

He leaned in. "Don't remind me. And don't you dare come home. Go to your father."

Her expression stilled and her own gaze narrowed. "Everything always has to be on your terms, doesn't it? Doesn't it? Well sometimes, Derek, your terms they...they *stink*. From the moment we met, you-you...expected me to mold myself into your arms as if I always wanted to be in them. And I'm sorry to say I didn't. I'm sorry to say Nasser was a far better friend to me than you ever were. Because you only see me as something to possess. Whilst he sees me as someone to understand."

It was as if she were proud of the fact that she had gotten involved with another man. His shock yielded to fury. "*Fuck him already and be done with it!*" he roared, unable to keep it in. "*Because I'm tired of loving someone who will never fucking love me!*"

Her eyes widened.

Lord Brayton stalked toward them, his gaze narrowing. "I suggest you and your fancy tongue full of emotions calm down before I send you through a window."

Derek rigidly pointed at the man. "If you come up to me, Hercules, I'll—"

"*Och, och, what is all this yelling?*" a French accented female voice called out from down the corridor. "A man who feels the need to raise his voice to the point of breaking my windows clearly knows nothing about control." There were several quick claps as if she were hoping to use her own hands to command attention and silence.

Derek paused as the clicking of self-assured heels echoed toward them.

An older woman pertly hurried toward them, her elegant ivory morning gown rustling with her quick movements. Her silver hair, which had been meticulously arranged in fashionable curls around her pale, aged face wobbled with each determined step.

The flirtatious scent of mint pierced the air as she came to a sweeping halt before them. The woman's blue eyes observed him. "Is your tongue always this foul?"

Derek swallowed, desperately trying to even his ragged breathing. He couldn't believe he had roared and sworn at Clementine. He never thought himself capable of it.

Clementine stared at the elderly French woman. "Why…it's you."

"Ah. We meet again. We know the same people. How beautiful." The woman stared at Derek, her pleased expression fading to contempt. "I am Madame de Maitenon," she offered in a firm, refined French accent, "and in this house no man will raise his voice to a woman or use vile words even if that woman deserves it. Now apologize to her." She waggled a finger in Clementine's direction. "Make it worthwhile. Impress her *and* me. Or I will call for the authorities and have them resolve this."

He felt like he had just been reprimanded by his own grandmother. He grudgingly turned back to Clementine, not because he wanted to but because he knew yelling and swearing was not who he was. She was making him into a person he didn't want to be. A person he didn't even recognize.

He swallowed and eventually offered in an even tone, "Raising my voice and swearing at you was uncalled for."

Clementine met his gaze. There was a lethal calmness within her eyes. "What is uncalled for is your inability to respect the love you claim to have for me. Because *this* is not how people love, Derek. And no one knows that better than I." She snapped out her gloved hand. "I would like my case of cheroots back, please."

How was it he was always the villain? He stuck his hand into his pocket and pulled out her silver case. He numbly held it out.

Plucking it from his hand, Clementine held his gaze, flipped open the casing, pulled out a cheroot, and stuck it between her full lips, flipping the casing closed with a single click. "I think I have earned the right to at least one, my lord. Be it in front of people or not. Don't you agree?"

He stared her down. "No. I don't agree."

"I wish I cared," Clementine tossed back. "Watch me smoke."

Madame de Maitenon sighed and plucked the cheroot out of Clementine's lips. "Whilst I admire your spirit that is dedicated to putting more coal into his fire, when a lady puffs merely to prove a point, she has overstepped her bounds."

Derek crossed his arms over his chest, holding Clementine's startled gaze.

At least *someone* was on his side.

Madame took the casing, opened it and delicately tucked the cheroot back inside with the nudge of a well-manicured finger before closing it and handing it back to Clementine with the swivel of a wrist. "I intend to put your pretty lips to better use. Now tuck it away, *s'il vous plaît.* Tuck it away."

Clementine quietly tucked the casing into her reticule.

Madame de Maitenon let out a theatrical breath and eyed each of them, her blue eyes brightening. "What brings all of this youthful passion to my door? Mm? It is rather obvious you two are married. How long has it been since you have both taken your vows?"

Derek widened his stance. "We were married yesterday."

"*Hier?*" A startled laugh escaped the woman. "You British do everything wrong. Wrong, wrong, wrong. You should still be in bed naked with your American bride, reveling in your newfound glory. Why are you both here? Why do you disrupt my way of life with your problems?" She stared at Derek.

Why indeed. Reveling naked in bed with his American wife would have been amazing. Though he damn well knew *that* wasn't going to happen any time soon. Not unless he stuck a sword through Nasser's oversized cock.

Madame quirked a silver brow. "Perhaps my age has seized my ability to hear." She tapped her ear, causing her diamond earring to sway. "I believe I asked you a question. Oui?"

He swiped his face. It wasn't even the afternoon and he was exhausted. "I needed to speak to Lord Brayton. I already did and now am leaving. Without her, mind you. She and I are getting a divorce. I apologize for the intrusion."

Those eyes snapped toward Brayton who was standing in the parlor behind them. Madame turned back to Derek. "Lord Brayton will understand my need to reschedule our appointment. I ask that you and your wife enter the receiving room at once. Do not worry about my naked men. They may be life-size, but they are not real. Now go. Go, go, go."

Clementine eyed the nude statues in the receiving room and edged back into the foyer and toward the door. "I'm not going in there."

Derek gave her a withering look. "What? You can go to your Nasser but not into a room full of naked statues?"

Clementine glared. "Nasser won't be naked when I see him."

He angled toward her, his pulse thundering. "Why do you seem to think I care?"

Madame breezed up a hand. "Heavens, your passions are exhausting even a woman like me. *Enough.*" Lowering her hand, she leveled a pert gaze at Clementine. "If my naked men irk you so much, I challenge you to go in and put a hand over whatever bothers you most. Go on. Show me. Are you not a married woman? Should you have not already touched everything you see?"

Clementine gasped and snapped a finger toward Derek. "I am holding you responsible for this entire situation!"

"And how is this *my* fault?" Derek pointed at Brayton. "He was the one who brought us here. *Bastard.*"

Lord Brayton held up both hands and trudged out of the parlor. Shaking his head, he grabbed up his wool cap from a red velvet pillow on the side table. "I will reschedule."

"*Merci*, Lord Brayton," Madame de Maitenon called. "Consider yourself admitted. I will have Lady Chartwell send you a missive."

The butler opened the door, letting Lord Brayton step out then promptly shut the door. Clearing his throat, the butler lowered his gaze and hurriedly walked past.

"Mr. Hudson," Madame de Maitenon said in a hardened tone to the man. "Do not think I am not aware of your *bouffoneries*. I will not tolerate it. No matter how many *petits enfants* you claim to support."

Mr. Hudson sighed, dug into his pocket and grudgingly held out the bank note to Derek.

For God's sake. As if he needed it. Derek pushed that hand away. "Keep it."

Mr. Hudson's gaze darted over to Madame, his features almost pleading.

She rolled her eyes. "*Oui.* Take it, you *coquin.* He is giving it to you."

Mr. Hudson grinned, shoved it back into his pocket and veered formally out of sight.

"Forgive him. His true age is closer to fifteen." Madame de Maitenon regally brought her hands together. "Honor me with introductions, my young people. Who is who?"

Why did he feel he was about to introduce them to trouble? He heaved out a breath. Not wanting to be rude, given they were standing in the woman's house, he quickly swept a hand toward Clementine. "This was my wife, Lady Banfield. And I am Lord Banfield. Now if you will excuse me, I have to contact a few lawyers and a—"

"*Non.* I cancelled my appointment with Lord Brayton for this. Your lawyers can wait." She extended a pale hand toward the parlor. "*Entrez, s'il vous plaît.*"

Appointment? What appointment could Hercules have with an older French woman?

Clementine eyed Derek.

Madame stepped between them. "Do not look to him, *ma chérie.* I am wanting to assist and will ensure there is no more yelling and swearing. Men are known for it. Especially when they are riled. It takes years to understand how their erratic minds work, but once a female understands it, life smiles upon a woman. And that is what we want. We want you to smile. Now do you wish to enter upon my invitation and end the yelling?"

Clementine stared at Derek. "No more yelling would be nice."

Derek stared back. "Words of love from your mouth would be nice."

Madame clapped her hands. "Do I need to separate your tongues?"

Clementine glared and turned. Gathering her morning gown from around her feet, she entered the receiving room, apparently no longer concerned about the statues.

He stalked in after Clementine, glancing back at the woman whose house they had taken over. "Madame, whilst I appreciate your concern, I can assure you—"

"Do not assure me, my lord. Assure *her.* For *there* is the problem. It is difficult for a woman to properly respond to a man when he is yelling and cursing like a sailor shouting at his peers over the wind." Madame de Maitenon followed him in with a lofty sashay. "Men do not usually bring their wives into my home given my *reputation.* So I will admit I am intrigued how both of you came to be here." She turned toward them, using her hand to sweep away the fullness of her gown from around her. Her delicate, older features mischievously brightened. "What brings you into the house of a courtesan and her School of Gallantry?"

Apparently, Brayton had a penchant for shagging pretty, elderly French women. And he thought his life was a mess.

LESSON ELEVEN

I will merely teach you to remember

what your soul already knows.

-The School of Gallantry

Judging by the wide-eyed look on Derek's rugged face, Clementine was fairly certain he was just as astounded as she was to know they were standing in a house of ill repute. She didn't realize elderly women were physically capable of entertaining men. One would think an older woman would use her age as an excuse to keep all the hands away.

"Maybe we should leave, Derek," was about all she could primly offer.

His gaze snapped to hers. "After you."

The elderly woman set herself between them and the door. "While I am pleased to see that you finally both agree on something, one does not come into my school, toss words, and leave. That is impolite."

Clementine blinked. School? Courtesans had schools? For what? She didn't even want to know. Because she was rather new to all of this. Heaven only knew what men *really* wanted outside of all things physical.

Madame lifted a prim forefinger into the air and shook it, rattling the gold bracelets on her wrist. "'Tis obvious you both require guidance and it is my duty to give it. Why? Because if I had been given proper advice when I had been at your delicate age, when my passions were ready and willing, I might have not only married but would have stayed married to the only man who ever mattered to me."

Clementine felt a knot tighten in her stomach at hearing that. There really weren't many independent paths for a woman to take in life if a woman didn't marry. This woman was proof of it.

Madame was quiet for a moment. "Given that you are both here the day after your own wedding, and there is discussion of other men, I am assuming your wedding night was a calamity." She pursed her lips, observing Derek. "How many times were you able to bed her last night? Did she ask for more of your *poom-poom*? If not, what did you do wrong?"

Clementine clapped a gloved hand against her mouth in disbelief. The woman was asking about their bedchamber life and what they did last night.

Derek's shaven face flushed as he swung toward the woman. "You have no right to be asking such questions."

Those silver arched brows came together. "Was the encounter that bad?"

A bubble of a laugh escaped Clementine from beneath her hand.

Derek glared. "Oh, *now* you have a sense of humor."

Clementine rolled her eyes in exasperation and lowered her hand. "I can't seem to please you no matter what I do. I'm amused at the wrong times and not amused at the right. If you ask me, your inability to control yourself is what brought us here."

He angled toward her and narrowed his gaze. "Perhaps my inability to control myself stems from the fact that you have given me *nothing* to control myself with. I was willing to forgive whatever happened between you and him. I was. But what I cannot and *will not* forgive is that you continue to allow this man to take something you never *once* allowed me to have: your trust."

Clementine felt her throat tighten. "Maybe if you weren't too busy trying to bed me, you could have earned that trust."

Madame de Maitenon tsked. "Let us cease arguing for a few breaths. *Oui?*" She sashayed over to the lone chair set in the middle of the room and tapped it. "The person who sits in this chair is the only person who will be allowed to speak. Anyone else left standing, outside of myself, must accept silence and listen. Who wishes to sit?"

Oh, she rather liked this idea of creating a controlled environment without verbal retaliation. Maybe she'd finally be able to say some of the things she wanted to tell Derek since she walked into this entire situation.

Clementine gathered her skirts to walk over to the chair.

Derek skidded over to the chair and sat in it.

Clementine gasped. "Oh, yes, go right ahead, *husband*. Your needs, after all, should *always* come first."

Madame pointed at her. "I am afraid he is already sitting. He was very rude about it, *oui*, but I prefer we address his rudeness first. Keep silent. No matter what he says that may irk you, please do not speak. This is his chair and his podium. You will have your chance when he is done. Do you understand?"

Clementine swallowed and then nodded. Heaven knows she already knew what Derek had to say.

"*Bien.*" Madame turned toward Derek. "We need to address that you clearly think your opinion matters more."

Derek set his shoulders, settling more stubbornly into it. "I think I earned it after everything she put me through."

Clementine bit down on her tongue to keep herself from saying anything.

"What did she put you through, my lord?" Madame prodded. "Share."

He angrily held Clementine's gaze, his nostrils flaring. "What *hasn't* she put me through?" His chest rose and fell as if he were still unable to steady his breathing. "For seven years, I wrote her letters that I poured out of my *soul* in the hopes of bringing her closer to me, given I was always here in England and she was travelling the world. The one and only time I *did* try to see her, to surprise her with a visit three years ago, I put myself on a boat and after almost twelve weeks of travel, arrived in New York only to find that she and her father had been called out for an unexpected political event in Spain. So I got the address and went to Spain to follow her. Only...they had already left for France. So I followed them to France. Only...they had already left back to New York. That was about when I decided I needed to cease chasing her and go home."

Clementine's breath hitched. She never knew that.

He shifted his jaw. "I never told her about it because I didn't want to come across as the love-sick pup I already was. I was pathetic enough. I was sleeping with her portrait. I was writing her letters every month that followed her around the world, and if I heard from her once every eight months I considered myself fortunate. For seven goddamn years, I stayed away from every woman who ever came to my door because I couldn't imagine myself in the arms of another. Seven. The only reason I finally *did* lay with a woman, whom I hired for a measly night, was to learn how I should pleasure the one woman I wanted to make my own: her. Why? Because I didn't want to disappoint her in my duty to give us children." He stared her down. "Only she doesn't want children. She doesn't want the joy of holding our child. Just as she doesn't want me."

Clementine closed her eyes, knowing his resentment was in many ways her fault. She should have told him more about her own life

NIGHT OF PLEASURE | 213

through those letters. The real life she had led. The one that had made her into who she was. She never told him because she hadn't expected to stay. Or to love him. Opening her eyes, she met his gaze.

He was no longer looking at her.

Madame was quiet for a moment. "Not to digress, my lord, but it *is* a woman's right not to want children."

Derek sat up in his chair and glared. "You think it a woman's right to deny her own husband a son? Or a daughter? Or a family? No, I'm sorry. I don't agree. She is denying herself the ultimate happiness and, in turn, denying me the right to ultimate happiness."

Madame tapped at his arm that was resting on the chair. "You are looking at it from the perspective of a man and not a woman. You men have so many expectations you pile onto the head of a woman and yet…what expectations do you pile upon yourselves?"

"Begging your pardon," Derek countered, "but the estate and my entire life has countless responsibilities and expectations. Do you have any idea how many nights I stay up well past three in the morning merely trying to ensure everyone right down to my own servants have everything they need day to day and month to month?"

Releasing a long breath, Madame continued, "Yes, but is it right to demand a child from a woman merely because she has a womb and you have an estate? I think it rather absurd society continues to think so. Not every woman is ready to embrace the power of cradling life. And *that* is what a child is, my lord. It is embracing the ultimate power of having control over someone's entire life until they are old enough to live it on their own. If your wife does not want that responsibility and power, it should hint to you that she fears taking it into her hands. You must therefore allow her to embrace being comfortable with the power of responsibility before you accuse her of being incompetent of it."

His brows came together. "And how have I not allowed her to be comfortable with—"

"Allow me to finish, my lord. Do not interrupt." Madame skimmed the back of his chair, rounding him. "How have you helped her embrace coming into her responsibilities as a woman? Mm? Have you had discussions about how she may recognize who she is and her competence? You demand to know all of her secrets but have you treated her as a friend so that she feels comfortable enough in disclosing them? Have you done *anything* to assist in empowering her into making a better decision as to whether she would or would not be capable of having children? What sort of discussions have you had? Have you introduced her to any children from your family and asked her what she feels about those children?"

Derek glanced up at her. His face flushed. "Well, no...I..." He winced. "No. I never thought of..." He swiped at his mouth, falling into silence.

It was the first time Clementine had ever seen Derek realize his way of thinking wasn't the only way of thinking.

Madame eyed him. "Discussions are important in making life-altering decisions, my lord. Don't expect them. Negotiate them. Is there anything else you wish to say before she takes the chair?"

He plastered his hand over his mouth for a long moment before letting it fall away. "Whilst I know I didn't approach any of this properly, I am not about to forgive that she lied to me. That she planned to be with another after all my years of devotion. I want a divorce, Clementine," he said in a low, definitive voice. "Because I'm done crawling for someone who has never once crawled for me. I may not be perfect, but I never expected you to be either. All I expected from you was some reciprocation of what I felt. What I have always felt. And you—" He got up from the chair and stared her down. "I will have the servants collect your belongings and have them delivered back to your father along with your three million. Because I don't need either. I hope you and Nasser are happy." Averting his gaze, he walked toward the open doorway leading out of the room.

Clementine struggled not to cry. What he didn't seem to understand was that this was already her crawling. Whilst he was always able to shout about his passions, she could barely whisper it. "Derek, please don't..."

Madame turned and called out, "You are not done, my lord. She has yet to speak."

He jerked to a halt but didn't look back. "Nothing she has to say will change how I feel."

"Is that so?" Madame tossed out. "Prove it. Stay and listen. If you hear nothing of worth, then you may go and hunt down your lawyers. The end result will be whatever you want it to be. *Oui?*"

Clementine glanced over at Derek's rigid stance, inwardly pleading he stay. Just long enough for her to share what she knew she should have shared with him last night: *everything.*

He swung back and strode back into the room. "Five minutes."

A soft breath escaped her. Five was better than nothing. Gathering her skirts with trembling hands, she made her way to the chair and sat. She was tired of hiding from a past she was ashamed of. She had almost forgotten she had a choice to be whatever she wanted and not what her mother had made her to be. She set her chin, in an effort to appear strong.

Derek widened his stance, his features stilling.

Madame de Maitenon peered down at Clementine. Her stern countenance wisped back into a beguiling, elegant French woman. "Do you love your husband, Lady Banfield?"

The woman *would* start with that.

Darting her gaze toward Derek, whose brown eyes intensely held hers, Clementine felt her knees wobble and her soul splash into a puddle at his feet. The way it had when she first saw him seven years ago and he opened a tin of candy, trying to introduce to her a world she had always shied away from: the sting of passion. "I have always loved him," she managed. "I fell in love with him through our letters."

Derek startled, his lips parting as he quickly walked toward them, his shaven face flushing to a hue she'd never seen. "*What?!*" He searched her face, his hands going up. "You never once— No. No, no, no. I don't believe you. If you ever loved me, Clementine, then why the hell—"

Madame snapped her fingers at him. "*Faire taire.* Stand away."

He glared. "No, I'm not—"

"You are *done.*" Madame glared. "She is in the chair. Not you. Did she speak once over your own words? *Non.* She did not. She respected your words by suffering in silence. And now we see what *truly* plagues this union. Do you not understand, my lord, that it is very difficult for a woman to breathe when she is constantly being talked at with such *intensity?* You are dismissing her instead of understanding her. If you want to understand her, you cannot bring your own emotions into this. You must set them aside. Now stand away. *Away!*"

Derek fell back and almost bumped into one of the nude statues behind him. His chest visibly rose and fell as he continued to stare at Clementine.

She knew Derek probably felt more betrayed than astounded by her admission of love. She averted her gaze.

Madame walked around Clementine's chair, her ivory gown rustling in the newly created silence. "Judging by your husband's reaction, he never knew you loved him. Which is odd. Women are usually the first to admit to the fluttering they feel for a man. Why did you never tell him?"

Clementine smoothed her hands against her skirts. "I have never been one to say such things aloud. I love my father but don't ever put it into words. Such words, I find, when tossed out are disrespected. So I prefer to hold onto them. Unlike some people who cannot hold onto anything."

Derek closed his eyes, his features sagging.

"Ah." Madame paused, fingering the back of Clementine's chair. "So Lord Banfield was suffocating you with his love. Much like a child does when it adores its pet. Some men do that. Might I ask, Lady Banfield, why you were able to admit all of this aloud to a complete stranger? Why admit to your love if you are not one to say it aloud?"

She knew why. "Because he is leaving me no choice. If I don't say it now, I may never have a chance to say it."

Derek's eyes snapped open.

Their eyes locked.

"So aside from his suffocating ways," Madame gently prodded, "what else made you hold back your words of love, *ma chérie*? There must be a reason. Love, after all, is a gift to revel in. Not push away."

Clementine swallowed, her eyes burning. Maybe if she said it aloud and made it real enough for Derek to understand why she was the way she was, he would finally set aside what he thought he knew and embrace what actually was. "I know love is a gift, but sometimes gifts can be cursed. Sometimes they turn into things we don't want them to be. And I have always thought it best to keep such things behind a door. So it doesn't fall apart."

Madame paused. "I am intrigued. Explain."

A tear unexpectedly slipped down her cheek. She swiped it away, trying to contain the quaking in her own soul. "My parents actually married in a similar manner. It was an arranged marriage by *their* parents. My father came from an incredibly wealthy family as did my mother. They were expected to join their estates, even though they had so little in common. My father confessed to me that the only thing they ever had in common was their physical attraction to each other. Which is hardly something to build a lasting relationship on. I never knew what he meant by that until I got older but it made a profound impression because everything about my mother involved being physical. I knew my mother loved my father, but she was erratic and irrational. One moment she adored him and did everything and anything to please him and the next she sought to destroy him."

Her voice wavered. "My father had always been a good looking man. And my mother had always been incredibly jealous when women noticed him. From what I understand, she would terminate servants on the basis of whether they glanced at him. He was always faithful, but she never believed him. So she would hurt him. She would take a fist to him. She would throw things at him and make him feel worthless. It made him drink. Which only made it worse. After she would rage at him, he would try to escape her by going into his room, only she would run through the house and follow. I would...I would run after them and stand outside his bedchamber door crying, thinking my mother was still hurting him, not knowing that their argument had turned into something else: physical pleasure. I didn't realize what I had been hearing all those years until...Derek pleasured me."

Derek's eyes widened from where he stood.

It was as if a weight had been lifted and it was no longer just her burden anymore but his.

Madame's silver brows came together. "To say so much, and in front of a stranger with a reputation like mine, takes courage. I admire you. Because I know you are saying all of this to try to save your marriage." Her voice softened. "Allow me to help in the only way I can by making you understand what you grew up with. There are two types of passions that exist in this world: the ones that create pain and drama and the ones that create a bond. Theirs was one that created pain and drama. Many, many men and women use their emotions and their anger to fuel their passion and, in turn, it amplifies their ability to embrace pleasure."

Clementine stared up at the woman. "I don't understand."

Madame sighed. "There are people who crush those they love. It is the only way they can love and the only way they understand themselves and life. I grew up with a father like that." She was quiet for a moment. "Did your father ever raise a hand to you or your mother?"

Clementine shook her head. "No. Never. He isn't that sort."

"But your mother did raise a hand to your father?"

Clementine half-nodded. "Yes. She did. Sadly, it was often."

"Did your mother ever raise a hand to you?"

Clementine shook her head. "No. Her anger was focused on him."

"Did she fight with your father in front of you?" Madame pressed.

Clementine swallowed. "Many times. But the governess always either took me for a walk outside or kept me behind another door. She would tell me to cover my ears if I was upset. To keep it out."

A breath escaped Derek as he tried to meet her gaze.

Clementine knew it was best not to look directly at him given all she was saying.

Madame's voice remained soft. "Your governess did well in protecting you. Might I ask if there were any times of happiness in your home? Anything worth remembering?"

Closing her eyes, Clementine drifted back to the days she did cherish. Their picnics, ice-skating together, and all of their toes in the sand on the beach in Boston with the wind blowing from the ocean. "There were many times of happiness, yes," she confided. "I remember them all. It was what my father and I clung to. My mother had the ability to be the most wonderful and charming person in the world. But charm never saved a marriage or made for a good mother." She opened her eyes in misery.

"You are not as broken as you think you are. And I am about to prove it." Madame hesitated. "What do you aspire to be? If you could be any one thing?"

Clementine swallowed and met Madame's gaze. "A stronger person capable of expressing what she feels."

"Ah. Imagine that. And your husband, whose inherent nature is to be strong, which you yourself recognize, intimidates you. But this is where you can help each other. You can teach him to be more humble about his strengths and he can teach you to take more pride in your strengths. But…the only way either of you can begin to understand each other is by eliminating all the doubts that have been created." Those full pink lips curved. "Answer me this: do the blind ever know when a glass is full without touching it?"

Clementine shook her head. "No. Of course not."

Madame tapped Clementine's cheek. "Put the glass into your husband's hand. For he is blind to what you feel. He is blind to what you hold. You must therefore make him *see* what you *feel*." She nudged Clementine's chin upward. "This afternoon, insist that your husband set aside this talk of lawyers. Find a place to talk and ask yourselves one very simple question: should you salvage what you have and why?"

Madame gestured toward Derek who quietly lingered. "Bless his misguided heart, he is *finally* listening. He did not have to stay and listen, but he did. He stayed beyond the five minutes he said he would. Why? Because, despite his rooster ways, he still wanted to hear what you had to say. Your words mean something to him." She sighed. "Men carry pride differently from us women. To them pride is everything. To us, it only amounts to what the world is willing to give. Which isn't very much."

Madame gestured toward Derek again. "This one speaks of divorce after only a day. To me, that whispers of a man who has emotionally endured more than he is capable of handling. I will assist in that by offering him an opportunity few men in London will get. The question is: does he deserve an opportunity to be reformed? Should I bother assisting him in becoming a better man and lover? Because I know nothing of his worth. Only you know of it. So look at him and decide. Should we let him go to his lawyers? Or are you willing to fight?"

A soft breath escaped Clementine. She veered her gaze toward Derek who still lingered. Those soulful and enigmatic dark eyes held hers. Those eyes reminded her of the fiery seventeen-year-old who had once leaned toward her in the corridor of his house and said, '*If ginger and licorice ever fell madly in love and married, their children would look exactly like this. It's an acquired taste.*'

He really was an acquired taste. "I'm ready to fight."

The line of his mouth stubbornly tightened a fraction more.

A sense of calm overtook her knowing she not only could win Derek back but that she would make them into the very thing they needed to be: *friends*. The sort of friends who would forgive each other anything and, in turn, become even more to each other than lovers ever could be.

Madame rounded the chair. "I think this particular session is done." She walked over to a small writing desk tucked in the farthest corner of the empty room, took up a quill from the inkstand, and wrote more than a few words on it. Using a sander to dry the ink, she plucked up the parchment and folded it against the desk. Placing a stick of red wax into the burning flame of a candle, she sealed the parchment with a dab and a twist of the wax against the parchment. Waving it about, to cool the wax, she swept back to Derek and held it out. "You are expected in class this Monday. You have quite a bit to learn if you intend to stay married. It will cost you ten thousand."

Derek choked. "*Ten thousand?* For what?"

Madame pursed her lips. "For a chance to save your marriage. After the amount you gave my butler, something tells me you can afford it. And as you can see—" She extended a hand toward their surroundings. "My school parlor could use some more furniture. My granddaughter would also like to go to Egypt. And I have *always* had very expensive taste in jewelry. I am not currently involved with any men who might normally pay the bills. So you will."

Derek shifted his jaw. "I am not paying ten thousand pounds to be insulted."

Clementine rose from her seat. Damn him. Even after everything she just shared and in front of a courtesan, no less, he still didn't think their marriage was worth saving? "If you think I'm the only one creating the problem here, Derek, I'm about to re-educate you." Marching over, she took hold of the sealed parchment and tucked it into her reticule. Facing Madame, she announced, "I'll ensure he pays and attends this school.

Because you have already proven your wisdom is worth investing in. We will invest in it."

The French woman smiled and inclined her head. "*Merci.* Sadly, wisdom is acquired through one's own stupidity. Which means...there is hope for him." She pointed at him in warning. "Roll back your tongue and your pride when it matters most. It will help. Also..." She turned and walked toward the doorway. "I will return in a few moments. I must fetch a few things for your wife." Once in the corridor, and halfway up the stairs out of sight, she called out, "*Lady Chartwell?*" There was a moment of silence. "I am in desperate need of a few items from the pleasure room. Where are the whips, shackles and ropes?"

Clementine cringed. She didn't even want to know why the woman was asking.

Derek muttered something and stalked over to pick up his top hat, which was still lying on the floor. He tugged it on and angled it.

They said nothing to each other.

Minutes ticked by and the quick steps returned, coming down the stairs and the corridor. Madame de Maitenon swept back into the room, carrying a sizable red velvet satchel. She regally deposited it into Derek's hands and announced, "When you are both ready to kneel to intimacy again, you, my lord, will open this satchel and allow yourself to be at the mercy of your wife. She cannot feel empowered in your relationship unless you give her the ultimate power of tying you down. If playful whipping is not to your taste, let her tie your arms and legs to the bedpost so she may explore domination. Whilst domination involves far more than that, you will keep it very simple: you will not be allowed to touch her or kiss her or do *anything.* She must and will conduct all of your intimacies for however long you are in my school."

Clementine felt her face burn as she glanced at the satchel. "*All?*"

Derek shook the satchel, causing what sounded like shackles to chink. He rolled his eyes and shoved the satchel at Clementine. "Be a good friend and give it to Nasser."

Clementine gasped and shoved it back at him. "Why not admit you're downright scared of giving me the sort of control you have no trouble taking."

He shoved it back. "I'm sorry, but I'm already paying ten thousand for a lecture."

Clementine glared and tightened her hold on the satchel. It was obvious where this was going. And she trusted her friendship with Nasser enough to know he would help her. "Go to Nasser. Tell your driver to take you to 14 Park Place. Go. And when you're done being an idiot, I'll be at home waiting with the ropes."

He paused.

Madame tapped at his arm. "You will learn how to kneel and she will learn how to stand. Let her stand." Madame inclined her head. "I will see you on Monday, my lord. If you do not arrive, I will send Harold to your door. Rest assured, he makes Lord Brayton look like a mere goat." She turned to leave.

Derek's mouth opened but nothing came out.

Clementine quickly hurried after her. "Madame?"

The woman turned back. "*Oui?*"

Setting a hand to the side of her mouth and lowering her voice so Derek wouldn't hear, Clementine asked, "What will he be learning in this school?"

"Everything a man thinks he already knows."

"Which is what?"

"Their understanding of women both in and out of the bedchamber."

Clementine let her hand fall away from the side of her mouth. "I will ensure he goes. Any last words of advice?"

Madame quirked a silver brow. "Learn how to showcase your love more. Some men need it more than others. This one clearly needs it. Hold his hand when he least expects it. Make him feel important. Also use your womanly intuition to herd him in the direction you wish your relationship to go. If you do not insist, it will never happen."

Derek cleared his throat. "I can hear everything you two are saying."

Showcasing her love at every turn was going to be awkward, but this wasn't about her. It was about Derek. It was about them. Not caring about social etiquette, for she doubted it applied to a woman like this anyway, Clementine embraced her hard, letting the scent of mint wash over her senses. "Thank you."

Madame pulled away, smiled and placed a soft hand against Clementine's cheek. "Make him regret his words."

Oh, she planned to. If Derek thought he was the only one who could chew spiced candy, he'd never met the girl who had shot a pistol, smashed vases over men's heads, grabbed her reticule, crawled out of a window bleeding and then watched the New York authorities take over while lighting a cheroot on the street.

LESSON TWELVE

The beauty of love is that it can wash away fear

and doubts. But only if you allow for it.

-The School of Gallantry

14 Park Place, early evening

Derek had circled the entire city of London twice trying to avoid calling on a man who would ultimately answer the one question that viciously clawed at his mind and heart. He decided he couldn't avoid calling on the man forever.

So here he was.

The double mahogany doors leading into the lavish private quarters of His Royal Highness were swept open by two dark-skinned men dressed in identical flowing emerald-green garbs bounds by thick, red sashes around their waists.

The wigged butler in livery announced, "Viscount Banfield, Your Royal Highness." The wigged butler moved backwards, head bent, until he exited through the doors.

Derek's jaw tightened as he strode against the gleaming white marble that the oil lamps and candelabras illuminated. A line of servants departed the large lapis lazuli colored receiving room. The doors behind him closed, leaving Derek to address the prince alone.

He paused at seeing a very good-looking, dark-haired gentleman of deep olive skin tone. The man slowly rose from a chair to greet him, dressed in formal black attire, save a blue silk cravat and blue embroidered waistcoat that amplified the dark coat and trousers he wore. His jet-black hair was swept back with tonic and his square jaw had been shaven to perfection despite it already being evening.

Set on a walnut table between his chair and an empty one were several decanters of various liquors, two crystal glasses, and various hors d'oeuvres.

It was as if the man had been expecting him.

Nasser skimmed his appearance and gestured toward an empty seat beside him with a large hand. "Be seated," he said in a heavy accent. "I was about to indulge in an evening repast."

Women probably found that accent and refined demeanor attractive. Derek tried not to think about whether Clementine found this man attractive. He stalked over to the chair and sat.

Nasser lowered himself into his chair and crossed his right leg over his left, shifting toward him. Intense, black eyes met his gaze. "I am honored to finally meet you, Lord Banfield." He reached out to the crystal decanter set between them, still holding his gaze, and lifted the stopper. With his other hand, he took up the decanter and poured the dark red liquor into each glass, before setting it back onto the small table and putting the stopper back onto the crystal.

Nasser took up his glass and lifted it to his lips. Taking a swallow, he offered, "Drink."

He damn well needed it after the day he'd had. Taking up the glass that had been poured for him, Derek took a long swallow of the tangy, spicy but sweet liquor. He lowered it and glanced at the dark red liquor-like substance he was drinking. It was like his gingered hard candy. Only better. "What is this?"

Nasser searched his face. "It is burnt wine. It originates from Italy, but I had it altered to my own taste. Do you like it?"

"It's tolerable," Derek muttered. He drank some more.

"I am very glad to hear you find my favorite drink tolerable."

They drank in silence.

Derek knew it would have been stupid of him to start fighting this man. He decided it was best to take a breath and calm down. He was still recovering from everything Clementine had said. She loved him. She said so. And if he was inclined to believe her, then why was he here? Maybe because he needed to better understand her through someone else. Someone who had become a part of her life.

When they were both finished with their wine, Nasser poured them each another glass.

They drank that. And the next one. And the next. By the fifth glass, Derek realized by the heat in his body and slight swaying of the room, he was already drunk. Which was hardly what he had come here to do.

He set aside the glass, which Nasser refilled.

Derek waved at it. "No. No, I...no more." He sat up, blinking rapidly against the strong wine. He was usually more than capable of handling any amount of spirits but this one...it punched him.

"So why are you here at this hour, Lord Banfield?" Nasser asked in a low tone. "It is rather late to be calling on a man. Do you not think?"

"Yes. It is. And it took me all day to get here. So just..." Huffing out a breath, Derek blurted, "Did you fuck her after I did?" It was the wine talking. But he didn't care. He was glad for it. The sooner he settled this, the sooner he knew what path he needed to take. "Did you fuck her or are you two genuinely friends? As in...real friends. Because I need to know. No matter what you say, I will not fight you. Because this isn't about us. This is about whether I can trust her. I need to trust her."

Nasser carefully set down his glass and eyed him. "Not all men look at women like you do, my lord. Some of us yearn for other things."

Derek leaned against the side of his chair, toward him, and rasped, "Let me repeat that. Did you fuck her after I did?"

Nasser also leaned against the side of his chair, toward him. "No. I did not."

A shaky breath escaped him. Trying to sense if this man was telling the truth or not, he edged in closer. Close enough for barely a hand to come between them to ensure they were eye to eye. "So you never once wanted to? It never once came into your mind? *Ever?* Not even randomly whilst sitting and having a conversation with her?"

Nasser lowered his gaze to Derek's lips before lifting his gaze again so their eyes met. "You are making it very difficult for me to focus. You may want to move away. Or I may take advantage of you. It is late and you are drunk."

Derek paused, the haze of the wine making it too foggy for him to concentrate. Was this man...? No. He was imagining it. This man wasn't advancing on him. Or...was he? He fell back into his chair, everything swimming, and grabbed the armrests to balance himself and his breath.

Nasser also leaned back into his chair. He set his shoulders. "Given we will be associating for as long as I am in London, as your wife is a good friend of mine, I suggest you cut your hair."

"My...hair?"

"Yes. I like it too much. I like it enough to consider doing something I never would. So cut your hair, keep your face away from mine and we will be fine."

Derek's eyes widened. Jesus. The man was a...Boretto man. "So you...you're...?"

Nasser sighed, took up an hors d'oeuvre, and pushed it into his mouth. He chewed and swiped at his lips, causing the ruby ring on his finger to glint. "Yes, Lord Banfield, I lie with men. Of course, I have not had the pleasure of kneeling to a man in years given who I am. Only five people in this world and in my circle know about my true penchant. Dalir, Clementine, my valet, a few of my lovers, my mother, and now you. The men who are tasked to stand outside my door at all hours are deaf and therefore hear nothing. I ensured it as I must protect my name. The only reason I am telling you any of this is not because I trust you, but because Clementine deserves to be happy, and you are clearly looking for excuses to terminate that happiness."

Derek closed his eyes in disbelief. He felt like an idiot. Clementine, bless her heart, had been protecting this man from getting lynched by the world for what he was. Not what they shared. That was why she had been unable to say anything.

Opening his eyes again, he cleared his throat. "I'm sorry. I truly am. I, uh...I overstepped my bounds. I'm still learning how to be in a...relationship and I...I'm done here. I should go." He rose and staggered, the room swaying.

Nasser stood, jumped toward him and caught his arm and waist, hefting him straight. "Maybe you should eat something." Nasser nudged his chin toward him. "Do you need to lie down?"

Derek froze, realizing the man was holding him and touching his chin as if Derek were a lady in need of fainting salts. "Can you...not...this is awkward."

Nasser released him and stepped back, holding up both hands. "I was only trying to assist. I meant nothing by it."

"I understand and...appreciate that." He cleared his throat. "I'll get used to this. Especially given you and Clementine plan to...*associate.* Which I'm fine with. No one in London would be fine with it, but I...it isn't their business. It's ours. If Clementine needs you in her life...then so be it." He hissed out a breath between teeth. "I...uh...I have some groveling to do at home. A few hours of it."

Nasser stared him down. "Clementine may be my friend but that does not mean you are. If you ever speak of this to anyone, and I do mean anyone, even your brother, I will send someone to kill you. If you think I jest, go ahead and try it. Tell someone."

Derek coughed out an exasperated laugh and swayed. "Oh, now, you...you needn't worry about me. I have no one to tell. And my brother he...have you ever met Lord Trent? Apparently he...anyway...my brother associates with your kind."

Nasser widened his stance and narrowed his gaze. "My kind?" he bit out. "Are you insulting my people or my preference or both?"

Derek winced. "I'm inebriated right now. So please don't...don't hold anything I say against me. I already have a woman I have to go home and grovel to."

Those sharp features remained unrelenting. "You women-loving men are too focused on being men. Focus on being human, for *fravashi* sake. Focus on being a friend. That is all she needs. The rest will fall into place if you recognize that."

Derek's chest tightened. Even in a drunken daze, he could discern good advice when he heard it. This was why Clementine had gone to this man in the first place. Because she needed a friend. Something he had never truly been to her. God save him, after everything she had shared about her own life, he was going to be that to her and more.

Nasser let out a breath. "Sit, Lord Banfield." He gestured toward the chair. "You cannot go to her in this state. Her father struggles with the cognac. You do know that, yes?"

"Yes. She told me." Knowing the man was right, Derek trudged back over to the chair and slumped into it. "I'm in love with that girl. To the point of being...blinded. I even threatened to divorce her over this. This. I...I'm stupid. Do you know that? I am...stupid."

Nasser smirked and seated himself back into his own chair. "We are all stupid when it comes to our emotions, my lord. Anyone who says otherwise is lying to themselves and their God. At least you're being honest about it and recognize what you need to do." He gestured toward

NIGHT OF PLEASURE | 231

the silver tray laden with hors d'oeuvres. "Eat and the dizziness will pass within the hour. Shall I call for some tea and honey?"

"No, no, I'm fine. But I will eat." Derek reached out over the side of his chair and grabbed up one of the small browned corn cakes dabbed with caviar. Shoving it into his mouth, he chewed on its savory flavor in genuine satisfaction, refraining from groaning about how good it tasted. He grabbed up another one and shoved it into his mouth. "Damn, I just..." He chewed in exasperation. "I just realized I haven't eaten anything all day. Not even at breakfast. No wonder that burnt wine hit me so hard." He swallowed and took up another small corn cake. "These are incredible. Amazing. Thank you."

Nasser smiled and nudged the silver tray closer to Derek. "Indulge." Taking up his glass of burnt wine, he leisurely tilted it against his lips. He observed Derek for a long moment. "You appear to be a man very comfortable with his surroundings. No matter who surrounds him. I like that. Very much."

Derek snorted and pointed at him. "Don't you dare start flirting with me. I'm a married man, you know."

Nasser grinned, his dark eyes brightening. "Yes. I do know. She is a very lucky girl."

Derek rolled his eyes and shoved another corn cake into his mouth. Whoever thought he'd be fending off the advances of a man. "If you make me blush, I'll punch your arm."

A playful low whistle escaped Nasser. "I believe you are now flirting with me. I rather like rough advances."

Derek choked and hit his chest twice. "Can...can you stop?"

Still grinning, Nasser inclined his head. "I am honored to welcome you into my close circle. It is an unexpected pleasure. May we all be friends."

Derek held up another corn cake. "I'll eat to that."

LESSON THIRTEEN

Groveling is an art form. Respect it.

-The School of Gallantry

Midnight

A knock at her bedchamber door made Clementine scramble up from the dressing table she sat before. She glanced toward the closed door, her heart pounding. "Yes? Who is it?"

There was a moment of silence. "It's me. Might I come in, love?" Derek's voice hinted he was no longer angry.

A breath escaped her knowing he had finally come home. After waiting hours upon hours, all while wondering if he and Nasser were clanging sabers against each other. Smoothing her long braid over her shoulder, she adjusted her silk robe. Sitting back down onto the long bench before the dressing table in the direction of the door, she set her ankles against each other to appear more collected and refined. She prayed Nasser cared enough for their friendship to reveal the one thing Derek needed to know: the truth. "Yes, of course."

The door edged open. Derek, who was still dressed in his morning coat and trousers, stepped inside. He closed the door behind him and adjusted his queue and lingered. He captured her gaze from where he stood, his brown eyes soft. "I'm an idiot and I'm sorry. I was treating you like an object instead of…instead of the wonderful woman you are. I feel like I have been chasing you all my life without even giving myself a moment to breathe. I failed to realize I wasn't honoring us but destroying us."

She could barely quell the fluttering in her stomach.

He cleared his throat and crossed the room, his pace slow. "I spent most of the evening talking to Nasser. I can see why you associate with him. He is very amiable and intelligent. I like him."

"You do?" She kept her voice steady and even, despite the fact her breath and mind were anything but.

He bit back an awkward laugh. "Not in that way, I assure you." He paused beside her and added, "I uh…I thought it noble that you didn't tell me. It wasn't your place to. I wish to apologize for my behavior. I wish to apologize for not trusting you."

This was the true beginning of their friendship, she knew. She almost set a hand over her own chest in awe of him. "Thank you, Derek. It means everything to me knowing you're willing to try. I know I wish to also apologize for creating an environment which you felt yourself incapable of trusting me. It wasn't fair to either of us. I'm…I'm not…I'm just not one to gush."

He turned and settled beside her on the bench. "I know that now."

They quietly sat side by side.

He nudged her. "So what should we talk about?"

Reaching into her robe, she pulled out the folded parchment she had earlier tucked into her pocket. She held it out to him. "You might want to read this. I already did."

He lowered his gaze to it and seeing it was the same parchment that Madame de Maitenon had given them, sighed, tugged it loose and unfolded it. He read aloud:

Your application has been formally accepted and selected by Madame Thérèse's School of Gallantry. Your studies will commence this Monday at the address you and your wife have already called upon. Be prepared to set aside Monday, Tuesday, Wednesday, Thursday, and occasional Friday mornings during the remainder of the Season. Hours of instruction will commence at seven in the morning and end at ten. Method of payment in full must be settled with Lady Chartwell during your first week of school.

He groaned and let it float to the floor. He set an elbow on each knee and stared down at it. "You don't actually expect me to go, do you?"

Clementine smoothed her robe against her thighs. "Aren't you at all curious as to what she will be teaching? After everything she helped us with?"

"While I do not doubt she has more wisdom to share, I am not paying ten thousand to attend a-a...French woman's idea of anatomy class. It's fairly obvious what she'll be teaching. I know how to roll my hips, thank you." He stood up and rolled them forward once and twice to demonstrate. "I'm good at it."

She gave him a withering look. "Yes, too good."

He sighed and sat down beside her again. "Are you saying you want me to go?"

"She said it would help us."

He threw back his head, stared at the ceiling, and whined in the manliest manner possible, "But what if I'm the only man there?"

"Are you really worried she might grab you by the queue and have her way with you?"

He leveled his chin. "No one is going to be grabbing it, I assure you. I'm cutting my hair."

Clementine quirked a brow. "Cutting it? Why?"

He tugged on it and shrugged. "It attracts too much attention from the ladies *and* the men. And I...I'm a married man."

She observed him. "Are you saying Nasser found your queue attractive?" She elbowed him. "Did he comment on it?"

He flushed. "I should embrace a new sense of style."

She poked his knee and sing-songed, "*Someone has an admirer.*"

"Yes, yes. Laugh about it. I earned it." He closed his eyes, a pained expression overtaking his rugged features. "Can I go to bed? I'm exhausted." He got up onto booted feet, heaving out a long breath between teeth and inclined his head toward her. "Goodnight, love." He trudged over to the door. "I'll see you in the morning." He held up a quick hand, opened the door, scrambled out, and closed it behind himself.

She sat up, astounded. Oh, now, he was taking this idea of friendship too far. He hadn't even—

The door opened and he leaned over the side of it with a lopsided grin. "I convinced you I wasn't interested in throwing you onto the bed, didn't I?"

She smirked. "No amount of schooling is going to educate you, my lord."

Still leaning over the side of the door he prodded, "Friends still get naked, right?"

She snorted and waved him off. "Go. We are done. I am not rewarding this."

He undid his cravat and flung it toward her from behind the door. "If I did this to Nasser he would wet himself."

Throwing back her head, she laughed so hard she thought her robe would fall open. She astounded even herself, because it wasn't that funny, but—

He tossed his coat onto the floor from behind the door. "Admit it. You want to strip me naked and tie me to the bed post and treat me like the naughty boy that I am, isn't that right?"

Laughing even harder and unable to catch her breath, she held up a hand. "Cease. I...I can't breathe!"

He unbuttoned his waistcoat and flung it across the room.

Still laughing, she stumbled up onto her feet and staggered over to him, holding up a hand. "Stop it. The servants will see you!"

He paused and momentarily disappeared behind the door before re-appearing again. "Nothing in the corridor but candles."

Letting out a breath she was just catching, she shook her head and walked over to him. Grabbing him by his arm, she tugged him inside and shut the door. Clementine took hold of his linen shirt and using the weight of her body, pushed him against the nearest wall.

His back hit the wall with a thud and she collapsed against him. "You exhaust me."

His hands jumped to hold her in place. "Good. I'm glad to hear it. I want to see you laugh like that all the time. Do you hear me?"

She lifted her gaze to his and bit back a smile. "I've never laughed like that before. So I guess there is hope for me."

His hands skimmed up to her face. "I think we're good for each other. We are simply still realizing it."

She nodded and smoothed her hands against the linen of his shirt, her palms curving against the hardness of his broad chest. "I agree," she whispered.

His jaw tightened. He grabbed her hands and drew them to her sides. "Don't do that unless you plan to follow through." He hesitated. "I'll wait for you to...invite me back into bed. All right? I'd love to go riding with you tomorrow and then the Diorama. You would love it. All of the paintings move in time to music. I haven't gone in years." Bringing her hands up to his lips, he kissed each one. "I'll see you in the morning."

She swallowed and half-nodded.

He released her hands and went around gathering up his clothing. He turned and headed toward the door, opening it. He glanced back at her from over his shoulder. "I love you, Clementine. I plan to prove it to you at every turn. Not just in bed."

Her heart squeezed. Despite having always denied it, this was why she had fallen in love with him through his letters during their years apart. Because he saw rainbows when she saw none.

He lingered.

She smiled.

He searched her face and quickly turned and left, shutting the door behind himself.

She pressed a cheek to the cool hardness of the wood and closed her eyes. He had been waiting for her to say the words. And all she had been able to manage was a stupid smile. She swallowed and opened her eyes. "I love you, too, Derek," she whispered. "Very much."

LESSON FOURTEEN

Dedicate yourself to bettering yourself and your life

will become what you need it to be: worthwhile.

-The School of Gallantry

Five weeks later

11 Berwick Street

After Madame de Maitenon's most unfortunate collapse at an evening event that led to the woman being bedridden, to Derek's surprise, the classes still continued under the rule of a different hand. Madame's own granddaughter, Miss Maybelle Maitenon. A petite, no-nonsense blonde who was merely a more civilized version of her grandmother.

At least that was what Derek thought.

He eyed the leather dildo in his hand as a line of four female models swept into the room, their red robes flowing around their slim bodies and long legs.

Derek tightened his hold on the dildo and sat frozen. They looked like gypsies. Their long dark unbound hair brushed against the fluid movements of their thighs and buttocks that were outlined by their clinging brocade robes. They all settled, standing in a row, each setting a bare right hand onto their hips as if they had practiced the art of standing before men holding dildos on a regular basis.

Miss Maitenon swept toward the row of four women and gestured toward them. "These beautiful women will be demonstrating the dildo."

Oh, now, shite. How was this educational? He highly doubted Clementine, who couldn't even manage saying 'I love you' would be able to manage a dildo.

Miss Maitenon's blue eyes brightened as she pointed to each beauty and the three other men in their seats then turned toward their newest student, the Duke of Rutherford. "Seeing there are only four women for the demonstration, Your Grace, I shall have no choice but to be the fifth."

Thank God she hadn't picked him.

Miss Maitenon continued, "An experienced and generous lover learns to keep a dildo at his bedside so that he can offer it to his lady whenever she pleases. The objective is to be creative. The more creative you are, the more pleasure it will result in. And as my grandmother always proclaims, 'A woman has more than one entrance to occupy a man's time.'"

"I'd say." Lord Hawksford stuck the end of the dildo into his mouth, waggled his brows up at his model and said through the dildo, "Do you think a woman will still respect me in the morning even with this in my mouth?"

Derek burst into laughter with the rest of the men.

Miss Maitenon rolled her eyes, hurried over to Lord Hawksford, and yanked the dildo out of his mouth using the wooden handle. Passing it over to one of the female models, who looked rather flushed, Maybelle glared at Lord Hawksford. "This is a classroom, my lord, not a circus-minded bordello. Allow me to demonstrate one proper use."

Derek sat up in his chair, praying to God she didn't intend to lift her skirts for the demonstration.

Making her way back to the Duke of Rutherford, she leaned down and took his hand, which already gripped the handle of the dildo. Gently, she repositioned his fingers around the wood handle, lifted the dildo to her mouth, parted her lips, and gently slid it into her mouth. As far as it would go. Toward the back of her throat.

Derek quirked a brow, noting that the duke's dark gaze was intently staring as if trying to measure how far it had gone. If he didn't know any better, he'd say there was something going on between those two.

Silence drummed within the classroom.

Guiding his hand, Miss Maitenon slid the dildo gently in and out, in and out.

Derek shifted in his seat and looked away. He'd never been much of a voyeur. While some of the classes had been surprisingly educational, this was ridiculous.

Miss Maitenon slid the dildo out of her mouth, straightened, and turned back toward him and the others. "Your purpose is to deliver pleasure. Being creative is always helpful with regard to this aspect. For in the end, it does not matter where this instrument goes, but whether your lover is receiving pleasure."

Derek gaped at her. His dildo slipped from his hand and down onto his lap, causing his heart to skid. Snatching it back up by the wooden handle, he cleared his throat.

She smiled. "There is no reason to be shy. If you can find it tolerable to insert a dildo into the lips of a complete stranger, I assure you, you will have no trouble inserting it into any part belonging to your lover. It is your duty to ensure that she is thoroughly sated." She turned back to the duke, leaned over, and patted his knee. "You were ever so brilliant, Your Grace. Do you require another demonstration?"

"No, thank you," the man bit out.

Miss Maitenon pointed primly to all of the ladies then to Lord Cald-well, Lord Brayton, Lord Hawksford, and to Derek, sending a dark-haired woman sashaying Derek's way.

Derek sank back against the chair. He hadn't had sex since his wed-ding night. Clementine hadn't asked for it. During these past five weeks, after taking walks together, shopping together, riding together, and at-tending events and parties, they always politely retired into their own rooms. He'd been patiently waiting for an invitation that still hadn't come.

He was a good friend. He was a fucking perfect friend.

One of the dark-haired women walked up to Derek and draped her-self onto his lap for the demonstration. "I understand you are married?" she casually asked, slipping her arm around his shoulder.

Derek half-breathed, looking past the slight opening of her robe that revealed the curves of large breasts pushed up by a corset. "Yes. I am." He hesitated and added, "She is gorgeous. Absolutely gorgeous. And we're happily married." Which was at long last true. Sex wasn't everything. Or at least that was what he kept telling himself.

Her dark eyes brightened and her mouth quirked. "If you're happily married, why are you here?"

He groaned. "Can we not interrogate the people who are paying you and this institution?"

She smirked. "Of course, my lord. Forgive me." She opened her mouth and tapped on it. "Before you put it in, ensure the dildo is well lubricated. Olive oil is best but we have none on hand, so we'll be work-ing with your own saliva. It's what a man always has at his disposition no matter where he goes anyway."

This wasn't right.

She tapped on the hand holding the dildo. "Lubricate. I will wait."

"I'm certain you will." He cleared his throat and prompted his own mouth to produce whatever saliva it could. Shifting his arm against the woman, he cupped his other hand beneath his mouth and spit a large pool into it. He eyed the dildo in his other hand.

"I'm waiting," the woman prodded.

"Wait some more," he muttered. The bad news was that he was lubricating a dildo. The good news was that it was a dildo, which was going to keep his cock flaccid. He tapped the dildo against his hand full of saliva, dipping it awkwardly.

She sighed. "You aren't dipping stale bread into gravy," she chided. Grabbing his hand, she enclosed it solidly around the leather dildo and forced his hand up and down its length. "Without proper lubrication, insertion is impossible. So lubricate."

He angled himself away. "Can you not...I'm intimidated right now. Which should say something." He couldn't believe he paid ten thousand pounds to molest a leather dildo that had been God knows where already. "I think I know my wife well enough to say she wouldn't be interested in doing any of this."

She smiled. "Nonsense. You don't know until you introduce it. If you can do this with me, a woman you just met, imagine what you can do with your wife." She lifted his hand. "Once lubrication is complete, insert slowly and ensure it is hitting her pleasure pearl." Directing his hand, she inserted it into her own mouth. She stroked it.

He drew in a ragged breath, watching that dildo slide in and out of her mouth. He was going home and fucking his wife. As a...friend.

****

Clementine tightened the bow of the apron around her waist, ensuring that her chartreuse gown was better protected. Once again taking up the large wooden pallet covered with an array of colored oils she had chosen, she dipped the tip of her brush into green paint and started moving the brush on different small angles across the canvas, her gaze following the small leaves she painted onto the trees lining the path of

Rotten Row where she and Derek had been riding almost every afternoon. Tilting her head, she drifted into replicating even the breeze that had rustled the leaves. She pinched her lips, trying not to get overly excited about how perfect it was.

The door to her painting room opened, making her glance over. She paused.

Derek closed the door behind himself, tossed a satchel onto the nearest chair and took off his morning coat then flung it to the floor. "I'm home."

Her mouth quirked, glad she only had a few leaves to finish on her painting. "How was class today?" She returned her attention to the canvas, dipped her brush again, and dabbed at a larger gathering of leaves hanging over the painted path.

"We studied dildos," he said matter-of-factly.

"How nice." She kept painting. "Why are they having you study extinct birds?"

He snorted. "I didn't say dodo, darling. I said dildo." He laughed.

"You're laughing at me." She kept painting. "Are you telling me I'm supposed to know what a dildo is?"

He cleared his throat. "No, you— We'll talk about it another time. When it's more…applicable. By the by, we got invited to a…risqué party by Lord Caldwell. One of the men at the school. Apparently, it became mandatory for reasons I don't know. I like Caldwell and the other men enough to want to go. Are you up for going with me? We can always leave early. We simply can't tell my mother."

"No worries. If you don't tell my father, I won't tell your mother."

"Agreed."

"By the by," she added. "I have officially stopped smoking."

His brows shot up. "Since when?"

"It's been five weeks now."

"Five? You mean you haven't…?"

"Not once. I thought about it, mind you, but never once gave in."

"Bravo. I get to finally kiss my wife without tasting tobacco."

She rolled her eyes.

He strode over and shoving his hands into his pockets, lingered for a long moment beside her. He eyed the canvas. "Is that Rotten Row?"

She nodded and kept painting. "Yes. Isn't it beautiful?"

He slowly crossed his arms. "The artwork is stunning, yes, but I never once rode down Rotten Row and thought to myself it was beautiful. Not when you can barely see over the heads of other riders and you're constantly veering your horse out of piles of manure." He glanced at her. "Out of all the things you could have honored, why Rotten Row?"

Oh, how she loved surprising him. "I always paint things for a reason, Derek. Aren't you going to ask why I painted it? You should."

He lowered his arms back to his sides. "Now I'm curious. Why?"

"Because something happened when we were on the path yesterday afternoon. Something I want to remember."

"Is that right?" He shifted closer to the canvas, his brows coming together. "I'm trying to remember what happened. We went riding, talked about the Diorama, I bought a flower for you off some random woman, and then I don't...what happened?"

She bit her lower lip, finishing the last of the leaves and set aside the wooden pallet. Stepping back, she gestured toward it. "I had an epiphany. Try to find it."

He tilted his head and squinted to better look at the painting. "I see a lot of riders, horses, leaves, sky." He glanced over at her. "What am I looking for?"

A breath escaped her. He probably hadn't noticed them yesterday. She hadn't said anything. She pointed to the stretch of grass off to the side where a woman in a bonnet cradled a babe while a man in a top hat leaned in and kissed the woman's cheek. "I decided I want that to be us. We can commence whenever you like."

Derek stared at the painted couple and the babe in the woman's arms. He snapped his head toward Clementine, his brown eyes searching her face in astonishment. "We've only been married five weeks. Are you...*really?*"

She set aside the wooden pallet and brush, let out a shaky breath and turned back toward him. "They have been the best five weeks of my life, Derek. You have proven to be...I can't thank you enough for making me feel part of a real family. Your family. I don't have to wait to know those happy weeks will turn into more months and then years. I saw myself holding that baby. I really did. That was us. I...you'll be a wonderful father. And I will do my best to be a wonderful mother. That is all that matters. That I do my best and you will help me do my best."

His lips parted. "Clementine...I..." He stepped toward her and grabbed her face with both hands. "I love you."

She pressed her hands against his. "I feel the same."

He smirked and wobbled her face against his hands. "It wants to come out. I know it does. Can't you say it just once? For the father of your unborn child? I promise I won't ask to hear it again."

She bit back a laugh and managed, "I love you."

He grinned. "Now I believe it." Capturing her mouth with his lips, he kissed her deeply, his tongue rolling against hers.

She melted into his arms and kissed him back harder. It was the first kiss they had allowed themselves in two weeks and she felt herself almost staggering against it, knowing they officially shared more than passion. They shared a life.

He broke their kiss and scrambled to remove his cravat and waistcoat, whipping them both aside. "We're not going to make it into the bedchamber. We're doing it here."

She untied her apron and tossed it at him. "Aren't you forgetting something?"

He gathered his shirt and yanked it off, the lean muscles of his arms and chest flexing. "On the chair in the corner." He tossed the shirt at her. "What do you want me to do?"

This ought to be interesting. "Bring over the chair and the satchel."

His hands paused on the flap of his trousers. "Just don't use the whip, all right? I'm really not into pain."

She tapped a finger to her heart. "I would never."

He jogged over to the chair, his trousers hanging low on his hips. Hefting it up onto one shoulder, he strode back and set it down. He opened the satchel and handed it to her. "Be merciful, my lady."

She reached into the satchel and pulled out the rope, tossing the rest of the satchel aside. It unraveled and coiled at her feet. She tried gathering the rope only to find it was excessively long. "Dearest Lord. She gave us enough rope to tie you to the entire building."

He grinned. "Not that it will hold me down." He purposefully flexed each muscled bicep for her, including his chest muscles, before sitting in the chair and adjusting his trousers. "I'll let you do the rest, heiress." He set his arms around the back of the cane chair. "Don't break the chair."

"I can do whatever I want, *husband*." She walked over to him, the rope dragging behind her. Coming around him, she bent over and tied his hands, looping and knotting and looping and knotting again and again, until his hands and forearms were bound with every last inch of the rope. She bit her lip and peered over his bare shoulder. "I actually used all the rope."

He tugged, hitting the back of the chair. "Something tells me I'll be in this chair a few hours."

She walked toward the paints. "If you thought I was sore after our first night together," she chided, "wait until I'm done with you. Ha."

He sat up against the ropes, trying to move. "Wait now. Where are you going? I'm over here."

She picked up the wooden pallet and paint brush and walked back toward him. "I've always wanted to have a *real* canvas to work with. Sit still."

"This masterpiece doesn't require any more paint."

"I disagree." She sat on his lap and daintily dipped the paintbrush into a random color. She painted a blue bird on the left side of his chest.

Then a yellow star. Then a red music note. Followed by an orange bonnet.

He glanced down at his bare chest as she continued to paint. "Couldn't you paint something a bit more manlier on me? In case it becomes...well...I don't know...*permanent?*"

"Oh, now, cease whining." She tilted her head and dipping her paintbrush in green, she drew a large dagger on his stomach. "How is that?"

He groaned and threw back his head. "It's pointing toward my cock."

She smirked. "I know. It's brilliant." She pertly got up and bustled the wooden pallet and brush back over to the table, depositing both onto it. She kicked off her slippers and slowly sashayed her way back toward him. "Now that I've properly marked you..."

He leveled his head and captured her gaze. "You're going too damn slow."

"Oh hush." She paused before him and let out a breath, trying not to embarrass herself. Everything they did was always such a blur. She dragged her hands up his thighs like he did to her their first night together. "How is that?"

His jaw tightened. "The legs are nice but go for whatever is under the flap."

She was officially nervous. She veered her hands inward, noticing that his erection was already sizably protruding against the wool of his trousers. With fingers that now trembled, she unbuttoned his flap. "I really don't know what I'm doing. Should I...sit on it?"

He tilted back against the chair, widening his legs and rasped, "Put your mouth on it first."

She paused. "Don't be ridiculous. How do you expect me to fit all of it into my mouth?"

He jerked his arms, but they remained tied behind him against the chair. "I'm not asking you to swallow the whole thing. Just...suck on it." He tried to move but couldn't. "Jesus. My arms are losing sensation."

She pulled out his rigid length and smoothed her hands over it. "You're just saying that."

His lips parted and his chest fell and rose more unevenly. "God. That...don't make me...it has to end with me inside you. Or those children won't be in our arms anytime soon."

She hesitated and then quickly lowered her mouth onto him, taking his erection into her mouth. Not knowing what she was supposed to do, she sucked on it. Hard. With her teeth.

He startled against her, jarring the chair against the floor. "*Jesus!* What are you doing?!"

She unlatched herself and glanced up at him, trying not to panic. "Did I do it wrong?"

His chest heaved, his face flushed. "No teeth. All right? No. Teeth."

It was obvious she'd hurt him. She winced. "I'm sorry. I don't know how you want me to do it. I can't readily remove the teeth from my mouth, you know."

A gargled laugh escaped him. "Can you untie me? Because this isn't going to work. I'll end up dead. We'll do this again when you're...more experienced."

Her cheeks got hot. "I'm sorry. I'm a terrible lover, aren't I?"

He captured her gaze, his features growing serious. "No. Don't say that. And don't you dare apologize." He dragged in a breath and let it out. "Use your lips to cover your teeth. That will help."

An exasperated breath escaped her. "Maybe I should just untie you."

"No. I'm..." He cleared his throat. "Teeth aside, I'm enjoying this. Really."

She hesitated. "Are you certain?"

"Quite. Try again."

Now she felt like *she* was in school. She awkwardly and carefully took hold of his erection again. Lowering her head, she molded her lips against it and pushed her mouth down onto it, pulling up and pushing down, ensuring her teeth weren't touching his length.

A groan escaped him. "Beautiful."

She adjusted her grip on him and continued moving her mouth against him, enjoying the feel of him. Hard and smooth. It was so...*erotic*. Everything about him was. She could feel herself getting wet. And he wasn't even in her. She moved her mouth more and more.

He pushed his hips against her, moaning. "Damn."

Something told her she was doing it right. She moved faster.

He gasped. "Not so fast...I..." He gasped again.

She knew what that meant. Releasing him, she hitched up her skirts and climbed onto him, slipping her legs around him. She reached between them and ensuring his erection was up, slid down onto it, letting out a breath. Grabbing his muscled shoulders, she slowly rode him.

Derek's eyes half-closed in between ragged breaths.

She leaned down and bringing her hands into his hair, kissed his forehead and rode him steady but harder, feeling her core tightening with each downward thrust. Her heart skipped realizing she was giving into more than just pleasure. She was giving herself over to making a baby. *Their* baby. She tightened her hold on him and pushed them both faster, losing herself to the moment. Her breaths, her heartbeat, his parted lips, and his heaving chest all blurred together.

Without realizing she had already physically lost herself, she cried out and trembled against the rippling sensation that erased her ability to control herself.

He bucked against her, jerking the chair beneath them. He yelled and stilled.

Knowing his seed was within her womb, she cradled herself against him, keeping his length within her. She closed her eyes and dreamily set her head against his. "How long before we know?"

A breath escaped him. "If you don't get your menses, we'll know."

Still keeping her eyes closed, she whispered, "I'll be more than my mother was."

"I know you will be," he whispered back. "You'll be amazing. Absolutely amazing."

She held him tighter.

After a long moment, he murmured, "I can't feel my arms. Would you untie me?"

Her eyes popped open. She paused, realizing she had smeared the paint all over her hands and gown in colors that resembled a rainbow. It was a sign. "I can't. I'm not allowed to move."

"What do you mean you're not allowed to move?"

She nuzzled him. "I'm not. We have to stay like this for a half hour."

"Uh…my arms might very well fall off by then."

"Derek?"

"Yes?"

"I'm seeing rainbows. Will you marry me?" she drawled. "Because I think I like you."

He groaned. "You aren't being funny. Untie me. Now."

She kissed his cheek. "I'm merely trying to ensure this baby comes."

"How? By making me suffer?"

She nudged him. "No. Your mother told me what helped her get pregnant was not moving for a good half hour after the act."

He paused. "I will disregard that my mother actually said that. But if there is any truth in what she is saying…I can wait a half hour. Don't move."

"I thought so."

EPILOGUE

The greatest gift is the one you do not expect: a child.

-The School of Gallantry

Nine months later, after midnight
Essex, England – The Banfield country estate

Derek swiped his face with a trembling hand, unable to listen to Clementine's sobs and screams that continued to echo through the house. "I can't," he rasped, his chest tight and his breaths uneven. "I have to see her. I have to help her. They can't keep me out here. I have to—"

A hand grabbed his shoulder hard. Andrew edged in. "You have the best doctors in Essex at her side."

Mr. Grey raked his hands through his hair and paced. "Her mother died giving birth."

Derek almost staggered. "Jesus, don't—"

Lady Banfield gasped and grabbed Mr. Grey's arm. "What are you trying to do? Send my son and all of us into a panic?"

Derek swallowed. He pointed at Andrew. "Have the footmen ready." Removing his evening coat, he whipped it to the floor. "I don't care what the doctor says." He jogged out of the room and down the corridor toward Clementine's bedchamber. Grabbing the doorknob, he turned it and yanked the door open. Going in, he closed the door.

One of three doctors gathered the linen from around Clementine's writhing body and assembled it over her large belly and bent knees like a tent.

Clementine's gaze darted over to him in between sobs. Her sweat-soaked black hair clung to the side of her flushed face. "Derek!" She held out a shaky hand. "The doctor says I'm close!"

Derek hurried over to her side and climbed onto the bed beside her, taking her hand. He cradled her head against his chest. "You can do this, love. I know you can."

"Push, my lady," the doctor insisted, bending in between the covered portion of her lower body. "Push. I can...I can feel the child's head. We might not need the forceps."

Clementine stiffened and letting out a shriek, leaned forward.

A tiny cry made Derek tighten his hold on Clementine in disbelief. His throat tightened.

The doctor lifted the small body and set the babe onto the waiting linen set on the bed. "It's a boy," the doctor announced, glancing up at them. "I won't cut the cord until I have your permission."

Derek stared at the tiny crying babe who was being bundled. He couldn't believe it. He was a father.

A sob escaped Clementine as she popped out both arms. "Let me hold him. Let me...hold him."

The doctor rounded the bed and carefully handed the baby over and into Clementine's extended arms, while one of the other doctors covered her legs with the linens.

Clementine gathered their child and tucked him against the crook of her arm, leaning back against the pillows gathered behind her. She tilted their son toward Derek, so he could better see. A breath escaped her as she touched a finger to that small glossy cheek and chin. "Love at first sight is real," she whispered. "It really is. Look at him, Derek. He is ours. All ours."

Derek swallowed and edged closer toward their son whose lips quivered as he cried. His tiny head shifted against the linen he was bundled in. Derek brought up a hand and delicately grazed that dark tuft of soft hair. A tiny hand flailed out toward him and hit his hand. A startled laugh escaped him. "A boxer. What do you know."

Clementine glanced up at Derek and tsked. "Don't be throwing him into boxing matches quite yet."

He kissed her forehead then her lips, before returning his attention back to their son. He touched that small hand. "Can we name him George? After my father? And Rupert, after yours?"

She nodded. "Yes. 'Tis rather fitting that the men who brought us together be honored. George Rupert Holbrook." She smiled and dabbing a finger to that tiny nose said, "Welcome to the world, George. I promise your life is going to be amazing."

Derek nuzzled his nose against Clementine's cheek and whispered, "I have a surprise for you. Do you want to see it now or when you wake up in the morning after you rest?"

She glanced up at him, her eyes brightening. "I want to see it now. What is it? You always have the most incredible surprises. What did I get? Jewelry?"

He laughed and kissed her cheek. "No. Something far better. I'll wait for you and the babe to get cleaned up." He gestured toward her lady's maid who lingered with a basin, soap, towels and fresh nightclothes.

The doctor asked, "Do I have permission to cut the umbilical cord, my lord?"

Derek glanced at Clementine. "Are you ready?"

She nodded.

The doctor snipped it with shears and quickly knotted a small piece of cloth around the babe's remaining cord.

"I'll let you wash up, dear," Derek said, angling toward her. "Are you up for seeing everyone after you get cleaned up?"

She nodded. "Yes."

He kissed her cheek again and skimmed his hand over George's small head, his throat tightening. It was surreal knowing this child was his. Pushing off the bed, he made his way over to the door and opened it. He glanced back at her, as her lady's maid set the basin onto the bed and took their child.

Sprinting down the corridor, Derek skidded into the room where his brother, Mr. Grey and his mother waited. "It's a boy!" he yelled, throwing up both hands. "The most dashing boy you've ever seen. You have to see him. He looks like me!"

Andrew burst into laughter. "Hopefully, he won't grow up to be as conceited."

Mr. Grey strode up to Derek, grinning. "Am I allowed to see her? When can I see her?"

Derek gestured toward the corridor. "She and George Rupert are getting cleaned up. You can go wait outside the door until they are ready."

Mr. Grey's lips parted. "You named the child after George and me?"

Derek patted the man on the back. "Two great men deserve to be acknowledged for their fabulous matchmaking skills."

Mr. Grey grinned, shaking his head and darted out of the room.

Lady Banfield bustled toward Derek, grabbed his face, and kissed him on the cheek twice. "May this boy give you the same adventures you gave me." She smirked. "I will leave it at that." She hurried out of the room.

Same adventures. Christ, he was going to grey early. Derek pointed at Andrew. "Are the footmen ready? Do they have every one?"

Andrew nodded. "Every one. They are all waiting. You want me to start this?

"In about a half hour. After she has time to get washed up with new nightclothes. Tell them to enter her room one by one. Like we planned."

Andrew walked by and punched his arm playfully. "I suppose I have to take you seriously now. What with you being a father and all."

Derek pointed at him. "Don't you forget it."

Andrew eyed him. "I'm an uncle now. Which means that boy will be in need of advice."

Derek shoved him, sending Andrew stumbling. "Whatever you do, don't give him female advice. Leave that to me."

Andrew shoved him back with a laugh. "By the time he is old enough to take advice on females, I'll be married with six children."

"You have to find a woman first, Andrew, " Derek drawled.

His brother smirked. "I'm all about respectable women now. Have you seen Lord Hawksford's sister, Lady Victoria? Damn."

Derek pulled in his chin. "Hawksford's sister isn't even eighteen."

"She will be next year. I'm waiting for her coming out."

"Can you stop scaring me and get the footmen in order?"

"Consider it done." Andrew disappeared.

Derek paused and seeing the life-size portrait of his father on the wall, walked up to it and touched the bottom of the gilded frame. His eyes fell on that bright jolly face that grinned. "Wish you were here," he whispered, half-nodding.

Sniffing hard, he swung away and knowing Clementine and his son were waiting, he strode away. Halfway down the corridor, he broke into a run and skidded through the open doorway and back into Clementine's room.

Mr. Grey was seated on one side of the bed and Lady Banfield on the other, both of them leaning in and talking in high-pitched adoring voices to the baby who was already dressed in a cap and garment.

Derek set himself against the nearest wall, quietly watching Clementine adjust their child in her arms as she talked to her father and his mother. Her hair was scattered around her shoulders and she, despite hours of pain, looked like a woman who had never known pain. She paused in between her soft chatter and captured his gaze from across the room.

She smiled. "Aren't you going to come over here, handsome?"

He shook his head. "Not until my gift arrives."

Andrew stumbled into the room out of breath. "I gathered every last one of them. They are all waiting outside. All thirty-two of them."

Derek grinned. "Tell them to come in." He pointed at Clementine. "This is for you, love. Don't think I ever forgot."

Clementine's eyes veered toward the open doorway.

One by one, footmen in their livery entered, each carrying a painting that had been scattered around the world since Clementine was a child. It had taken Derek a touch over six months to gather them after he had Mr. Grey disclose every location of every home her paintings had been left in.

Clementine's eyes widened. "My paintings!" A choked sob escaped her.

Derek let the paintings continue to walk in until there was barely any standing room and they were all surrounded by every painting Clementine ever created as a child.

Weaving through the footmen, he came up to the side of the bed, leaned across his mother toward Clementine and said, "I brought them home. Where they belong."

Gently handing off George to her father, she grabbed Derek by his linen shirt and tugged him closer. Until they were nose to nose. "You are the best thing to have ever happened to me. Do you know that?"

Derek grinned. "I knew that well before you did."

"Are you bragging?"

"I'm trying not to."

"I love you, Derek."

Feeling as though he might burst from the perfection of his own life, he kissed her.